Sandra J. Paul

THE GIRL WITHOUT A VOICE

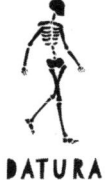

DATURA

DATURA BOOKS
An imprint of Watkins Media Ltd

Unit 11, Shepperton House
89-93 Shepperton Road
London N1 3DF
UK

daturabooks.com
Silence speaks louder than words

A Datura Books paperback original, 2025

Copyright © Sandra J. Paul 2025

Edited by April Northall and Travis Tynan
Cover by Sarah O'Flaherty
Set in Meridien

All rights reserved. Sandra J. Paul asserts the moral right to be identified as the author of this work. A catalogue record for this book is available from the British Library.

This novel is entirely a work of fiction. Names, characters, places, and incidents are the products of the author's imagination or are used fictitiously. Any resemblance to actual events, locales, organizations or persons, living or dead, is entirely coincidental.

Sales of this book without a front cover may be unauthorized. If this book is coverless, it may have been reported to the publisher as "unsold and destroyed" and neither the author nor the publisher may have received payment for it.

Datura Books and the Datura Books icon are registered trademarks of Watkins Media Ltd.

ISBN 978 1 91552 338 9
Ebook ISBN 978 1 91552 339 6

Printed and bound in the United Kingdom by CPI Group (UK) Ltd, Croydon CR0 4YY

The manufacturer's authorised representative in the EU for product safety is eucomply OÜ - Pärnu mnt 139b-14, 11317 Tallinn, Estonia, hello@eucompliancepartner.com;www.eucompliancepartner.com

9 8 7 6 5 4 3 2 1

*To my family.
You are everything to me.*

"I'm dying."

Dad dropped his travel bag and briefcase to the floor and sat down on his favorite kitchen stool, barely looking at us as he spoke.

"Give me a cup of coffee."

Mom and I shared a glance before she walked calmly to the coffee machine that she had bought just the other day and started a fresh brew. Soon, the scent of coffee filled the kitchen, providing us with some sense of normalcy in a world that had suddenly changed.

Mom set a mug down in front of him and filled it to the brim, spilling a bit over the side onto his hand. He hardly noticed. He drank the scorching-hot coffee as if it were a cold milkshake. Perhaps dying did that to a person.

"How come?" Mom asked, emotionless.

"How do you think?"

"The cancer."

She stated it as fact, revealing in that very moment that she had known that he'd been sick. I had noticed the gray pallor of his skin before but never really thought about it. I didn't know what sick people looked like.

"Yeah. The cancer."

"How long?"

"Not long."

"Okay."

"I'm going to have to make some arrangements. I need to call the office first."

"You mean they don't know yet?"

"Nope."

Dad finished his coffee and got up, not even looking at me or Mom as he walked over to the phone hanging on the wall. He tapped the office's number, dragging the long cord of the phone with him as he stepped into the hallway to speak to whomever.

Mom looked at me. I looked at her. I sighed and scratched an old scar on my wrist that I'd had for as long as I could remember. Was I supposed to do something now? Cry? Whimper? Jot down how sad I was in my journal?

But I wasn't sad. I was devoid of any feelings, and I knew that it wasn't normal. He was my dad, and he was dying, and I felt absolutely nothing.

PART ONE
Life

1

I've never lived a normal life, at least not in comparison to people in all those books I've read over the years. Or to the characters in those soaps I secretly watch when mom runs off to the grocery store. I manage to catch about one and a half episodes before she returns, anxiously peeking out the window, only really half-enjoying what I'm watching.

She's always fast. Her trips take no more than an hour, but it's enough for me to sneak a glimpse of the real world out there, no matter how twisted television's version of reality may be. I like it better when she goes out for other things like appliances, clothing, the hardware store. That takes more time, but it's also more unpredictable. I linger behind the heavy drapes while I sit in her rocking chair, ready to fly out of the seat as soon as I hear her old, battered car roll up the driveway. That thing makes so much noise you could hear it from a mile away. By the time she's inside the house, I'm already upstairs in my favorite reading chair, apparently lost in whatever world it is I'm reading about.

Everything I know of life comes from books, and only the ones Dad – and occasionally, Mom – gives me. I'm not allowed to choose my own. So I end up with an odd mixture of romance novels, children's books, and thrillers. The latter are my favorite; I love reading about murder mysteries and how to solve them. *Murder on the Orient Express, Murder on the*

Nile, the Endless Night... or stories about detectives in New York who solve crimes.

My books are my pride and joy. I have titles that are over seventy years old, like the one about Gulliver, who traveled to the strangest countries and returned with the oddest tales about tall and small people.

And all of my books are used, often torn and tattered. The oldest ones have notes in them, written in handwriting I can't really read. I've kept them in my bedroom for as long as I can remember, and I've read them all multiple times.

Reading those books has shaped my vision of what life out there must be like. I sometimes imagine those huge cities with millions of people, all cooped up together in small apartments, sharing the crowded but dangerous streets.

I also dream of places like London or Paris where, according to my books, life is so wonderful that everyone wants to live there. I have a few picture books with images of the Eiffel Tower and Big Ben, and I know what Tower Bridge looks like. I've also seen pictures of the Twin Towers in New York, and the Brooklyn Bridge. It's all so perfect that I yearn to go there some day and see it for myself.

But I am not allowed. My home is this house, with its four bedrooms, its huge basement, and the dusty, dark attic I never enter because it gives me nightmares. Kids should never be in attics anyhow. They're dangerous places, but then so are cold and damp basements. I just stay on the ground floor, with its old kitchen and unpleasant living room, where my mom usually hangs out.

I'm not allowed in my parents' bedroom, nor in the guestroom, where the only piece of furniture is a spare bed. I don't even know why we have a guestroom, since I've never seen anyone visit us.

Most of my life is spent in two rooms. The first is my bedroom, with its four-poster bed, large cupboard and closet, and two windows. The largest one is shut; I am able to see part of the street, but most of my view is hidden behind a huge oak tree that must have been there forever. I have a book about trees, and given the width of it I figured out it must be at least a hundred years old. There is a massive drape in front of that window that I'm not allowed to fully open, so that part of the room is always dark.

The other window looks out on the neighbor's house, but since they're hardly ever there in winter, and always in the backyard in summer, I don't have any contact with them. I can pry that window open just a bit, which allows some fresh air in – something I'm often in dire need of. I don't like shut windows or closed drapes. Darkness scares me no end, so I sleep with the lights on.

The second room is adjoined to this one by a blue door I always keep open. At first, it was just a room with some boxes and junk, but when I turned twenty something changed. It was my birthday, the one day each year that I get a gift from Mom. A cake, some books, a furry animal or a doll. Every year, she brings me something, but it's never something I wish for. I wanted to see New York or London, or the magical city of Paris, but I knew I could never have that. People like me aren't allowed to go anywhere.

But the present I got that year was different. She came into my bedroom, wished me a happy birthday, and took me to the adjoined room, which she had been clearing out over the last few days. I had heard her going through things and dragging stuff down the stairs. She never asked for my help, and I never offered.

The room was now completely empty, and it was larger than I had remembered. Since there was never anything of my own in there, I hadn't been inside for a long time.

"This is yours from now on," she said. "You can have it for your books and things."

I looked at her inquisitively, using my hands to speak, even though she hardly understood.

Mine?

That she did comprehend. Her signing skills weren't great, but they were developed enough to communicate about the basic stuff.

Food.
Hungry.
You.
Me.
Downstairs.
Mine.
Yours.
Sleep.
Why?
What?
Who?

That was about all she understood – or what she was interested in. She spoke verbally to me since I wasn't deaf, and I communicated back with my hands and on notepads. It worked, but it was damned lonely.

"I figured you could use some space for your books," she said, pointing through the open door to the stacks and stacks of books, new and old, that I couldn't fit anywhere but on the bedroom floor.

"You will need to move out of your bedroom for a couple of days. Choose the basement or the attic, and take enough bits to keep yourself occupied. You can use the spare basement bedroom. You can sleep in your own bed in the evening, but during the day, I don't want you around. A couple of guys are coming by fix up the room, and I don't want them to see you."

The thought enthralled and scared me at the same time. I grabbed my notepad and scribbled down, *basement*. She nodded.

"Get to it, then. They'll be here in half an hour."

I quickly gathered some things – a couple of books, a blanket, warm clothes, a few of my furry companions – and headed downstairs, past the kitchen, to the basement. I hadn't been there in years, not since Dad had punished me for snooping around his bedroom. He had come home early from a trip and caught me sitting behind his desk, staring at his things. Mom had gone to the grocery store, and I was bored out of my mind because the television had broken and she hadn't gotten a new one yet.

Dad was so mad that he made me spend two days down there, at the far end of the basement, locked in the dark with nothing but my own silent screams. I just sat on a mattress in the cold dark, wondering why I was living this life, and why those people were my parents.

On Sunday evening, Mom came to get me, which I only found out about after as I had gone into a sort of catatonic state and woke up in my own bedroom with Mom sitting frantically by my side.

That was the only time she ever cried in my presence or seemed to care enough to worry about me. Dad had left by that time. He came back a week later as if nothing had happened. I never told him about the horrible nightmares it gave me.

My heart sank as I walked down the basement stairs, horrified of what I would find. I was sure the nightmares would return. But I was relieved to see that the rooms had been changed. The walls were painted in a brighter color, and the far end had been turned into storage space with shelves and a decent light.

The basement bedroom had a proper bed now too, along with a cupboard and a closet, and the walls were bright yellow. There was a small window that overlooked the garden, but it still felt claustrophobic and every alien sound triggered my senses. I was not allowed to see my new book room until it was finished, so I spent that night upstairs in my bedroom wondering what it would look like. I had no expectations.

On the second day, late in the evening, after the workmen had left and I was allowed back upstairs, I knew in a heartbeat that those two days of fear had been worth it.

The room had been turned into a massive library, and Mom had even installed a reading nook, some cozy lamps, and posters with book quotes. It was the most beautiful room I had ever seen – not that this was saying much – and I loved it more than anything in this world. At the same time, it was a reminder of my solitary life.

I spent three days organizing it just the way I wanted, sorting all my books per genre and color. I dragged it out, changing bits here and there, until I was finally happy with the result – and exhausted, because my body simply wasn't used to work like that.

When Dad came home that night after five days on the road, he became upset with my mom when he saw what she'd done. I heard them arguing downstairs.

"How much money did that cost?" he barked.

"Not that much," she said. "The child needs something to occupy herself. I've run out of topics to teach her."

"But a *library*? Are you insane?"

"I had two guys do it. I paid cash. It was nothing. I used some of the savings; you'll hardly notice."

"Two guys?! What the fuck did you do? Let strangers in here?"

"Who else?" she said, sounding sharp. "Someone had to do it. It wasn't as if *you* were planning on doing anything nice for your daughter for once."

They took the argument into the kitchen and shut the door so I couldn't hear the rest, but the next morning Dad came up to the room with two bags of books and dropped them on the reading table.

"Here," he said. "For your collection." And he was gone. He had given me some Stephen King books. *Carrie. Salem's Lot. The Shining. Firestarter. The Rage.* I had never heard of the author before, but that marked the beginning of a new addiction. Stories of odd ones out, living bizarre lives and going through strange events? Yep, that was me. I have my own King cupboard now.

2

For twenty-four years, I had only known this house and my parents. My world was limited to this place and the adjoined yard, surrounded by massive trees, hedges, and gates. I wasn't allowed to go beyond our property, and I wasn't allowed to communicate with anyone other than my parents.

And all this for one simple reason: I couldn't speak. But I wasn't deaf. I was born without a voice, or at least with an inability to use it.

My parents called it mutism, stemming from a complication at birth. That's all they ever said about it. I was unable to produce one syllable, as if someone had cut my vocal cords. People with a hearing disability can often still speak, if only a little, and can often emphasize what they want to communicate. I couldn't. I couldn't produce a single sound.

I couldn't recall ever seeing a doctor or having tests done. I asked my mom about it when I was thirteen years-old, wanting to know where my condition came from and if I would ever get better. She said they examined me when I was little, and that the doctors had called my medical condition irreversible. That was the only time we ever spoke about it.

"The doctors have done everything in their power, but we were all forced to accept that you will never be able to speak."

And so I can't live a normal life? I scribbled down the words rapidly, almost incomprehensible.

"It's more complicated than that, Alice."

How?

"The doctors believe that your mutism is a symptom of a larger problem. You won't be able to live on your own, not ever, even when your dad and I are gone. They said that you are... well. That you don't have the abilities it takes to live like other people."

I'm stupid. I didn't write it down or sign it, but that was what she was saying. I was too stupid to live a normal life.

Was I too stupid? I must have been. If that was what the doctors said, who was I to question them?

"So your dad and I decided we would protect you from the outside world. That was our obligation to you, especially since it was our fault that you were born this way."

Your fault?

"I did some foolish things while pregnant," she said, but she wouldn't elaborate on that. "It may have impacted your health."

Drugs. Drinking. Something terrible. Again, I didn't actually ask, but I knew that had to be the reason.

"You should be happy you have such a nice house to live in. You've got everything you need right here. That's enough."

But it wasn't normal. She didn't know how I had learned my life was so different. She could only guess that it came from my books and brief moments of watching TV. But, I wondered, if I had figured that out on my own, should I still be considered stupid?

We lived in a cul-de-sac in Hays, Kansas. Our house didn't stand out from the others. It was decent, albeit one of the eldest amongst most of the homes in our street. The front yard was overgrown, as was the outstretched backyard. Dad didn't care about gardening, and he didn't want to spend his scarce free time fixing up the place. Mom hired a couple of kids once a year to do some work instead. It still looked terrible, especially the front. It was a telltale sign of the wacky life my parents led. Sometimes our next-door neighbor would come by with a lawnmower and do the overgrown patch so it wouldn't look so ugly, but it didn't help much.

In the yard behind our house, there were a number of trees that bowed under the weight of apples and pears in the fall and then stood naked in the winter. The fruit was impossible to eat. The pears were hard and apples sour, and by the end of the season loads of them hung rotting on the trees, spreading a pungent odor. The fruits were as useless as I considered myself to be.

I was allowed in the garden because no one could see me, and I couldn't call out to anyone. My visits were brief, and always supervised when I was little. But as I grew older, Mom would leave me alone once she was satisfied I wouldn't escape.

I didn't have any friends and wasn't allowed any pets, even though I yearned for either. Mom was allergic to cats, and I couldn't go out and walk a dog, so what was the point in having one?

I kept track of my boring days in notebooks Mom gave me, scribbling down the books I'd read or what I had seen outside. I would jot down special moments, like my dad coming home with a gift. I didn't tell my parents. They had no clue that I was registering my odd life in this house that I knew every inch of. I kept my notebooks hidden in a black box under the bed, barely visible.

The days were long, the months crept, the seasons felt like an eternity. In summer, I would sit outside and listen to the excited screams of the kids living a few doors down, plunging happily into a swimming pool. Sometimes it would be too hot, and I would head back inside to seek the coolness of the kitchen.

I hated summer. Fall and winter were my favorite seasons. When it was cold, I would spend my days in my bedroom, counting down the minutes from the moment I woke up until the second I was finally able to go to bed, hopefully without lying awake most of the night.

I was never tired and always restless, wondering how I was supposed to spend the remainder of my life like this. I was trapped in a world where life had come to a standstill, where every day repeated itself. The date on the calendar changed, but each day felt like the previous one, the passage of time only marked by the changing of the seasons and the books I read.

I often believed without a doubt that nobody knew of my existence. If there were a house fire, I would certainly die. Firemen would stumble upon my burnt corpse and wonder who the heck I was and why I was there. I was nonexistent. Invisible. Unseen and unimportant, trapped in a narrow world with a mother who didn't love me and a father who didn't care.

Despite having two rooms filled to the brim with things to do, I was bored out of my mind. Every day dragged on from morning to midnight, with nothing to do but read. Perhaps some people would kill to live this life, but to me, it didn't matter whether it was Monday or Friday.

Mom was my caretaker, but I often wondered if she was more my watchdog, judging by how little she allowed me to do. Then again, she didn't do much either, except rummage around the house, going through the motions.

She occupied herself with cleaning, cooking, watching television, reading, sewing or knitting, grocery shopping, or the occasional outing to the department store. She repeated this routine daily, except when Dad came home during the weekends. I honestly believed she hated the weekends the most, and that she would have preferred him gone forever. She always seemed scared and cautious when he was around.

We had a phone downstairs, but she never used it, apart from when Dad would call to say when he would be arriving home. That was usually on Thursday nights, and she would be sitting by the phone waiting anxiously for his call. Before he arrived for the weekend, usually late Friday afternoon, the house would be squeaky clean. She would have a homecooked dinner ready – something she never bothered with when it was just the two of us – and she would make sure that everything was as he liked it.

Friday night dinners were the worst. We would sit together and eat without even looking at each other. Dad didn't know sign language, so he couldn't be bothered watching my hands move. I had stopped trying to teach him, so I used notepads to ask him questions, if I bothered to at all.

Dad would barely ask how Mom's week was, nor would she inquire about his. They would make small talk about things he had seen on the road, and she would say things she had heard at the store. Nothing that held any meaning. They both seemed careless of each other's wellbeing, and I often wondered why they stayed married if they hated each other so much.

On Saturday mornings, he would usually leave the house. I never knew what he was doing, but Mom told me once that he would go to the new shopping mall on the outskirts of town, see a movie and have beers after. He would come home late at night, usually drunk, and sleep in until noon Sunday. When he left later that afternoon, she would sigh with relief, happy to have the house to herself again. I shared her feelings; having Dad around felt like keeping a loaded gun in the house, even if I had never actually seen a weapon in my life.

Mom, devoid of any friends or family, was just as lonely as I was. She never invited anyone to the house, nor did she bother to go out to meet people. She was always home, always doing something. The sounds she made around the house made me feel that I wasn't alone in this world. Not that it mattered much one way or the other; she hardly ever spoke to me.

The one thing she did do was turn on the radio or play records. She had a stack of albums that she listened to on repeat, from artists whose names I only learned when I secretly went through her stash of LP's. The Jacksons, Elton John, Derek and the Dominos, Pink Floyd, The Rolling Stones. I loved her taste in music, and it became mine, too.

I loved when she played records, but I liked the radio more. Those were the moments I heard other people's voices: DJs talking about whatever was going on in the world, commercials about shampoo and detergents and make-up, all mixed into one. The radio was where I heard a lot of new music, too, from up-and-coming artists or those who were already famous.

There was always sound in the house, either from the radio or the television standing in the living room. Mom would keep the volume up high, even while watching her soap operas or crime shows. She loved shows like *Columbo*, about this weird detective who solved mysteries that were shown from the point of view of the killer, or *Happy Days*, with The Fonz, or *The Little House on the Prairie*, a family-themed show that always made me sad because it showed me how oddly twisted my own world was. The characters spoke of family values my parents didn't have.

After the changes to my rooms, I would always open the library door so I could catch the sounds and imagine what those people on television looked like. They never broadcasted *Little House* when Mom went to the store, so I got stuck with *All in the Family*, which was okay too.

On Friday night, Dad chose the shows. He had a thing for political debates and true-crime documentaries. He would watch them for hours, listening intently to whatever the reporter was saying about person X or killer Y. Recently, he seemed fascinated by a man called Ted Bundy, who I had never heard of until he started watching news reports about his crimes. That was the first time I ever heard the term "serial killer". When Mom caught me listening from my room, she scolded me and shut the door in my face.

Mom was something of an enigma. I always believed that she was jealous of my dad's freedom, even though she never said. I could tell by the way she wandered around the house. Dad could go wherever he wanted, do whatever pleased him, had no one watching over him. All the while, Mom was stuck in the house, keeping close supervision on me.

We had never been close. Our relationship was quite strange. She took care of me, but she seemed to hate me for it at the same time. I didn't have a single memory of her holding me or even touching my hand or my face. We lived at a distance, as if some strange disease forced us apart. I blamed my lack of speech, but there was more to it. If she had wanted to, she could have communicated with me, but she rarely bothered.

She had tutored me for years, but stopped when I had turned eighteen. I couldn't remember when the teaching had started, but I must have been very young, as it's part of my earliest memories.

"You need to know things," she would say when I didn't feel like listening.

Sometimes, I'd get fed up with her teaching and would just want to read, which I had learned to do at a very young age, and I would tell her so through gestures and quickly scribbled words. She would reprimand me for being lazy, but in reality, I hated calculus and geometry, which she insisted I should know. I did like History and Geography, a combination that taught me about the world we lived in.

"One day, you will be alone in this world, and I want you to be able to read, write, and do math, so you can find a job somewhere and be useful. Even though you'll never get a degree. When the time comes and our lives here are over, you'll have to fend for yourself."

I never understood why she would say such horrible things, like, "when the time comes", or "when this is over", or "when I'm gone". What kind of mother would talk about these things with their children?

During those years, she gave me plenty of books about our world's history, what our planet looked like, and about different cultures and races. I picked up a great deal from science books. Sometimes she would bring me magazines that she had bought at the local supermarket, always about "topics of value", as she called them.

She never told me why getting a degree was an impossibility, but I knew it had to do with the fact that I was invisible to the rest of the world. Or maybe it was because I was simply useless.

The future scared me. Without my mom, I thought wouldn't be able to survive for long. I would starve because I would be too scared to go outside or walk to the local supermarket. I knew the value of money because she had taught me, but I had never bought a single thing for myself.

I couldn't drive a car or ride a bicycle. Physically, I was weak. My body wasn't used to long walks or workouts. I barely left my room. I was skinny because I didn't eat much, and I lived on unhealthy food, since Mom never bought any fresh products. Photos of apples and pears made me salivate, even though I had hardly ever tasted them. We lived off chips, junk food, and pasta. Mom was also skinny, probably because she cleaned so much. She kept the house tidy out of fear that Dad would come home early and find a mess. Or so I believed.

"When we're gone, you'll need to find a job," she always said. "The world is changing, and your dad isn't making as much money as he used to. Not anymore. People like him are becoming obsolete. I want you to prepare for an uncertain future. The heartache will come, Alice. Don't think that it won't."

By the time I turned eighteen, I had learned all that she could teach me, or so she said. So her gift to me was the end of her tutelage. Despite my growing reluctance towards it, I felt like I was being pushed into a black hole with no end in sight. At least those hours spent studying kept us both occupied. And when that stopped, life became even more unbearable.

Mom never laid a hand on me. But I think, in a way, never being touched was worse. Sometimes I wondered what it would take for her to notice me enough to hit me in the face. She wouldn't even touch me to help me, or place a hand on my shoulder in comfort, or even in anger because I hadn't put in enough effort. Sometimes, I slacked on purpose in a futile hope that she would pinch me. She never did.

And then, all of a sudden, after she had stopped tutoring me, she started drinking. Or perhaps she had been drinking for a long time and had kept it hidden. She would still listen to music, and watch TV, but I started noticing large gaps between those moments, where she would be alone with a bottle in her bedroom, drinking until she passed out.

I only discovered this when I went looking for her one evening, starving because it was way past dinner time, and she hadn't called me yet. I eventually found her in the master bedroom, out cold on the bed, an empty bottle beside her. When I tried to wake her, she looked at me bleary-eyed and told me to "fuck the hell off."

She must have remembered this, because the next day she told to stay the hell out of her business and never to enter that bedroom again.

As time passed, she started drinking downstairs, too, and didn't bother hiding the evidence. She kept empty bottles in the kitchen, scattered around the sink or in the bin. She also started neglecting the home. Her cleaning routine went from daily to three times a week, and then to once a week.

By the time Dad would be expected back, she'd have all the empty bottles cleared out. She took them outside and made sure that the house was clean, and that the lingering smell of alcohol had evaporated. She started burning scented candles to disguise the smell.

When Dad was home, she managed to stay sober for two days straight, probably counting down the minutes until he'd take off again. She didn't dare drink while he was out on Saturdays or Sundays because she never knew when he'd be back. I wasn't sure if he knew, or if he simply ignored the signs because it didn't suit his agenda.

But he did know.

A few months after she started drinking, Mom purchased a brand-new television after placing a half-full bottle of wine on top of the old one only to knock and spill it, causing the old TV to "short-circuit", as she called it. She brought the new one home and installed it before Dad returned without telling him. Of course, he found out when went into the living room to watch his shows. I was still downstairs, at the time, and witnessed the whole argument.

"What the fuck did you buy that thing for?" he had snapped.

"The old one broke."

"It was two years old! Do you think I've got a money tree in the backyard? Take it back. You don't need a television."

"TV is the one good thing I have in my life, and it's staying."

"Why? You're always too drunk to know what's going on anyhow."

She was shocked to silence.

"What? Did you really think I was too stupid to notice? You've been using grocery money for booze. There's hardly any food at the house and *she* –" he pointed at me "– is skinnier than ever. Do you even bother feeding her anymore?"

She swallowed, and then snapped, "Why don't *you* feed her then?" And left.

Whenever I'd get a chance to watch part of a soap opera, it was all over-the-top drama and tragedy, with people leaving and coming back, dying, killing each other off for money or another lover. There was one long-running soap about a twisted family where everyone seemed to die multiple times and then always come back through some strange event. Actors would play their own twins; characters would return looking completely different. It was ridiculous and funny. But my life was more dramatic than any soap I had ever seen, and now it didn't seem so funny anymore.

Dad chased after her. He raced up the stairs into their bedroom, and they started yelling at each other. Then, suddenly, it stopped. The sound was muffled. I no longer heard their voices, but the bed creaked. When they came back down as I finished cleaning the kitchen, Mom was subdued and Dad was flustered, and I knew they'd had sex.

Yes, I knew about sex. I'd seen it on television and read about it in books. But I never thought of it occurring in this house, not between two people who hated each other like my parents did.

"You can keep your television," Dad said, glancing at me. "Perhaps you should get one for her too and put it in her room."

"No."

He threw money on the table.

"Get her one. She deserves to know what's out there. I'll expect one up in her room when I come back next week."

Mom picked up the money, put it in her pocket, and glanced at me without really seeing me. There was something broken in her eyes, but I didn't understand. She got her television, didn't she?

By the following Friday, I had my own television up in my bedroom.

At first, the TV was on my cupboard, facing the bed. But I didn't like to sit there all the time, so I dragged it to the library and positioned it so I could watch from my favorite seat. For the first time in my life, books no longer interested me. There was a whole new world out there, and I was eager to see more.

At first, Mom tried to force me to watch silly children's shows or comedies where people would overact to the point of it becoming stupid, but as the months passed and she was drunk more often than sober, her monitoring stopped altogether. She was drinking daily now, binging until late in the evening and sleeping off her hangovers most of the day, which meant I had the house to myself. I still didn't go downstairs unless it was to get some food that I then ate in my bedroom, watching television.

Mom also stopped drinking in her bedroom, which was just at the end of the hall. She didn't drink in the living room either, where the new television now sat unused on the table against the wall unless Dad came home and turned it on.

Instead, she claimed the basement room with the yellow walls, where she installed a second fridge stacked to the brim with wine bottles, something I had discovered during one of her daily trips to the store.

She no longer hid her problems. Not from Dad, and certainly not from me. She had given up, as if she didn't give a damn about the world anymore. We no longer spoke, and I barely saw her. There were days she didn't even come up for food. Sometimes she forgot to go to the store – unless she was running out of booze, then she was out the door in a flash. She drank and drove, and I often wondered what would happen if she crashed her car, leaving me alone at the house. She locked the doors from the outside when she left, so I couldn't get out on my own. I had the phone, but who would I call? What would I even tell them without a voice?

My food became dry sandwiches and water. Occasionally, there would be a TV-dinner, or some Spam or something else that vaguely resembled meat. There might be some dry pasta, or, with any luck, some premade tomato sauce. And if I got *very* lucky, there would be cheese too.

I had trained myself to listen for the telltale signs of Mom heading to the basement, bumping into walls and doors as she went. As soon as the door closed, I would sneak downstairs and get whatever food was available, hoping and praying that she would be sober enough to go shopping soon and bring back something edible.

She grew very skinny during those days, like some of the drug addicts I saw on police shows, but heroin was not her crutch. She simply forgot to eat or take care of herself.

Television became my escape. There was this cop show about policemen on bikes in L.A. which I loved, called *C.H.i.P.S.*, and even though the storylines were always the same, it made me feel as if I were part of a city far beyond my reach.

I avoided the news, since everything out there seemed so horrible. There was always war and murder and drama, and I had enough drama to last me a lifetime.

Sometimes I'd catch a glimpse of that Ted Bundy guy and get an idea of what he'd done. Apparently, he had murdered a number of young women, and they seemed to believe that there had been a lot more than that. It struck me as odd that someone could murder people for years without getting caught.

Death was something that scared and intrigued me at the same time. I often thought of death as a release from this life I was forced into, but I was also scared to find out what being dead actually meant.

I often wondered what would happen to me if Mom died. She was my sole caretaker, and with her gone I wouldn't even know how to buy clothes. I just wore what she gave me, a wardrobe consisting of T-shirts, sweaters, and sweatpants. I wore thick socks over my cold feet, day in, day out, even during summer. During winter, I would wear three layers of clothes because Mom didn't heat the house. She said it was too expensive and that I had to make do with clothes and blankets. Sometimes I could see my breath in the room.

Mom never bothered to dress up, either. She went through life wearing the same things I did: plain T-shirts and sweatpants. She looked old for her age, with tons of wrinkles that she didn't bother covering with make-up or lotion. Her grayish-blonde hair ran in strains down her shoulders.

She only showered once per week. Her body odor grew fiercer each day, a mix of sweat and alcohol. All of her days were the same, and she became emotionless. Her voice was bland, her actions slow, her words scarce. Not too few, not too many – just enough to say what she needed to. She didn't ask me what I wanted for breakfast, like those moms in those soap operas did. I was lucky to find a pop tart, or maybe some bread. When she still cooked, she would make mac and cheese or spaghetti. We would eat some of it and she would freeze the rest, or keep it in the fridge until it started smelling sour.

She had used to stack the fridge with microwave meals, but those days had passed. I dreamt of peanut butter and jelly sandwiches, because people on television talked about them all the time. She never bought peanut butter or jelly. She just bought bread and butter, and I had to eat the same loaf until the bag was empty and it became tasteless and hard to swallow.

She was a mystery to me. She hated me, but sometimes, she seemed to love me too, like when she gave me my library room, or – as reluctant as she was – a television.

I didn't understand why she hated me so much. I mean, I didn't ask to be born. She was the one who had brought me into this world. Why would she have wanted a child if she seemed to dislike the concept of motherhood so much?

3

When I was sixteen years old, I found a picture of Mom while rummaging through her bedroom.

I was in a rebellious state of mind after an argument with her about my education. She wanted me to do math, but I hated it, so she took away all my other books except for that textbook and told me to do my assignments.

I used sign language to tell her to *fuck off*. There weren't actually any swear words in my sign language book, so I had invented my own.

She still understood, and she was so upset that she left me there and took off to the store, threatening to not come back until late in the evening, and that I'd better be ready to apologize for my behavior.

I ran after her and tried to pry the door open before she could lock it, but she was faster than I was and slammed it in my face, bolting it from the outside. I pounded the wooden door hard while silently screaming that I wanted to leave.

Of course, no one could hear me.

I ran back upstairs, locking myself in my bedroom until my heart stopped pounding so hard and I felt I could breathe again. When rational thinking returned, I decided that I needed to escape this hell my parents had forced upon me, even if I didn't have the key to my own front door or any means to get out.

I knew that running away would be stupid. It would

probably mean certain death, especially in a world where there seemed to be so many human monsters snatching children off the streets. I wouldn't survive a day without money, but I couldn't stay.

So, while Mom was out, I snuck into her bedroom to search for money. I figured that I just needed a couple hundred dollars to get me to a major city, like Dallas or Chicago, where I could find a job waiting tables or something.

Instead, I found a photo of her in her nightstand, and it shook me. This was undoubtedly mom, but she looked completely different. It was a black-and-white picture from a beach somewhere, and she was smiling broadly and carelessly into the camera. On the back of the photo was a year scribbled down. *1954.* I could hardly believe that she had once seemed so carefree. What happened to her to turn her into this dark and brooding woman?

Her name was written on the back: "Eileen Harris, Miami, Florida."

At that moment, I saw her as more than just a mom, more than just my caretaker. She was a person just like me, with hopes and dreams, with fears and regrets.

I never ran away. I placed the photo back where it was, vowing to do better from now on. I wanted her to love me, to treat me like I was the most precious girl in the world. And in return, I wanted her to be a carefree woman. A loving wife. An amazing mother.

I naively told myself that we would find common ground, so that we could become a real mother and daughter, best friends. Perhaps that would make her life better too. Maybe she would finally learn how to love me.

But that never happened.

That photo was the one thing that kept me at home. It

gave me some ridiculous hope that things could get better if I set my mind to it.

Today, I no longer believe in miracles. I know now where her disdain for me stems from. And that it all started with him.

Sometimes I wonder if I should just call him Father, if he would prefer that. It sounds too religious in my head, so I stick to Dad. The outside world called him Jack. Mom did too. Jack. *Jack Jenkins.* It sounded like a news reporter, or one of those guys that babbled on about sports.

Dad was a man of routine. A traveling salesman with a strict itinerary, provided to him by the head office in Dallas. He worked for a company called Brightsweep Industries, which employed over five thousand people countrywide. Or so Dad said.

Every Sunday afternoon, he checked in with Dot, the company's secretary, who gave him the following week's schedule. They would go back and forth about the products, and he would double-check if there were any particular items he needed to sell more of that week if they had leftover stock of product X or Y.

In the past, all of this happened by fax, and he needed to head to the post office downtown to get the necessary documents, but things often went wrong, and he would spend hours fretting over whatever mistakes had been made at HQ. He thought the Sunday afternoon calls an improvement, even though I was pretty sure that Dot didn't approve of her time being interrupted by calls from various traveling salesmen, of which there were plenty.

Mom asked at some point why the hell Dot had to work

on a weekend, to which Dad said, "The new guy wants it. He wants us all to start selling as early as 8am Monday. 'No time to waste, folks,' he'll say. 'Time is money.' The guy is a bloodsucking vampire. He always wants more. More this, more that. More new products to learn about. He's a fucking lunatic. When does he ever sleep?"

Dad avoided the Dallas office, except for the annual Christmas party. He also avoided his managers, and he'd had many over the years. He was one of the oldest traveling salesmen at the office, having started as early as 1947.

He mailed his weekly sales invoices from the local post office in a big brown envelope with CONFIDENTIAL stamped on it. When he had signed a big contract that needed urgent attention, he would use the fax machine so the office clerks would have it on Monday morning.

There was a local sales office in Kansas City, but he never bothered to go there, either. There was no need to, as everything he needed to sell was shipped to our house, from samples, brochures, files, invoicing sheets, and travel journals. Everything came in brown boxes that were stacked in his office upstairs or in that part of the basement Mom and I never used.

Sometimes, a new product would be delivered to the house that would set him off about "the stupid things these idiots come up with", but he always ended up in the top ten sales ranking anyhow.

He never spoke to or of his peers, and I doubted he even knew who they were. They all had their own assigned areas, and they never interfered with each other's customers. The competition was tough, but no one ever crossed the line.

Sometimes, when someone passed away or retired, he would take over their area, since no one else wanted to do it. He often disparaged young people for being lazy and stupid, contemplating how messed up the world would be after his 'hard-working' generation died.

My dad loved the travel; he thrived on it. For a little over thirty-three years, he had been going to the same towns on the same week of each year, adjusting easily when taking over new routes. He would stay at the same motel, talk to the same people, sell an updated version of whatever product they already had in their homes, or sell something new that was claimed to be revolutionary.

He always mocked his customers when he came home, using those strained Friday night dinners to go off about one or another in particular. He called his clients idiots with too much money. But those idiots paid for this house and my life, as bleak as it was.

He usually left on Sunday evening or, on rare occasions, Monday mornings, depending on the distance he had to travel. We had two cars, one old and battered, and one paid for by the company. He might drive up to six hours on a Sunday evening with light traffic to reach his destination.

He didn't like to fly, but sometimes he had to, mostly when he went out to the East or West Coast. He didn't like the West Coast. He said the people over there were arrogant sons of bitches who considered people like him idiots for still doing door-to-door sales. But once he got a foot in the door, he would sell more to them than he ever did anywhere else.

"They are the moneymakers," he would say. "They don't give a rat's ass about price. They just buy whatever they want."

Lately, though, there had been a change in him. He was getting older, and it showed. The hours and distances had started to wear him down. Since he never took a day off, or spend time with his family, or booked a vacation, the months and seasons didn't make a difference to him. He just kept at it.

He hated the festive season. He called it "a bitch" to work then, when people were too occupied with their damned turkeys and stupid family visits. If it were up to him, he would call the whole thing off and just keep on going. He was home for two days during the Christmas period, and on the road again before the end of the year. We didn't have a Christmas tree or presents; he called it a waste of money.

The day before Christmas, he went to the annual party at Dallas HQ, showed his face for a couple of hours, and headed back home. Christmas Eve was the same as every other day, as was Christmas Day. We had nothing to celebrate.

New Year's Eve was just Mom and I too, but we didn't spend it together, nor did we celebrate the end of one year and the beginning of the next. In our routine, none of it mattered. Dates were of no importance.

I imagined Dad spending the end of the year sitting in some motel, watching television while eating burgers. I couldn't imagine people inviting lonely traveling salesmen into their homes while counting down until midnight.

Apart from telephones and faxes, my dad also hated computers. He said they would rob him of his freedom one day, and he predicted that sometime in the future they would be in everyone's homes, and people would be hooked on them.

HQ had installed something called a "server", and he didn't like the fact that his superiors were now using computer data to collect and analyze their sales figures. I only understood half of it, and Dad wasn't good at explaining.

Up until then, secretaries had calculated all the sales

manually, not caring much about the total figures. They just took a look at the results, made the invoices, and went about their routine. Since most salesmen did okay, there were no evaluation meetings or changes made to the process. Not until computers entered their lives.

Those days of freedom were now gone, especially with the younger managers on board, who knew a lot about the new technology.

The company knew everything about everyone now, and they were starting to use it against them. Challenging them to do more, to earn more, to work harder. It worked on Dad's mood.

His talks with Dot became longer and harsher. He seemed flustered and upset, going on and on about how it was never good enough anymore, and how he wanted to head over to Dallas and give them all a piece of his mind. Dot challenged him to do so, but he never did.

He knew that he could be rendered obsolete at any time, and it would leave him without a job or the luxury of travel. Despite all the things he had to say about it, I knew that if he were to lose his ability to travel, he would never be the same person again.

Dad started traveling for Brightsweep Industries in 1947, when he was twenty-two years old, barely two years after World War II. He had never worked anywhere else. Brightsweep Industries was his life.

He had started out selling cleaning products, and then halfway through the sixties, electrical appliances were added to his product list – from vacuum cleaners, to coffeemakers, to whatever new electrical household appliance the company would offer next.

He always seemed to know what would sell and what

wouldn't. He was extremely good at his job, and according to his own stories, people trusted him. He just had that face.

He was invited into their homes, into their lives, and easily sold whatever he wanted. He had a huge list of steady clients he frequented annually, but he did mention that many of them had died, and their children weren't as easy.

Now, thirty-three years later, at the age of fifty-five, he was obviously unable to switch companies. He still had over ten years to go before retiring, but the constant stress was taking its toll on him. He was stuck between a rock and a hard place. I had seen him change over the years from a relatively attractive man to the person he was today.

He told me once how he used to take care of himself. He ate healthy foods, worked out, even while traveling, and always made sure that he got all the vitamins a man needed.

That all changed a couple of years ago. His black hair was gone, except for a few streaks. He started wearing glasses and stopped working out. He no longer ate well, and chose fast food instead, making him bulky around the belly.

Overall, he looked worn down. He appeared to be in his seventies instead of his fifties. He no longer had the appeal of a younger man, and his customers noticed that too. His sales numbers had gone down significantly – even though they were still higher than most. He didn't put the blame on himself though, but on society.

Even I, in my room with only a television as a window to the outside world, knew how things were changing fast. There were computers everywhere now, in all the television shows I watched. Kitchen appliances changed rapidly, and coffee wasn't just coffee anymore; it was now "café latté".

"Everything's going too fast," he said. "These things are going to replace people, and when they do, there will be futuristic robots and artificial intelligence that will wipe us all out."

I didn't understand what he was talking about until my mom reacted.

"You're watching too many science fiction movies," she said. "It won't go that fast."

"Won't it? I'm not so sure about that. I'm telling you this now, Eileen: In a hundred years, this planet will be ruins. It's a good thing we won't be around to watch it happen."

Mom rarely said anything. She mostly sat and listened while he went and on about his life, as if he had the lousiest job in the world and we should count our blessings that we had such a wonderful life.

"Always more," he ranted. "They always want more, and more, and more. More hours, more sales, more revenue. They blackmail us, tell us that our kind of job is becoming obsolete, that we can be replaced by someone cheaper. And if we don't bring in more, we're going to be finished."

Mom looked pale when he said that. I could tell she was scared that this might become our reality. I was afraid too, since all my life I had heard how Dad was the sole breadwinner of the house, and how we wouldn't survive without him.

"We're extinct. Old. Too expensive. They complain about motel costs, and gas. Focus is shifting to the local stores. Door-to-door sales is no longer the way to go, so now they're considering sending us to the stores directly. No more personal customer contact. Which is ridiculous. Do you know how many people they see a day? How hard it is to get an appointment? The small-time owners don't want us standing in the way. They want to make money; that's all that matters to them. Every dollar counts to survive. And I'll tell you what, Eileen, doing this job is no walk in the park. I hardly sleep anymore. There's always noise, and motel beds suck. I wonder if those white-collared bastards would survive one week on the road. I'd like to see them try."

"You're tired from all the traveling. Maybe it's time to call it quits," Mom proposed reluctantly.

"And do what, exactly? Yeah, I'm tired of the travel. Sick of the miles and the airports, and the fucking rear airplane seats. But what am I supposed to do if I don't have that? I'm no good working in an office. I don't even have a degree. Work at the local grocery store and lose all my financial benefits after all the hardship I put in? No way. Besides, they'd want that, wouldn't they. They'd be happy if I gave up on my own. Out with the old, in with the new. Fat chance of that happening."

Mom was clearly relieved that Dad waved off her proposal. She never made the suggestion again.

4

To this day, I'm still not sure if Dad loves me, or even likes me. I've never been able to tell. There were times he was nice to me, like when he brought me stuff from his trip. And there were times when he was completely cold towards me, as if I reminded him of something he had long lost.

My parents weren't teenagers when I was born. They weren't forced to get married. In fact, they had been together for many years before I came into this world. And they both had one thing in common: they would gaze at me bewildered sometimes, as if to figure out who I was and why I lived in their house.

It was the oddest thing to live with people who obviously didn't like or care about their daughter. And I had no one who I could ask questions about them, so I relied on their scarce stories.

When I was about thirteen, if I recall correctly, I asked Mom how she and Dad came to be a couple. I had written down my question, curious about their relationship and how it all began. She shrugged and didn't say anything until one day shortly after, while we were sitting at the kitchen table having mac and cheese.

"You asked how we met?" she said, and I could tell she'd had a bit of wine. A bit tipsy, she'd become loose lipped, and I took advantage of that moment.

I nodded excitedly, wanting to find out more about them.

"To be honest, I barely remember. Your dad and I met back in Florida. We were both living in this small town near Miami. It wasn't much, just a couple of houses, some shops, a supermarket, you know. It was tiny. Anyhow, since there were hardly any kids living there, the few that did tended to hang out together. We kind of became an item because that was what people expected of us."

And? I signed. *Love?*

"Oh, God no," she said, laughing, as if I had said the oddest thing. "We married because we had to."

Why?

"He knocked me up when I was eighteen."

I stared at her. This was the last thing I had ever expected.

I had a... sibling?

She didn't understand the word sibling, so I wrote it down. She looked at it, stared at me and tried to comprehend what I was asking. Then it dawned on her.

"Oh, no, no. I lost the baby when I was six months pregnant. We got married when I started showing, which was about three months before that. In those days – well, I suppose it's still the same – pregnant girls were pressured by their family to marry. So we got married and moved here. In the end, it didn't even matter. My family kicked me out once I got married, because the whole town knew about it and my father lost half of his clientèle. See, he was a banker, and I was the town's little princess. Until Jack, a fisherman's son, came along and fucked my life up."

I was startled. Sad. Shocked.

It also explained a lot.

I'm so sorry.

"Well, I'm not," she said harshly, while stirring her dinner. "I wasn't ready to raise a family."

Until I came.

"What?" She looked at me bewildered, until it dawned on her what I had said. "Oh, yeah, right. Until you. But that was some time later. It took a while. I had three miscarriages before you came along."

I felt sorry for her, but I also didn't understand why she would treat me the way she did when she had lost four children, no matter how far gone she was. Would I not be her dreamchild? Would she not pamper me to compensate for all she'd lost?

Do you miss the baby?

"What?"

Again, she couldn't follow my hands, so I wrote it down for her.

"Why would I? It was stillborn. A freak of nature. Something was wrong with it, and it didn't have a right to life. It wouldn't have survived its first year. Nope, better off dead, I'd say."

I didn't want to point out the obvious, that I was a freak of nature too. That I was born without an ability to speak and would probably spend the rest of my life this way. But I didn't write it down, nor did she say it herself. My poor mom, stuck in this loveless relationship, had been trapped twice in her life.

And Dad? Well, that was his story to tell, but he never did. I was at a loss when it came to understanding him. He was strict, firm, sharp, often harsh, always rude. He must have hated his life as much as Mom did, but he still took care of things.

There were times he would come home, sit at the kitchen table, and then look at me and smile.

"You look just like your mother," he would say. "I should have paid more attention to you. I'm sorry."

Love you, Dad, I would sign. But he didn't understand a single word of the language, and he would always look away when I used it.

"Notepad," he would murmur.

I love you, Dad, I'd write, and he would smile and lean forward, almost touching my hand. But he never did. He never once touched me, just like Mom. The only times they must have was when I was a baby. You couldn't care for a child without holding it, after all.

Sometimes I wanted to cry and plead with him to take me away from this place, but I never did. He kept me locked in here with Mom, and he even told her that I was never to go outside.

"She has all she needs in the house. Don't let her see anyone."

"You know I won't," she would say.

My upbringing seemed to be the only thing they had in common. They both sucked at it.

Dad came home unexpectedly on my twenty-fourth birthday. Mom had given me some books and a few records, since I didn't need anything more. She also brought me a record player. My own record player. I was ecstatic.

She was bleary-eyed and apologetic. "I'm sorry that I can't take better care of you. It'll get better someday. Just you wait and see."

I didn't respond. I was at an age at where I wasn't expecting anything more from life than what it had given me so far. It was a perfect birthday really, with my new record player and albums, even if I hadn't chosen them myself.

I was lying on the bed listening to the music when Dad

suddenly burst into the room. He walked straight to me, sunk on the bed, and stroked my hair. His thumb brushed past my face. It was the first touch I'd felt in as long as I could remember, but it didn't seem right.

His eyes were dilated. There was an odd scent on his breath. He pushed me down on the bed, lying on my back, and kept his hand on my neck. I couldn't protest with words, and he had pinned both hands, so I couldn't sign, either.

"You're so pretty," he slurred, while his hand slid from my hair to my back. I didn't dare move.

"My beautiful girl."

The gentle whisper of his voice sounded as if it was meant to be comforting, but I only felt fear. It was so physical.

"You're the reason I still come home, Alice. Just you. You're extraordinary; remember that always."

He leaned forward and kissed my cheek while his hand roamed down my back and between my legs. I cringed. It was the worst feeling ever.

Mom flew into the room and pulled him away from me. Her actions were so out of character that both Dad and I were shaken.

"What the fuck do you think you're doing?" she screamed as she threw him out of the room. My bedroom door remained open.

He nearly stumbled down the stairs but managed to stop and compose himself. She pushed him again. He stood steady on his feet.

"What the f– You're stoned." Her words sounded sharp as a knife. "You're disgusting."

He tried to find the right words to calm her down, but nothing would come. "You're one to speak. You're drunk again," he muttered.

"At least I know I am. Why are you back? Did you drive like this? You could have killed someone, and then what, huh?" she shouted at him.

I sat up on the bed, watching them, and felt tears drip down my face. They were supposed to protect me, but all they did was hurt me.

Why did I continue to exist?

What good was this life if nothing made sense?

"Go downstairs. Sober up. You won't come back upstairs until you've got your senses back," Mom snapped. "Do you hear me?"

"Yeah, yeah," he mumbled, before stumbling down the stairs.

To my surprise, he did what she said, no questions asked, no further remarks given. Instead, he left the house, slamming the door.

Mom walked back into my room and looked at me, noticing my tears.

"That will never happen again," she said, and she shut the door.

I looked at the record player on the shelf and the stack of albums she had given me and knew I could never play them again. They would always remind me of the moment that my dad became a threat to me.

PART TWO
Hailey

5

"We're getting new neighbors. They're moving in soon," Mom said, two weeks after my twenty-fourth birthday.

Since *that* day, we had returned to normal life, as if none of it had happened. Dad didn't come home that night. In fact, he didn't come back for three days. And then Friday night came, and he showed up as if everything was 'normal'. All we could do was pretend it had been a bad dream.

He hadn't tried to touch me since. He hadn't even spoken one word to me. He avoided being in the same room as me as much as possible, and when we were together, Mom was there.

We only had neighbors on one side of the house, and I hadn't even known that they had moved out. It was September, at the end of a long, hot summer, and people were back to their regular routine.

"Shit," Dad said.

"Do you want me to do something about it?" Mom asked.

"What can you do?"

"Nothing, really. Just tell them from the start to mind their own fucking business."

Dad glanced at me briefly while running his hands over his balding scalp. "Just make sure they don't wind up standing on our doorstep with a stupid cake or something," Dad said. "No exchanging baked goods or any other crap. Why the fuck didn't Tom say he was moving out? Fucking asshole."

"It's not like we were friendly with each other."

"He could have at least warned us. Who's moving in?"

"Some young woman. I'm guessing she's about twenty-five, twenty-six? Pretty girl."

I wondered where Mom could have picked up that information. The grocery store, perhaps, or she might have met the new neighbor while getting the mail from the mailbox.

"She's working downtown in some clothing shop."

"And she's here all by herself? Can she afford it?"

"I guess so. I didn't ask."

"You talked to her?!" Dad exclaimed.

"Of course not. Margaret told me all about it. She's from out of town and rented the house before it even came on the market. She had some inside information."

Margaret was the store clerk. She freely threw around gossip, or so Mom said.

I kept my thoughts to myself, but I couldn't hide my excitement that something new was happening, even if I was already sure I wouldn't be allowed contact with our new neighbor. At least we had something to discuss other than Dad's job or Mom's desire for new drapes.

Suddenly, Dad looked at me, for the first time in days, and scowled. "Why are you acting so smug?" he said, leaning over. "Don't think for a moment you'll be allowed to talk to her."

I nodded meekly.

Dad shoved his chair backwards and moved his plate to the sink, with only half of his meal eaten. He was visibly angry, standing there with his hands balled into fists, gazing at me as if he was contemplating hitting me.

Mom immediately stood up, tense and ready like a guard, looking at him with warning in her eyes.

"Don't." That's all she said. But I knew what it meant. *Don't you dare touch your daughter.*

For the first time in my life, I realized that she wasn't just watching me: She was watching *him*.

He blinked. "I need to head to the post office; I've got some things to send to the company."

We both knew he was going there to find out more about the girl moving in. He wouldn't rest until he was certain she would not try to connect with us.

Mom and I gazed at each other after he left. My hands shook, but so did hers.

"Finish your dinner," she said. "You need to eat more. You're all skin and bones."

I ate every last bite of her tasteless meal as quickly as I could, shoving the food in my mouth and swallowing it so fast that it hurt. I put the plate in the sink and fled the kitchen, ran up the stairs, escaped into my room and shut the door.

I walked over to the smaller of my two bedroom windows and stared past the trees to the neighbor's house, wondering who was hidden behind the glass. Someone normal. Someone with a *life*. Someone who probably had a normal family.

I longed so badly for a friend, someone real. Someone I could communicate with, who could give me some respite from this life I had been forced into. But that would never happen for as long as my parents were alive.

Even if I had wanted to, I wouldn't have been able to contact the stranger. The trees would forever block my view; our property would remain as secluded as ever. No one would ever know I was here.

But I was wrong.

* * *

I woke up the next morning to find a bunch of men climbing into the trees, taking down all the branches one by one. The men hadn't seen me yet, but it was just a matter of time before they noticed a girl in the window.

And then, for the first time, I suddenly had a view of the neighboring house.

Mom ran into my bedroom and shut the drapes.

"Be very still," she warned me. "Don't you dare draw attention to yourself."

I sunk down onto the bed in the darkness of my room, and Mom stayed with me as my watchdog. We listened in silence to the work until the sounds stopped. We heard vehicles leave.

"You stay put," Mom ordered, and she left.

I debated between reading in my library room and staying in the bedroom, and finally decided that television was the only thing that could alleviate the strain, but I couldn't focus on anything other than what was going on outside.

Hours later, long after the noise had subsided, I opened the drapes once again and peeked at the two large windows of the house on the other side of the fence.

But there also was a change within my own room. For the first time, I had sunlight streaming through the windows. Mom came in, obviously startled by the bright light.

"Goddamn," she said, and stomped out of the room again. She came back an hour later.

"You're moving to the basement bedroom. Pack up your things. Take only what is necessary."

Noooo!!!!!!!

I made furious gestures.

I won't go. I won't go! You can't make me go!

She looked at me as if I had lost my mind.

"I don't know what the fuck you're trying to tell me, but I won't take 'no' for an answer, Alice. You're moving."

I took a pen and a notepad and scribbled so fast the pen broke in half.

I won't go. You can't make me.

"You have to."

I'll kill myself.

She stared at me in shock, rattled by my words. My mom was always a harsh and cold person, but this time she looked at me with something that could be described as pity, and she caved in immediately.

Her shoulders sagged. She looked defeated.

"Alright," she said. "You can stay upstairs during the week. For now. But your dad can never know. Do you understand?"

Yes, I signed.

"Good. You'll have to sleep in the basement when he's home."

I nodded furiously.

Thank you, I signed. *Thank you, thank you.*

"Don't thank me yet. If he finds out, he'll kill us both."

I didn't care. I flung myself into her arms and hugged her impulsively. She pushed me away so fast and hard, that I stumbled backwards. She glared at me coldly.

"From now on, the drapes remain shut. Is that clear? I don't want to catch you opening them. *Ever.*"

I nodded my agreement, but I wasn't planning on keeping that promise. It would just become another one of my many secrets.

Over the course of years, I had developed sensitive

hearing, so I knew when Mom was coming up the stairs before she even set her foot on the first creaking step. Plus, her drinking came in handy. She constantly wavered on her feet, lurching and stepping heavily.

From that moment on, whenever I heard her coming upstairs, I would close the drapes quietly, as if darkness was my best friend. She would find me lying on the bed, reading under a light, or in the library room, far away from the neighbor's windows. The moment she walked out again, I reopened them, all too eager to bask in the sun.

Every weekend, I would move downstairs and pretend it was my new room. Dad had never bothered to come down there before, but now he did. He saw some of my things scattered around the room, took a quick look at the book in my hand, smiled briefly, and said, "Good girl. This won't be for long, I promise. I'm trying to figure out a way to put up some high privacy screens. That damned landlord should never have taken down those trees."

The trees were on their property, not ours, so it wasn't his call to make. But Dad could do whatever he wanted on *his* turf, and he was planning on doing just that.

All that time, there was still no sign of our new neighbor, and I started to believe that I would never get to see her at all. How wrong I was.

6

It was a warm Tuesday afternoon in September, and I was sitting in my favorite rocking chair by the window with my legs pulled up, engrossed in Stephen King. The drapes were open; Mom was out cold in the basement bedroom, and Dad would be back on Friday, as usual.

It became so hot in my bedroom that I put my book down and pried open the smaller window to let as much air in as possible.

Just then, my eye caught something. A moving shadow, a figure out of place. And there she was, like a vision of an angel, standing in front of her bedroom window that suddenly didn't seem so far away anymore.

I could have been watching a goddess; the sight of her felt that special to me. She was the first living creature I had seen for so long. She had a beautiful face, long, dark hair, and a slim figure. She was simply stunning in her white T-shirt that read *The Cure* underneath the face of some pale guy with makeup and pitch-black hair.

I could have watched her there forever.

It felt as if my television had come to life. Like those folks on talk shows or game shows who played to win a big amount of money, who looked so smart and radiant and happy.

They were normal people. People who had the best lives, who had family to celebrate with them when they won – or to support them when they lost.

People who wore normal clothes that fit them. Who went to hairdressers, instead of having their hair cut by their mother with a pair of kitchen scissors.

People who didn't spend long hours reading and rereading books in their rooms, as if there was no world outside.

People who didn't look pale, almost translucent.

People who ate normal food and were able to go to supermarkets to pick out whatever they wanted.

People who ate meals they enjoyed, instead of ones they despised, that all looked and tasted the same.

People who had a normal father, and a non-alcoholic mother.

The woman next door was all that, and probably more.

Or perhaps, a part of me thought, she was like me and just hid it better. Perhaps she, too, didn't belong in this world.

Who are you? I signed, but she didn't see. When she turned around and shut the drapes, I was out of sight. She didn't look at my windows once.

The next morning there was no movement in the other house. The drapes were closed. There was no light inside. She could have gone out early, or maybe she was sleeping in late. Either way, it was none of my business.

I forced myself to ignore the house, just like I had always done. The other neighbors hadn't cared about us at all, so why should she? We were just a house full of people she didn't know. Why would be interested in us?

I spent my day watching television, switching from soap operas to game shows to talk shows. I loved watching people talk. I loved commercials, too. People could talk for hours about detergents or whatever new kitchen appliance would make a woman's life so much better. I loved seeing conversations between parents and their children.

The day crept by until the evening arrived. There still hadn't been any movement in the other house. I had kept the drapes open all day, hoping to catch a glimpse of her, should she ever come back.

I had dozed off in front of the television, so I forced myself into the bed for a decent nap, but any chance of further sleep seemed to evade me.

And then, there was movement. The drapes were open, and there she was again, standing in front of her window, undressing. I saw her bare back as she removed her bra and slipped a dress over her head. She pulled her hair together and then let it slide down her back, shaking it a bit so it fell perfect again.

I couldn't pull my eyes away.

But then she turned around and caught me standing in front of the window, watching her.

Her expression betrayed her surprise. It carried a mixture of curiosity and shock, as if she had just noticed our house for the very first time.

I thought she was going to flip me the finger, like people did on TV when something happened they didn't like, but she didn't.

She smiled gently.

She waved.

For a split second, I felt so dizzy I thought I might pass out. I was *not* invisible.

I waved back.

For years, I had obeyed every single rule my parents had made for me. That day I defied them all.

That day, I smiled at a complete stranger.

7

I had once read this book that stated that things always happened for a reason. That one door opens when another one closes. Perhaps this was such an event. Maybe our former neighbors leaving and giving way to someone new was going to be a life-changer.

But I was not ready for it.

On impulse, I closed the drapes but left the window open. I caught one final glimpse of the girl next door, and that was it. I returned to the dark with shaking legs and a pounding heart.

Stress and panic washed over me. I sunk back in my rocking chair and dropped my hardback on the floor. A hard thud resounded through the house. I waited in panic for Mom to come flying up the staircase, but she didn't. It remained quiet.

Nothing happened. There was no change in the room, no sudden crumbling of walls and ceilings. I hadn't been caught in this horrible act of disobedience. The panic died down quickly.

I picked up the book and ignored the dent in its cover while I held it on my lap, rocking gently back and forth.

Mom didn't need to know that I had waved at someone. How would she ever find out? If I didn't allow this to happen again, we could forget the whole thing.

The woman next door wouldn't think anything of it. She

had merely seen a shadow, an image, a vision of someone living here. This brief encounter would not send her knocking on our front door to become my new best friend.

I kept the drapes shut and pushed every thought of her out of my mind. For the rest of the day, I watched television, listening at the same time for any foreign sound.

Nothing came.

The next morning I was up early. I had forgotten about the open window, and the sound of the garbage truck on its weekly route woke me up.

I opened the drapes not expecting to see her, but there she was, with her back towards the window. She was getting dressed again; I could see her bare back and white underwear before she pulled a dress over her head.

I closed the drapes feeling embarrassed.

That evening, I left the drapes open on purpose so I could watch her coming home. Her car pulled in around 7pm and she walked into the house. It seemed she lived there alone.

A few moments later, lights turned on upstairs and she walked into her bedroom, throwing her bag on the bed before pulling her dress over her head and replacing it with a T-shirt and trousers.

She turned around. I didn't flinch this time. I stood there, watching her watch me. She must have known that I saw her get changed. I felt flushed, caught.

She waved again.

I waved back.

I had been skulking around my two rooms all day, cleaning the bookshelves and rearranging my extensive collection, secretly hoping she would come home sooner, but she never did.

Of course she wouldn't. She would probably be working or studying, or enjoying whatever it was that people my age should be doing. And she would have forgotten about me, just like she would forget about me now.

But instead of closing her curtains, she opened her window and leaned out, waving once again. We were still many yards apart, but that didn't stop her from calling out to me.

"Hey," she said. "What's your name?"

Her voice was sweet and clear. I closed my eyes briefly, taking in the sound of someone else's tone. It was strong but not intimidating. It had a softness without being too gentle. Composed, perhaps. Self-assured, like those women who performed in soap operas. It sounded trustworthy.

"Did you hear me?"

I nodded.

"What's your name?" she repeated.

I couldn't respond, so I waved my hands, making gestures that may or may not have made sense to her.

She seemed to understand.

"Are you using sign language?"

I nodded enthusiastically.

"But you can understand what I'm saying?"

I nodded again and touched my throat.

"Ah! You can hear, but you can't speak; is that it?"

I nodded again, ridiculously happy she understood and didn't slam her window shut.

"Open your window further," she said. "Can you do that?"

I nodded again and pried open the window, shoving my

skinny form through it. Every movement was thrilling, and I wondered if I would pass out from pure excitement. Did people do that? They did in movies, but in real life? I wouldn't know.

I leaned outside, while at the same time trying to focus on any sounds coming from inside the house. I was alone. Or so I felt. Mom was out cold down in the basement; I hadn't seen her since lunch. Still, I kept my ears open.

I studied the young woman carefully. She must have been about my age, but the differences between us couldn't have been greater. I had red hair, but not the beautiful glossy red I always saw on TV. My skin was almost translucent from lack of sun, and my face was sunken and small. I didn't wear makeup, and I had no clothes that could make me even remotely beautiful.

I considered myself plain, especially when I compared myself to actresses, who were always gorgeous. I knew that their beauty was mostly due to the magic of makeup, but still... There were people out there with tanned skin and curled highlighted hair. Girls who wore skirts and wide blouses with wavy sleeves. Girls who looked like they could command the world with a wave of their hand. Who could flash their teeth and draw any boy's attention.

Those girls really existed, and this one was living proof. She was stunning. She had gorgeous, light eyes that contrasted beautifully with her dark hair. She had a small nose and a beautiful mouth with full lips. She was wearing makeup, and she wore that *The Cure* T-shirt again with the scruffy pale guy's face on it over light-blue jeans with wide legs. Big looping earrings, that I had also seen on television, completed the look.

I wore my regular, dark – way too big – sweatpants that

hung loosely around my hips, and a T-shirt that was narrow around the waist and chest. I had worn that thing for years and I refused to give it up once my chest started growing because I loved it so much. I didn't even know why it meant so much to me. I preferred to wear my older clothes instead of the newer things that never seemed to fit properly. I suppose there was something familiar about them, in how they looked and smelled. When I asked my mom where they came from, she said they were hers, and she had kept them for me to wear someday.

"I'm Hailey," the woman called out. "What's your name? Can you tell me somehow?"

I thought about her request and retreated into my room, where I grabbed a marker and a piece of paper. In big, bold letters I wrote *ALICE.*

She smiled. "Alice; that's a beautiful name. Were you named after Alice in Wonderland?"

I shrugged – I didn't know where my name came from. I knew the story, of course. Alice who follows the white rabbit down the hole, and of the vicious Queen of Hearts. Of the potion that shrunk her, and the cake that made her taller. I had read it years ago from an old, tattered copy in my room. It had felt oddly familiar, as if someone had read it to me years ago.

I didn't really like the story; it was psychedelic and bizarre. Plus, the queen frightened me to death. I'd often had dreams about her where she screamed at her guards to cut my head off. The story felt like a representation of my life. I was running through mazes too, trying to find an exit that didn't exist.

"Can you do sign language?" Hailey asked.

I nodded.

"I'm taking that as a yes," she said, laughing.

I pointed at her. *You?*

She understood. "Unfortunately, no, but I'm willing to learn. It can't be that hard, right?"

I shrugged; I had mastered it when I was a kid.

"Got it," she said. "I mean, if someone starts to learn a new language, it's hard to predict how long it will take to communicate, right?"

I stuck my two thumbs up. She laughed.

"I'll learn," she said. "But be patient with me, alright? Don't laugh at me when I mess it all up."

I stared at her dumbfounded. Why would a total stranger want to spend time learning a new language in order to communicate with someone she didn't even know?

She started talking, and I listened. She said how important it was to communicate in this world, and how it should be her making the effort, not me.

I couldn't help but stare. She was radiant, like a sole star in a dark sky. I made a gesture that stopped her chattering, and used my marker and paper to write, *I will teach you.*

Her smile lit up her face.

"Thank you," she said. "I would love that."

8

I had never been happier in my life.

Everything changed when Hailey moved in next door. She was the missing link in my existence, my means of experiencing what regular life was, even if she still had no idea what mine was like. I only told her bits and pieces.

Every single day for two weeks – except the weekends when Dad was home – we communicated through our windows. She used her words while I used my hands, which was a painstakingly slow process, but I really didn't care, nor did she seem to. She was enthralled by my use of sign language and absorbed every gesture like a sponge.

After a few days, she had mastered the same basic words Mom had taken years to learn. She understood when I asked things like *How are you?* or *How was work?* or *Television?* That would send her into a whole rant about how good of a show such-and-such was, or how bad a talk show this-and-that was.

She liked to talk about her job. She worked in a high-end retail store I'd never heard of. I hadn't seen the inside of a store in my life, but I hadn't told her that yet. I just nodded and smiled when she went on and on about whatever brand she was selling. I couldn't distinguish anything expensive from anything cheap anyhow.

She talked about her manager, who was apparently a local celebrity. They had won a pageant – I knew what that was from TV – but they obviously hated people and looked down on everyone who came shopping in the store. Still, she hid it pretty well, because customers meant money, and she loved having money to spend.

Hailey was a fast learner, obviously quite bright. When she didn't understand me, I wrote down what I meant, which I later tore up into the tiniest bits possible before burying them at the bottom of the trash bin.

If Mom had known that we were communicating, she would have sealed my windows shut before moving me into the basement bedroom forever. She would have killed me.

But she didn't know.

Mom's hours were spent binging. I didn't know why it had gotten so bad. It all seemed to lead back to the night of my birthday. Something had clicked in her head that day. Or maybe her pain had always been there, and now she had simply given up.

She barely went to the store anymore. She mustered the strength to go once a week, didn't buy a lot of food, and when she did, it was mostly jam and toast, and – if I was lucky – some butter. Our hot meals were reduced to twice per week. Once on Friday, when Dad came home, and once on Saturday, which consisted of Friday's leftovers.

I was so hungry all the time, and I lost a lot of weight. I could tell by the way my clothes hung off my frame. Hailey seemed to notice it too. She soon started asking questions. I knew that would happen at some point. I couldn't blame Hailey. She was just curious; I was mostly surprised it had taken two weeks for her to start prodding into my life. Then again, our conversations had been sparse to begin with, since she was always away during the day and came home after our dinner. Which was perfect, really, since Mom would be downstairs drinking herself to sleep.

"Can I ask you something?" Hailey said.

Anything.

"I was wondering about your condition."

Yes?

"How come you can't speak?"

I don't know.

"Are you sick?"

I don't know.

"But there must be a reason why you don't have a voice."

I don't know.

"You must have seen a doctor, right?"

I shrugged. *I guess.*

"Hm."

When Hailey thought about things, she became quiet and withdrawn, and bit at her fingernails.

"What did your parents tell you?"

Nothing.

"Nothing?!"

Yes.

"Do they..." She stopped. "Do they... I know it sounds crazy saying it out loud, but I've been wondering about this for a while. Alice, do they keep you locked up?"

My expression must have betrayed my feelings. I had kept my life under wraps, not wanting her to believe I was an incarcerated lunatic. But she must have realized that something was wrong with me. Everyone would.

Not locked up.

"Then, what?"

I don't know.

"Why can't we meet outside? I've asked you a couple of

times. It would be so much easier than hanging out of our windows. Why won't you come to the front door? I could come over."

No!!!!!!!!!!

I shut the window frantically and closed the drapes. This could *not* happen. I had taken it too far.

My heart raced; panic overwhelmed me. If she were to come over now, my mom would find out we had been talking. She would tell my dad, and I would be sent to the basement bedroom for the rest of my life.

I ran to the library room, shut the door, and paced so fast I got dizzy. When I ran out of steam, I dropped to the floor, heaving and feeling so heavy I thought I would never be able to get up again.

I had lost Hailey.

I had lost the one person in my life worth talking to.

She would never speak to me again.

Lying on the carpet, tears dripped from my face onto the wool surface. I fell asleep.

9

I didn't open my drapes for three days. I was too scared to find out Hailey would ignore me from now on, that I would be forced to watch her from afar and mourn the talks we'd had, realizing I would never have them again.

Thankfully, she hadn't come knocking on the door. She hadn't inquired if I was okay. I wasn't so sure if that was a good or a bad sign. In the end, I took it as an end to a friendship that had barely begun.

But when I opened the drapes again on the fourth day, trapped between grief and hope, she was there. She stood in front of her window watching me, as if she had been waiting all this time.

She opened her window, but I kept mine shut. My eyes were puffy and red from crying, and I had lost some more weight having not eaten, and I knew I was a mess. I didn't need a mirror to tell me that.

She called out to me, but I barely heard what she said. Then, to my surprise, she made gestures with her hands that formed words. She had been studying!

Please open the window.

I hesitated.

Please.

I opened the window.

"I'm so sorry," she said. "I'm so fucking sorry for asking you to talk about things you weren't ready for. I am really, really sorry. Please forgive me."

I was in shock. Hailey, asking *me* for forgiveness?

Thank you, I signed back. *I'm sorry too.*

"Can you please forget the whole thing and go back to the way we were? I've missed you so much. You're my only friend in this town and I missed talking to you. I've had to resist knocking at your door, but I figured your parents would be pretty mad."

Thank you.

"Are you okay?"

I nodded.

"You look so sad."

I raised my hands to sign but stopped. If I told her what I was thinking, she'd run away screaming.

"What?" she asked.

I've missed you, too.

Her smile broke. She was so beautiful. I wanted to hug her so badly, and tell her to come get me out of this damned house. But where would I go? I didn't want to be a burden to her.

"I won't ever ask about your parents again."

But I did want her to know. I *had* to tell her. But how? It would take forever to explain my situation to her. And would she even want to hear it all?

"Alice...?"

I looked at her.

"Do you want me to know?"

I took a deep breath. *I do.*

"Can you tell me?"

Yes.

"How?"

I thought things through and signed, *I will write.*

"You'll write it all down?"

I nodded.

"That would definitely help," she said, sounding relieved. "I would love to find out more about you. You're so wonderful, Alice. I don't understand why you're cooped up in that house as if there's something wrong with you. There isn't, you know. You're so nice, and you're obviously extremely intelligent. So what if you have no voice? There are plenty of people out there with a disability who lead normal lives. Why do they keep you prisoner?"

Not a prison.

"Yes, it is. You just don't realize it," she said fiercely. "This is not living, Alice. Your parents aren't treating you right. This is abuse."

Hailey got all worked up, and she didn't seem to expect a reply from me. I was aware of what she was saying. I had always known. I just didn't know how to change it.

"You obviously need a friend. I feel goddamn useless. I'm sorry."

You are my friend.

I drew a big red heart with a smiley mouth and eyes on a piece of paper and showed it to her. She laughed. Relief washed over her face.

"I'm so happy we're talking again. Talk again tomorrow?"

I waved goodbye with a smile, but felt empty and frustrated. This was not her fault; it was mine.

The next morning, I started writing down my story. I began by explaining about my mom and dad, about the house, the homeschooling, the isolation, the lack of friends. I wrote everything down and it felt like instant therapy.

It took me two days and about a hundred sheets of paper, which I hid in a black box in my bedroom. I was slim enough to slide under the bed and remove a floorboard without even moving the furniture.

When I was done, I took the box and the tattered American Sign Language book, intending for her to have it. I just needed to wait for the right moment.

She was home on Thursday afternoon, the one day she didn't have to work. My mom was drunk out of her mind again, passed out in the downstairs bedroom. I had told her that late afternoon was the best time, and she had gone up to her bedroom to wait for my sign.

I gestured for her to head downstairs, to the backyard. All the way in the back, there was a small, locked gate. *Meet me at the garden gate*, I wrote in big bold letters, pointing down. She knew what I was talking about. It was the only place our gardens met.

I ran outside and hurried to the gate and waited for her eagerly, all the while convincing myself that she wouldn't show up. That she would finally admit to herself that this whole thing was a farce, and that she had kept me around for fun.

But she did show up.

We couldn't open the gate; it had been sealed long ago. But we did catch a glimpse of each other through the cracks in the wood, and we were able to exchange the book and the black box through a gap in the fence that she tore open.

Our fingers touched briefly.

"Thank you," she said. "This will definitely help."

I had marked the most important signs for her, and I knew that she would catch on really quickly now. But more importantly, I wanted her to know everything. It was time that someone knew.

I ran back to the house and waited in fear.

If she read my story, there would be two possible outcomes: either she would think I was pathetic, sad, and messed up, or she would understand.

I had no regrets about telling her. She was the first person outside of this house to learn that I existed, and it felt good that someone finally knew. If there was ever a fire, at least I might not burn to death now. She had given me a reason to hold on, to continue living. Now, all I could do was hope she wouldn't use it against me.

She didn't.

Hours later, she came to the window with a shocked expression on her face. She was silent and hesitant.

And then she used sign language to tell me how she felt. Slowly, but correct.

I will forever be your friend.

10

I was having an off day, and Hailey felt it the moment she opened her window. It was October 1st, and the weather was awful, a sign of bad days to come. Winter was upon us, and I was dreading it already. But that was not all that bothered me.

"What's wrong?" she called out to me.

Nothing.

"Yeah, there is. I know you better than that. What is it?"

I hesitated.

"Alice?"

I looked at my hands, unable to sign what was bothering me. It would take too long, and she wouldn't understand.

"Can you write it down?"

I shook my head while contemplating the right words. I took a deep breath and concentrated.

Dad.

"Dad?" she repeated.

Coming. Home.

"Your dad is... he's home?"

I shook my head.

Coming. Home.

"Ah, hang on."

She always put the book on the windowsill and used it to translate. She was picking it up so quickly now that we could have easy conversations.

"He's coming home? As in early?"

I nodded.

"Why? It's Wednesday."

I don't know, I signed. I made a sign like I was using the phone.

"Ah, he called?"

I nodded.

"Okay. Is he sick? Did something happen?"

Sick.

"That sucks. I hope everything's okay."

I shrugged. All I cared about was that him coming home early would ruin the rest of my week. Him being home meant no communication with Hailey, no chats in the morning or evening, or on her days off.

I often felt like a dog, suddenly able to communicate with a human being. If that were ever possible, I imagine it must feel just as significant for the animal.

"Listen, I have to get to work soon, but I'll be back tonight," Hailey said. "Will you be okay?"

Yeah.

"Are you sure? I could cancel. Make up some lame excuse."

Don't. I'm fine.

"Okay. Well, if you're sure. Just… you know, if you ever get fed up with your parents, you can stay with me. I mean, I've got plenty of room, and you're an adult, so you could just them tell them to fuck off and come here. You know?"

I was stunned. This wasn't the first time Hailey told me I had a choice, but I had never even considered this option. I didn't want to ruin our friendship or give her the impression I was using her to get out of my situation.

"You're not alone, Alice," she added. "You've got a friend now."

I burst into tears.

"Aww, don't cry."

Thank you, I signed.

"Love you," she said. "I have to go."

She waved and shut the window, and I sank down on the bed, stunned. She *loved* me? She... wait, *what*?

Of course she didn't love me *like that*. Girls didn't love each other that way... did they? I was so confused.

People used the word "love" all the time. It was as common as "bye" or "hello". It meant nothing. Of course it didn't.

But what if it did?

I had never loved someone before in my life. I didn't even know if I loved my parents. What did love mean, anyhow?

I thought about the gestures that spelled out, *I love you*. I knew them by heart. I had taught myself how to sign these three words, hoping that someday my parents would tell me they loved me, and I could say it back.

They never did.

PART THREE
Dad

11

Dad came home that Wednesday night.

It was dinnertime, which consisted of toast and jam, as was common these days. But Mom was there, and she was sober because we knew he was on his way. She still hadn't bothered cooking, and she reeked of booze because she hadn't showered for days.

As he walked through the door, I stood upright with my plate in one hand and a slice of toast in the other. Mom sat at the kitchen table, eating hers slowly. The TV in the living room was on, some game show I didn't really like.

He shed his raincoat on a chair, leaving it to drip water onto the floor. He didn't say hello, and barely even noticed me leaning against the countertop. He ignored Mom, too. He just stood there, bags in hand, looking at nothing.

"Why did you come back so soon?" Mom asked, her voice strained.

"I'm dying."

Dad dropped his travel bag and briefcase to the floor and sat down on his favorite kitchen stool, barely looking at us as he spoke.

"Give me a cup of coffee."

Mom and I shared a glance before she walked calmly to the machine that she had bought just the other day and started a fresh brew. Soon, the scent of coffee filled the kitchen, providing us with some sense of normalcy in a world that had suddenly changed.

Mom set a mug down in front of him, filled it to the brim; it spilled a bit over the side onto his hand but he hardly noticed. He drank the scorching-hot liquid as if it were a cold milkshake. Perhaps dying did that to a person. Maybe he didn't feel anything anymore.

"How come?" Mom asked, emotionless.

"How do you think?"

"The cancer."

She stated it as fact, revealing at that very moment that she had known he'd been sick. I had noticed the gray pallor of his skin before but never really thought about it. I didn't know what sick people looked like.

"Yeah. The cancer."

"How long?"

"Not long."

"Okay."

"I'm going to have to make some arrangements. I need to call the office first."

"You mean they don't know yet?"

"Nope."

Dad finished his coffee and got up, not looking at me or Mom as he walked over to the phone hanging on the wall. He furiously tapped the office's number, dragging the long cord of the phone with him as he stepped into the hallway to speak to whoever it was.

Mom looked at me. I looked at her. I sighed and scratched an old scar on my wrist that I'd had for as long as I could remember. Was I supposed to do something now? Cry? Whimper? Jot down how sad I was in my journal?

But I wasn't. I was devoid of any feelings, and I knew that

wasn't normal. He was my dad, and he was dying, and I felt absolutely nothing.

When he came back into the kitchen, he sighed.

"Beer," he barked.

Mom dove into the cupboard and retrieved a bottle. Some American brand he liked. He wasn't into foreign beers. She handed him the bottle and sat down opposite him. He downed it as if he hadn't drunk anything in months. He belched after, which I found disgusting. His stale breath filled the room.

"This is it," he said. "The end. I told them."

"How did they react?"

"I don't know. Passive. Uncaring."

"They should care after all these years you've put into that job."

"I'm sure they're happy I've solved their problem for them. Now they don't have to fire me, but I'm sure as hell gonna make them pay every damn dollar they owe me. Well, at least you'll be well off with my insurance policy and retirement money."

"Do you care?" Mom reacted bitterly.

Dad glanced at me.

"*She* needs it."

"Are you saying I don't?"

"Not if you're going to drink it all."

"I won't."

"Yeah, right."

I stood frozen while my parents had this conversation, horrified at their mutual indifference, unsure whether I should weep or celebrate.

Dad got up, picked up his bags, and left the room. We could hear him stomp up the stairs, followed by the familiar click of his bedroom door. Mom hadn't been in there for months, and it hadn't been cleaned in a long time. Why bother? He only slept in that room a few nights per week. The last time she walked in there when he was at home, he started yelling at her about privacy and personal things. The desk inside was always locked. She probably could have pried it open while he was gone, but she never bothered.

Mom shrugged and threw the rest of her cold toast in the bin. She took a tootsie roll from the kitchen cupboard and started chewing on it furiously.

"I'm going downstairs," she barked.

She left me alone in the kitchen. Her withdrawal symptoms had already set in; her hands had started to shake, and she seemed unsteady on her feet. Mom was just as bad without booze as she was drunk.

I cleaned up the kitchen and threw the rest of my toast in the trash, unsure of what to do next. I wanted to tell Hailey, but what would I say?

Soooo, Dad came home and announced he's going to be dead soon, but my mom doesn't care one way or the other.

By the time I'd finished in the kitchen, Dad came back downstairs and stood quietly in the doorway, watching me.

"Did you get what I just said?" he asked.

I stared at him for a moment before nodding.

"Do you know what it means to die of cancer?"

I nodded again, even though I had no clue. I suddenly realized that I had ignored the obvious. How he had lost a lot of weight lately, his sunken eyes, his gray, pale, exhausted appearance. He was sick. And he really was going to die.

I started signing, before realizing he didn't understand. I grabbed my notepad and scribbled the words.

I'm sorry.

"No, you're not. You'll be happy to be free."

I really am sorry.

"Don't be."

He studied me, probably wondering what was going through my mind.

"You've always been so quiet, Alice. I wish you would find your voice again."

Again?!

"There was a time you could talk, you know. A long time ago. But that was before shit hit the fan."

I didn't know what to think. My entire life I had thought I had been unable to speak. That this condition of mine had been a part of me since the day I was born. I didn't understand.

When?! I wrote down.

"I don't remember. Like I said, it was a long time ago. I – We used to get along, you and I. But your mom didn't like that. She stopped us from being friends."

Dad leaned against the kitchen table so casually that I wanted to shake him. He had never spoken to me about our lives together, and now this?

I want to know more, I wrote down. *What happened?*

He shrugged and smiled. "It doesn't matter. It's all gone now, everything we've ever had. I'll be dead soon, so what's the point dwelling on the past?"

It matters!

Dad smiled. He moved forward with his hand stretched out. He wanted to touch my face. He kept moving towards me, his fingertips almost touching.

But I took a step backwards and looked away, remembering what Hailey had said. *He is an abuser.*

My gesture shook him from his reverie. He sighed and dropped his hand.

"You're just like your mother," he said, and left the kitchen.

12

Mom and Dad sat at the kitchen table the next morning when I came down in search of breakfast. I hadn't slept all night. Hailey had had a fashion show event at the store last night, and she had warned me ahead of time that she wouldn't be home until way past midnight. She didn't know what was going on yet.

Dad's news lingered amongst my thoughts as I tried to tire myself enough to fall asleep. At some point, I had convinced myself that I was trapped in a vivid nightmare and that this couldn't possibly be true. But when I walked downstairs and saw them, obviously waiting for me, I knew that it was.

"Please sit down, Alice," Mom said. "We need to talk about your dad. Things are going to be changing around here, so be prepared."

I took my notepad and pen, but decided that I wouldn't write anything down until I knew more.

"So," Dad said, looking at me. "Your mother and I have decided that it is best that we tell you together what's going to happen. I know you'll find it difficult to grasp, but here is my situation."

I looked at Mom, who didn't look at me. She was sober and calm, which was a miracle on its own.

"As I said last night, I am going to die. I have stage four cancer. I've got weeks left, a month or two maybe, but that's it."

I didn't react.

"This has been going on for a while. Your mother and I have been hiding my illness from you, as you may have noticed yesterday, so this didn't come as a surprise to us. I've been taking pills for over a year, but when I was first diagnosed, I refused to undergo chemotherapy."

I was stunned. He had refused medical treatment that could save his life? Why?

"I've always known I would die young," Dad said, understanding my confusion. "Just like my father, and his father before that. It's a family thing."

He glanced at mom.

"The company's health insurance policy will cover all medical expenses, so that's one thing you don't have to worry about. I've also made sure you don't have to spend time worrying about bills and insurance and all that bullshit. The life insurance money will come once I'm dead, and the house has been paid for, so you'll have plenty of money for the rest of your life. I'm actually worth more dead than alive. Isn't that great?"

Mom looked him dead in the eye. "Yeah, it is."

I couldn't believe what I was hearing.

He got up. "Good. That's it, then. Well, apart from the fact that you'll be stuck with me until I'm dead."

It was all so matter of fact that it made me wonder for the thousandth time who he really was, and why he took everything in life so casually, including his own death. He was dying for goodness's sake, and it didn't seem to matter to him.

"Will you tell anyone?" my mom asked.

"Tell who what exactly?"

"You know."

He looked at her bewildered.

"Who would I tell? I don't owe anyone anything."

"Yes, you do. You owe many things to a lot of people, including me."

What were they talking about? I was lost. His job? His knowledge of the company's products? What?

"End of conversation," Dad said, but Mom didn't give up easily.

"You really need to–"

"Shut up!" he yelled, banging his hand on the table. "You will never speak about this. Not once, do you hear me? Not after I'm gone, and certainly not now."

Mom fled the room, leaving me alone with him.

I had ached for his death on multiple occasions, but now that he would truly leave us, I was stunned, shocked, stuck between feelings of disbelief and absolute liberation.

I scribbled on my notepad and shoved it in his face. He barely looked at it.

"'Will you really die?'" he read aloud. "Yes, Alice, I'm going to be dead soon. But guess what? You shouldn't really care about me, so why should you care whether I live or die?"

I didn't react. He smiled slyly.

"You'll miss me, I'm sure, but you will forget about me too, like you should. You don't need me to survive in this big, ugly world. You can finally start living, without ever having to look back. Be happy that I'll be gone soon; you deserve to be free."

I am not happy, I wrote.

He was obviously surprised. "You're not?"

I shook my head.

"Why the hell not?"

You are my dad.

He softened a bit. "Maybe I am," he said, "but I'm also a lousy shit who deserves what's coming. I've hurt so many people in my life. They always say karma's a bitch. I guess that's true. We'll see."

He retrieved a small bottle with pills from his pocket. Mom came back into the kitchen and stood still, watching him. Or was she watching me?

"The doctor gave me these. They'll numb the pain, keep it under control. They're part of my final stage of life. I'm scared that once I start taking them, I'll lose who I am altogether. I'll be a zombie, Alice. Alive without living. A walking, talking corpse. They'll kill my soul. I might as well be dead already."

He looked me in the eye.

"I've planned one final good day for myself before I start taking these. The pain has been unbearable for months, Alice. I can't do this much longer. But before my time comes, I want to tell you some things about who I am and what I've done with my life. You have the right to know."

"No," Mom said sharply.

He ignored her, got up and took another beer from the cupboard. He opened it and drank until it was empty. Then he took another.

"Alice, go to your room," Mom said. "*Now.*"

I looked at Dad, who nodded.

"Go to your room, Alice."

I left the kitchen, headed into the hallway and went up the stairs, knowing they would listen to the sound of my feet. But when I turned around, they weren't there checking up on me. They had already continued their argument.

I crept back downstairs and sat on the first step, listening in on their conversation.

"I'm going to tell her," Dad said.

"No, you won't."

"I will. Who's going to stop me?"

"I am."

Dad laughed. "Seriously? You've done shit to stop me before, so why start now?"

"You're talking about our daughter."

"*Our* daughter? That's rich. Since when do you care about her?"

Mom became upset. "I've always cared. Why do you think I've put up with you? While you were out there doing your thing, you've left her with me. I took care of her in every way possible. I've raised her, tutored her, fed her. Where were you all this time, huh?"

"You know why I wasn't here."

"To avoid her, so you could avoid what you've done to her."

What has he done to me? I balled my fists. I wanted to run into that room and confront them both, but I stayed put.

"I protected her by *not* being here!" Dad yelled. "Don't you get that, Eileen? I've done right by her."

"No, you haven't. You fucked up, Jack. You've taken away every chance for her to lead a normal life."

"I've kept her *safe*!" he screamed. "I saved her goddamn life! I gave her a home. I gave her everything she needed. She grew up just fine. She's lived a better life than most kids. She doesn't know sorrow or pain, she doesn't know hate or fear. And she's smarter than anyone I know, thanks to her books."

Mom snorted. "Do you honestly believe your own bullshit? You've created a defenseless young woman who will never be capable of holding a job or experiencing a normal relationship. Do you realize that?"

"That is on you, Eileen. I told you to raise her well, and what did you do? Treat her with disdain. Just confess you hate her, and you're already looking for ways to get rid of her once I'm gone."

"I love her," Mom said softly. "I've done all I could for her."

"Is that why you hardly feed her anymore? Why you've stopped cooking meals? Why you're downstairs binging while she's in her room doing God-knows-what?"

Mom didn't say anything. For a while, it remained silent until she spoke again, her voice hoarse and tired. "At least I've kept her away from you. God knows what might have happened if you'd had your way with her."

A harsh slap startled me. Mom hissed. I heard a thud. She had fallen to the ground. I could imagine Dad hovering over her.

"Enough!" he barked.

I got up and ran up the stairs, not caring if they heard me. I slammed my bedroom door and barred it with a chair. I fell down on my bed and clutched the duvet, searching for warmth.

Dad's heavy footsteps were audible in the corridor. He came upstairs, but didn't knock on my door or try to enter. He walked past my door, into his bedroom, but I never heard it close.

Mom stayed downstairs.

After a couple of minutes, I got up and removed the chair. I walked to his room, mentally preparing myself to hear what he had wanted to tell me.

He was seated behind his desk, crying. His shoulders shook, his body trembled. It was the first time I had seen him act so emotionally.

In front of him lay a closed leatherbound journal. I recognized it. He used those volumes while traveling. An old brown suitcase lay wide open on the floor. In it were several other journals, scattered around. There must have been at least thirty, one for each year he had traveled. I never realized he had kept every single one.

He saw me, stood, and walked over. I thought he was going to ask me in, but instead he looked at me strangely and shut the door in my face.

I walked back to my room, closed the door, and opened the window only to realize that now Dad was home, I wouldn't be able to talk to Hailey. He would hear.

She appeared in front of the window and opened it, but I put my finger against my mouth as a sign to remain quiet.

She understood immediately.

She looked around her room and then came back with a large notepad and a marker.

Your dad is home?

I nodded.

How long?

I signed, *I don't know.*

I saw her lips form the word *Fuck* and smiled lightly. Fuck indeed.

She closed the window, as did I. I shut the drapes, and when I turned around, Mom was there. She had seen the whole thing.

13

My dad had given up on life and almost seemed eager to die; the sooner the better.

All through Thursday – the last day of his life, as he called it – he wandered around the house, busying himself with whatever. I heard him rummaging through his bedroom cupboards and closet. He shuffled stuff around the living room and kitchen next. Then he was in the basement, and finally, in the attic.

After I had eaten lunch in my room, he left the house. I had no idea where he went or what he was going to do, and I honestly didn't dare to ask Mom after what had happened before.

She hadn't spoken a word to me about it, and she hadn't demanded to know if I had contacted our neighbor. If she knew, she definitely hadn't told Dad about it either, which was odd, since he seemed to know almost everything else.

I was in my room when Dad came back and started making noise around the house. I could tell by the way that he wandered, stomping his feet loudly, that he was intoxicated. This wasn't the first time' his behavior was similar to Mom's when she got drunk.

I heard their voices resonate loud and clear, even though Mom tried to shush him several times. The argument was about me again, and she won. Again. She wouldn't allow him to tell me what it was that he wanted to share.

Even with death on our doorstep, nothing changed between my parents. They were still waging their cold war. My mom was stoic and often angry, but she also seemed relieved, as if his death would mean certain freedom for her. In a way, that was true, I guess.

On Friday morning, Dad started taking the heavy drugs that he had shown me. We sat at the breakfast table, which felt like we were at a wake for a living person. He ate a bagel and the pills lay on the table before him.

"Go to your room," Mom told me.

I left the kitchen and sat on the stairs, not obeying her – again.

"You need palliative care," she told Dad. "You can't die in this house."

"You know why I can't leave," he said. "I can't take that risk. What if I say things when I'm out of control?"

"But you're willing to risk staying here with her?" she remarked snidely. "Unless that's what you want to happen. It'll give you an excuse to tell her the truth, and you'll blame it on the drugs."

"I have to die somewhere. And no, I won't tell her. She'll stay in her room, and I'll take the basement, so I'm afraid you'll have to drink yourself into a stupor in the spare room upstairs." His voice was dripping with disdain.

"Why are you so mean?" she asked, obviously hurt. "You'll need me taking care of you."

"No. I don't need you."

"Yes, you do."

"No, Eileen. I don't want you near me."

"Fine. Suffer on your own, then, if that's what you want," she said curtly. "But stay as far away from her as you possibly can."

"I will. Happy now?"

After a short silence, she sighed.

"Yeah. Just… don't take too long dying."

He laughed, leaving me in shock. "Don't worry. A couple of days at the most, and then you'll be rid of me forever. Sound good?"

"No."

"Oh, really? I thought you'd be thrilled?"

Mom sighed audibly. "Don't get me wrong, Jack. I'm relieved that you're going to die, but I'm also worried you'll do everything in your power to stick around for as long as you possibly can to make my life even more miserable than it already is."

"You'd rather I just off myself, wouldn't you?" Dad remarked.

"Yes," Mom said.

"Now, why would I do that? The only person benefiting from that is you."

Silence.

Dad laughed. "If you want me gone so desperately, why don't you do it, then? You could easily give me an overdose, and no one would be any the wiser."

"And miss the chance to watch you suffer?" Mom said. "You can't take that away from me."

"My, my, aren't we feisty today," Dad said, humming. "Well, I'm afraid you'll have to be patient. I won't overdose by accident, and you aren't going to do it for me, so that leaves us in quite a pickle, don't you think?"

Mom remained quiet, creating an odd silence between them. Then she said, almost inaudibly, "It's her I worry about. And what you'll do to her in your final hours."

"She'll be fine," Dad said. "I won't change my mind. We have an agreement."

"You really should consider going sooner," Mom said, softer now. "Suffering won't do you any good."

"I've suffered my entire life," Dad said.

"Yeah, maybe you have," Mom whispered. "In your own way."

"Yeah."

"At least you dying will do some good, too. You'll be free at long last."

"I'm not so sure about that. The doors of Hell will be standing wide open to welcome me home."

"At least then you'll finally understand what it means to live there," Mom said.

Her footsteps moved to the hallway. I hurried upstairs as quietly as I could and hid behind my bedroom door. She didn't come upstairs though. Instead, she went to clean the basement, preparing it for him to suffer in.

And suffer he did.

14

As of that Friday morning, when he started taking the zombie medicine, as he called it, Dad was bound to bed, unable to get up even to use the bathroom. He was relatively okay one minute, and a dying man the next.

Even though I didn't go downstairs until way past dinner time, I knew exactly what was happening. I could smell it even with my door shut and two floors between.

The scent of Dad's decay pervaded the house. At first only slightly, but as the day progressed, it became worse. His urine and feces must have been scattered all over the bed, because Mom had to clean up several times per day. It made her vomit and gasp the whole time. I didn't want to imagine it, but I couldn't help it.

Despite the fact he had told her to fuck off and leave him alone, it turned out to be impossible for him to suffer on his own. He started screaming whenever his bowels threatened to betray him, crying out her name and ordering her to come help him.

Mom, who was busying herself downstairs without a drop of liquor in her, had to rush into the room to help him. Sometimes she managed to get him onto the toilet in time, but often he had already soiled himself.

I felt sorry for him. I also felt sorry for her. He yelled and screamed at her, but she still went, because she knew it would only become worse if she didn't. The rooms reeked of his stench; we didn't even have any scented candles to cover it up.

I opened the bedroom window, while keeping the door closed, and pretended it wasn't stone cold outside. Hailey was at work, so I could stare at her window for hours, pretending I was living in that house instead of mine.

I spent my day there, wearing two sweaters over my frail form and mittens on my hands, and reading a book that I could barely hold on my lap. I didn't know what I was going to do when Hailey returned, but I would deal with that later. Right now, there were other things to worry about.

That evening, my dad began to lose all self-control. He screamed for more drugs and became lost in a world of pain.

I didn't go downstairs to see him, but his agonized voice carried though the house, telling me that he was barely sleeping. That zombie-like state he had predicted wasn't coming. He remained lucid through his suffering, which I didn't understand. Shouldn't those drugs have knocked him out?

Hailey hadn't returned home yet, and even if she did, I didn't dare contact her out of fear Mom would catch me. My dad's illness had brought her back to her senses. She no longer drank, even though I could tell in the sparse moments I had seen her throughout the day that it was hard on her.

Around 11pm, I finally walked down to find something to eat. My stomach had been painfully twisted all night from the lack of decent food. I needed to find something.

I walked slowly, hoping no one would be around. There was no screaming coming from the basement, but I still heard noises. He was mumbling, grunting, groaning, complaining.

When I walked into the kitchen, Mom was sitting at the table, a cup of coffee in hand. She barely looked up. Before I even set foot near her, she began to speak.

"It's the cancer," she said. "Stage four bone cancer. It's spread to his organs and brain. It won't take long. Every day will get worse and worse, and he'll finally reach for his medication and overdose, just to be rid of it."

She took a sip of coffee before placing the mug down. I sat down across from her, waiting for her to continue.

"He probably won't sleep much in the coming days, even though sleep would be a relief. The ache will cut through his bones like a knife slashing flesh. He'll age by the minute."

Why won't you help him? I wrote.

She smiled. "He doesn't want my help."

Maybe he does now.

"He should have thought of that sooner. He should have listened to his doctors when they told him to stop working and get the chemo. He didn't want to. Well, now here we are."

I remembered a couple of things that I had not really paid attention to over the past year. He'd constantly complained of the cold and how his body had ached. Sometimes he would shiver uncontrollably. He had lost a lot of weight and hair. I had always thought it was his age and exhaustion from traveling.

"This disease didn't start overnight," Mom said. "It slowly crept into his system, taking control. But he still continued working. Ah, well."

What next? I wrote down.

She looked at me.

"What do you mean?"

What happens to us?

"Nothing. Once he's dead, I'll clear the house of his stuff, and we can decorate it. Get rid of his presence here. I'd like that, actually. Maybe I could move downstairs, and you could have the entire top floor. Would you like that?"

He wasn't even dead yet and she was already daydreaming about what would happen after he was gone. But that was not what I meant. I wanted to know how we were going to survive.

He had spoken of a life insurance policy and the house being paid for, but would that be enough? Mom never bought any extras or luxury products, so I had to assume that Dad hadn't earned a lot of money with his job. Could we last on that?

"Or maybe you wouldn't want to stay with me at all," she continued. "Maybe we should sell this damned place and move elsewhere. Or we can split up, live separately. I'm sure you'd like that. I mean, I would, if I were you."

Live without my mom? Could I even do that? I was hopelessly helpless. How would I manage?

I thought of the mix of good and bad days, the times where she did stuff like organize the library room. And then I thought of the days when I didn't know we were living in the same house.

I couldn't survive without her. Whatever happened next, that was one thing I was certain of. No matter if Hailey believed I was capable of living without the woman who had raised me, I just knew that Mom was the one constant in my life that I needed to hold onto. She was not a terrible mother. She was a confused one. If anything, these past few days had proven to me that, despite it all, I loved her.

I wrote, *I will find a job.*

She looked surprised. "Why?"

To help support us.

She understood. She looked at me in shock.

"You want to stay with me?"

I nodded.

She stood, walked to my end of the table, pulled me up and hugged me. And then she cried.

On Saturday morning, Hailey opened her window and looked at me. I had been waiting for it, eager to see her.

She had made a couple of signs on a notepad that she had used over the past few days, since I still didn't dare to make a lot of noise with Mom being clearheaded and Dad downstairs. She lifted her notepad, because she wasn't good at signing herself, even though she understood quite a lot by now.

Are you okay?

I nodded.

Your dad okay?

I shook my head.

Your mom?

I shook my head again.

How can I help?

I smiled and made the signs I knew she understood. *You already are.*

She smiled broadly.

I love you, she signed.

I felt my heart lift and signed back before I could stop myself. *I love you, too.*

Her radiant smile told me all I needed to know. This time I knew she didn't mean it as a friend. This was the real thing.

15

Late in the morning, Mom came upstairs to my room. I'd kept my window ajar so that some of the smell would leave my room. I had gotten used to the new smells in the house, but I still hated them.

"I need to run to the store and get some food and other stuff for us," Mom said, hesitating. "I wish I could take you with me, but that's impossible. Are you okay staying here on your own for a while?"

I must have seemed puzzled. I was always alone, so what did it matter?

"I mean, with him downstairs. He's loud and annoying, I know, but I can't put off shopping any longer. Plus, I'm in desperate need of some candles and stuff to get rid of the smell."

Me too, I wrote down. *Please.*

"I'll take care of it," she said with a faint smile. "Alice, whatever happens, do not go downstairs. No matter how much he yells or pleads, don't go there. You can't see him like that. It's too weird. Promise me you'll stay here."

I promise.

"I mean it, Alice. Don't go down there. He's in a strange state of mind and he'll say things that are... out there. So don't listen to him. Okay?"

I won't.

Mom smiled, hugged me quickly, as if that's what she had been doing my whole life. "I'll come back as fast as I can."

She closed the door, but as soon as I heard her leave, I opened it again to listen to the noises coming from my dad. The basement door had to be open, because I could hear him clearly. His calls for help were like faint cries, but they still seemed to pierce my skull.

The pleads became yells. The yells became screams. He started screaming as if his life depended on it, calling out for anyone to hear. I wasn't sure if he realized Mom had left the house, because he would scream her name.

"Eileen! Eileen, help! Help! I didn't mean to hurt you. Help me. I need you. I'm sorry."

This went on for a while, and finally I heard my name. He was now calling for me.

"Alice. Alice. Alice, come. Come here, Alice. I need to tell you something."

I couldn't bear listening to it anymore and shut the door, but my sharp hearing still distinguished his screams which became wails of anguish. I couldn't ignore them any longer.

"Alice, come here!"

He yelled now, and I wondered for a moment if he would actually pull himself from bed and make his way upstairs, even if he were at death's door.

I didn't want that smell in my room. I didn't want him polluting my sacred space. So I decided to go to him instead. I walked downstairs, making sure my feet didn't creak on the stairs.

I waited a moment at the basement door before pulling it further open. I stood at the top of the stairs, debating whether I should pretend that I didn't hear or go downstairs to help him. I didn't really want to go, but what else was I supposed to do? I couldn't take him screaming anymore.

I walked down the stairs. The basement bedroom door was

open. The smell of decay invaded my nostrils immediately. This wasn't just shit and piss anymore. It was the smell of cancer wreaking havoc on his body, and it was getting worse. These were his final days or hours. Minutes, maybe.

This had to be hell for him. He should not be here, but in the hospital, in a drug-induced sleep, biding his time until death came to claim him. Why wouldn't Mom call an ambulance? If they put him in a coma, he wouldn't even realize it. He would just slip away.

But did she not say that she wanted him to suffer? Maybe she wasn't giving him enough medication on purpose. Perhaps this insufferable pain was her revenge. Maybe she wouldn't allow him to fall into a welcoming, hazy sleep.

Giving him more drugs could end his life faster. An accidental overdose, none the wiser. It seemed inhuman not to help him.

I walked hesitantly into his bedroom and saw him for the first time in the final stages of his life. He wore a white T-shirt, soiled by vomit and blood, and boxers that showed he had wet himself once again. He was running a high fever and had thrown off all the blankets. He was sweating profusely. He had lost even more weight than before.

I stayed near the door, unable to bring myself to move closer. My eyes searched for the pills that he was supposed to take. They were sitting on the nightstand within his reach, but he would still be unable to get them himself. He was that weak.

His eyes opened. He stopped panting and screaming. It became awfully quiet in the room. I couldn't ask him what he wanted, and he probably wouldn't be able to read my written message.

At first, he didn't see me, but when he noticed, his

facial expression changed. He wasn't happy to see me at all, despite the fact he had begged me to come. He started screaming in horror, as if he saw something or someone that he dreaded. It was a different kind of scream now, no longer coming from agony, but from fear.

"Get out. Get out!!!!!!!"

I fled in panic, shut the door, and leaned against the wood while I tried to control the fear that rushed through me. My heart pounded in my chest, my fingers cramped together, and I was in agony too, just like him. I could feel the horror and pain he was going through, even if I wasn't the one dying.

After a while, he became quiet. He didn't scream anymore, but I could hear him panting heavily. He was alert, lying on that bed, bathing in his own piss. The smell was god-awful.

My mom still hadn't shown up. I pushed my ear against the door and listened to his noises, realizing that he had fallen asleep at last. The panting had subsided, and he had become deadly quiet. Maybe this was the end, the moment he gave up.

I opened the door for the second time.

He wasn't asleep. He was wide awake. He saw me, and whatever it was that haunted him remained. It was gruesome to watch, especially since he'd always been so self-composed.

He clearly recognized me, but I wasn't so sure that it was me that he saw. A mixture of disgust, fear, and everything that had nothing to do with me was visible in his expression. His hands grasped the bedsheets, his fingers dug into the fabric.

This was no longer my absent, distant father who never showed any emotions, but a man scared for his life. I didn't know what or who he was so afraid of, but it was obvious that something had warped his senses.

He flinched as I approached the bed, and everything changed in that instant: A sudden rush of power, that seemed to make up for all the shit he had put me through, swept through me.

I made him scared. *I* did this to him. *I* was in control now. *I* was in charge.

That power made me move even nearer to him, to show him the person he had to fear. When I stood close enough, he grabbed me by the wrist and pulled me closer.

I didn't flinch. His grip on me was weak; it wasn't hostile or aggressive. If I wanted to, I could have choked him.

His imminent death reflected in my pupils. I represented what he feared the most: eternal damnation for all that he had done wrong, whatever that may have been. He had told us that the doors of Hell would be opened for him. Not a single prayer to whatever god he believed in would grant him forgiveness for his sins.

Even though I couldn't speak, my eyes told him all he needed to know.

You've kept me prisoner.
You've deprived me of a normal life.
What did I ever do to you?
Why? Why???

My dad let go of my wrist. He sunk back deep into the old and tattered mattress looking paler than I had ever seen him. His withered form resembled some uncanny mix of old man and frail child. He was already dead; his mind simply hadn't accepted that fact yet.

I reached for the bottle of pills and contemplated feeding him enough to end his life, but my hands refused to open the lid. I put the bottle down again. Maybe Mom was right. An easy death would be too good for him.

Dad grabbed me by the arm again and pulled me closer.

"Speak, goddammit," Dad snapped. "Just say what you have to say. Use your fucking voice!"

I couldn't say anything. He knew that. Every word hurt.

"Use your voice to tell me how much you hate me. Come on, Alice. Say it!"

I tried to pull free.

"Tell me how much you want your freedom back. Come on, let's hear it. You won't get out of here if you don't ask."

I was shocked by what he was saying. I had never spoken a single word to him, but now he was demanding that I use my voice?

He swallowed heavily; his grip on my arm increased. It was so firm that I winced without making an audible sound. Even though he was hurting me so badly, I couldn't talk.

"I know you want to run. You're trying to get out, aren't you? But I *will* find you again, and I'll kill you with my bare hands when I do. You're mine, and you always will be."

He wasn't seeing me. He was seeing someone else.

"Get used to me, like the others," he muttered. "You really think you're special because I keep you close, don't you? Do you think you don't have to abide by my rules?"

I tried to free myself again.

"Stop fighting me! Stop crying. I'm so tired of you bawling like a baby. Stop staring at me like that! You think you're so much better than me."

He shivered and finally let go. The fever made his body tremble. I stood, unsure of what to do next.

"Don't go," he whispered. "Stay."

I debated between running away forever and helping him. I reached for a blanket and threw it over his chest. He clutched it as if it were a lifeline. The warmth of the blanket calmed him down. He was no longer trembling; his body relaxed. His voice faded away. His eyes closed.

I turned around and left the room.

"Don't go," he called after me.

I stopped.

"Don't you want to know what happened to the others?"

I turned.

He swallowed thickly and pulled the blanket further up. "Don't you want to know what I did to them?"

I stood frozen to my core. Then, my mom came in and pulled me out of the room. She slammed the door shut and pushed me hard against it.

"What have you done?!" she screamed.

I pushed her away and ran upstairs into my room, shut the door, and propped the chair against it. She didn't come running after me.

Tears streamed down my face as I slid against the wall until I sat on the floor and stared at my hands.

Don't you want to know what I did to them?

What had he done?

Mom came to my room later that evening. She knocked on the door, not a habit of hers. I could tell she was still distressed.

"How are you?" she said.

I shrugged.

"I'm sorry you had to go through that. I knew I should have stayed home. I figured you were probably still upset, so I brought you a sleeping pill for the night. You haven't slept much, have you?"

I shook my head. I wasn't sure if that was because I didn't want the pill, or because I hadn't slept. It was obvious that she wanted me to take it though, and maybe that wasn't such a bad thing.

I already knew I wasn't going to sleep tonight, so why not? It would knock me right out, and maybe, just maybe, I'd be okay in the morning.

I took it without protest and drank the glass of water she handed me shortly after. She watched me as I crawled into bed with one of my books.

She hesitated.

"Goodnight, Alice."

I said nothing and opened my book.

I didn't get far. Within minutes, the letters started dancing before my eyes and the drawings looked like they'd been created in Wonderland itself, as if the White Rabbit was toying with them – with me. As if I'd become part of his crazy world.

16

Sunday. Five days since his return.

I woke up with a heavy head, bothered by the aftermath of the medication. I felt oddly rested. My sleep had not been disturbed by strange dreams. It almost felt as if last night's events hadn't occurred at all.

But they had, and we all knew it.

His words, his expression, his disease had me confused and irrational. I had avoided communicating with Hailey last night, too horrified to share this with her. If I revealed this, all hell would break loose.

Don't you want to know what happened to the others?

What others? And what had he done to *me*? It didn't make any sense at all.

I heard Mom stumbling up the stairs. She knocked on the door, rattling the knob.

"Alice, open the door."

I didn't react.

"Alice, come on. Open the door."

I got up from the bed and removed the chair. She looked at me inquisitively, but she didn't mention yesterday.

"The end is near," she said. "You need to see him one last time. Despite everything, he was your father. This is not a request."

Was. She said *was* your father. As if he was already gone.

Her words made me shiver. I didn't want to go, but I knew

had to. I walked down the stairs first, with her breathing down my neck. Down in the basement, I entered Dad's smelly bedroom for the last time.

Mom stood right behind me, hovering like a shadow, and she didn't say a single word. She placed a hand on my shoulder to support me, but I hated her touch.

There had been a major change in him. The screaming had died down; the pain was gone, or so I suspected. Maybe she had given him more meds. Or maybe his mind had finally come to realize that he was better off dead.

The other horrible symptoms of his illness remained. The groaning and heaving, the panting and wheezing, gasping air into his ruined lungs. His eyes were glassy, his complexion gray. All blood was drawn from his cracked lips.

I imagined Death entering the room in the shape of a horrible monster, sent from Hell by the Devil himself. It had a gruesome head, and a body covered in boils, and it waited patiently in the corner for my dad to release his last breath. And then the Devil would deal with him, if such a creature really did exist.

Dad wasn't religious. He had never prayed, never spoken about churches or priests or God. I'm not sure if he believed in any such thing. Mom hadn't called for a priest to give him his last sacraments, either, although she had plenty of time to do so. I guess he just had too many sins to confess.

I imagined Death approaching the bed and leaning over Dad's scrawny body to suck his dying breath from his mouth. I closed my eyes while I envisioned their final conversation.

"Are you ready?" Death would say.

"No," Dad would reply.

"That's too bad."

"I'm scared."

"You should be."

When I opened my eyes again, Dad had stopped breathing.

The light in his eyes was gone. His mouth had stopped moving, and his chest no longer heaved. His fingers had been clutching the bedsheet, and now they had eased. His toes were no longer curled; his legs were relaxed and stretched out. His entire form was slack.

He had pissed himself one last time; the stench permeated the air.

I turned around and looked at Mom, signing my question furiously, even if she didn't understand.

What did he do?

She ignored me.

Did you know?

She looked at me without understanding what I was trying to tell her. "Use your notepad, Alice."

There wasn't one in the room, so I hurried outside and ran up the stairs, not even waiting for her to come after me. I heard her close the door behind her, and I knew that this was going to be the one and only time I would get answers from her, before Dad would be taken away.

I scribbled down my question.

He did something to me.

Mom read it and reacted stoically. "He did a lot of things to many people."

Who?? Who are the others?

"I don't know what you mean."

He had another life!!

"Of course he did. Everyone does. Or do you think that there's nothing more to us than what we share with those around us? We all have secrets, don't we, Alice?"

I stared at her in shock.

Mom cleared her throat and wiped a handkerchief past her mouth, licking her lips while she folded the white cloth. She had not shed a tear for him. She was relieved that he was finally gone.

"I told you not to go into that room, Alice. There was a reason for that. Some things are better left unspoken. Forget what he said, for your own sake."

I can't!!!!

I couldn't scream it, but she knew that I was upset.

"I have to go get things done," she said. "Call some people. Get him the hell out of here as fast as I can. The whole house stinks of him now."

The smell of my father's remains haunted me, too.

Mom sighed heavily, rubbed her face and seemed twenty years older. It felt as if my father's sickness had shortened her own lifespan by decades.

Tell me who he was! I wrote down.

"He was your father."

More than that.

She glanced at my words and sighed. "You're never going to let this go, are you?"

I shook my head.

"Alright then, Alice. I will say this only once, and then we will never speak of it again, do you understand?"

I nodded.

"Your father was many things, but he had his good moments. He took care of us. He loved us in his own way. He was our caretaker, and he gave us this house, this life. It wasn't all bad."

But?

"But he was also scary, awful, and evil. He never let that version of him inside this house, or at least he tried not to. He kept who he really was outside these walls, and we should be grateful for that. If he hadn't, we would not be having this conversation right now. We would have gone a long time ago."

What did he do?!

"Nothing you will ever find out. Let him rest in peace, Alice. Forget everything else. Let the dead go, and allow their sins to go with them. What does it matter?"

It matters to me.

"Not to me. What I know is that we're free. You and I are finally free."

She looked at me with her face relaxed. Part of her youth had come back, or at least the reflection of the age that she really was. My mom still had a life ahead of her. She had been waiting for this moment to come, and it had arrived sooner than she could have ever imagined.

There was a new shine to her eyes, she had less wrinkles, appeared less unsteady and angry. She was a normal person for once, a mother. Or at least, what she thought a mother should be. She placed her hand against my face. Her touch was soft and warm but felt unnatural. I flinched.

"There are so many things that I want to tell you, Alice, but it doesn't matter anymore. You and I are all that's left now, and we'll spend the rest of our lives together. But things will be different from now on."

She looked at her hands.

"I know I've made a lot of mistakes, but they were all made to protect you, to keep you safe."

What?

"Now, then, why don't you go to your room and get some rest? I'll take care of everything that needs to be done. As soon as he's gone from here forever, I will sell this terrible place and we will move to another town, to a new house, with a new library room. You'll finally be able to lead a normal life. But as long as we're here in Hays, you are not to show yourself to anyone. Do you understand that?"

I nodded.

I didn't want to go, not really. I wanted to stay here, where Hailey was. The thought of losing her was almost too much to bear, but I couldn't tell Mom that. She would force a wedge between us, have us move out immediately.

I almost hoped she would start drinking again. Right now, there was no chance I would get to speak to Hailey and explain all that had been going on. I had to escape this house, and Mom.

Mom stopped by the door. She hesitated.

"You are so beautiful, Alice," she said. "You're gorgeous inside and out, and I am so proud to be your mother. Whatever else happens in life, or whatever else you might want to believe about me, at least trust in that."

I was left in the kitchen alone with my thoughts, with the knowledge that Dad may have committed atrocities that would never be exposed, and with a future that would probably turn out to be just as bleak as the legacy that died with the man in that basement.

PART FOUR
After Death

17

Dad's body remained in the downstairs bedroom. Mom and I had left it until some people in suits came a few hours later to take him away.

Mom told me to stay in my room, and only unlocked the front door once she was sure I was up there. Before long, the house was flooded with people. I rubbed the scar on my wrist, like I always did when I got nervous, and waited for something – *anything* – to happen.

Mom had retrieved some of Dad's clothes for the coroner to take and dress the body in. She had chosen one of his business outfits, a charcoal suit with white shirt, a black tie, gray socks, and black, shiny shoes. He always dressed nicely when he was out working. No one would invite a guy looking like a drifter in their home.

"If anyone should go upstairs, even though I don't think they will, you need to stay in the library room," she had instructed me. "You don't show your face, or they will tear us apart, Alice. You don't want that, do you? To be taken to some institution?"

She hadn't spoken these words in a long time. When I was young, this was the common threat she would use to reel me back in whenever I was disobedient.

"People don't like children who are different. They'll lock you up. No more books, no more fun."

I had left my bedroom door ajar so I could follow what was going on.

A doctor came to confirm Dad's death.

A coroner came to take away his corpse.

The police came too, but I don't know why. I heard them say something about *standard procedures* and *deaths at home*, whatever that means, followed by a reassurance that it was pretty obvious he had died a natural death, and that these were just routine questions.

Eventually, Dad's body was gone.

Nobody came upstairs to search for me or to look for anything unusual around the house. Why would they? Dad's death, obviously due to cancer, made no room for suspicion of foul play or questions regarding his behavior. To them, he was just a guy who died after a long battle, and who had been taken care of by his loving wife, who had nursed him and provided palliative care at home.

I had never left this house in my life, so no one wondered where I was, no one expected to see me. No one other than Hailey realized that I existed. I hadn't been able to call out to the visitors, but I could have gone downstairs and showed myself.

But I didn't.

Something held me back. Maybe it was Mom's urgent insistence that I keep quiet so they wouldn't take me away and lock me up. Which was, in my mind, something that could really happen. What else would they do with someone like me?

The officials left and my mother came to talk to me. She seemed more relaxed, her breathing was regular. She came upstairs to tell me.

"We're safe," she said. "We're good. Everything's fine. The worst part is over."

I was relieved that my dad's body had been taken away

from the house, as it meant that the stench would also finally be gone.

I walked downstairs with Mom. We opened all the doors and windows, and she went downstairs to clean the basement room and bed. She opened that window too, despite the fact it was quite cold outside.

"It'll never really go away," she said, "but maybe that's just my imagination."

I shook my head, because I felt it too.

I helped her clean up. We stuffed the sheets, blankets, and pillows into big garbage bags. She put them in Dad's car, which had plenty of space. The company hadn't retrieved the vehicle yet, and I wasn't even sure if Mom had told them.

All of his medication was thrown out. The mattress was stained with wide patches of yellow. We pulled it off the bed, but it was too big to fit in her car, so we dragged it to the back and threw it on the terrace floor.

"I'll take the bags away and head to the post office to send out some letters to people that should know. I'll call his office, too, but not today. Tomorrow, maybe. I have to get the financial stuff out of the way. There's a lot to do, and I want to get it over and done with."

I nodded.

"I'll be back in an hour. I'll pick up some food as well. How does hamburgers sound?"

Hamburgers?! I hadn't eaten those in years. She smiled when she noticed my confusion.

"Freedom is a wonderful thing, don't you think? I'll be back soon. Don't open the door to anyone, you hear? I'm trusting you to stay inside."

I nodded again, wondering what was going on. Was this still the same mother, or had something happened to her, too?

Before leaving, she opened the kitchen cupboard and dug out four bottles of wine and liquor.

She's going to drink again, I thought.

But she didn't. She stuffed the bottles inside another garbage bag and tied it closed before adding it to the trunk of her already overloaded car.

She didn't even flinch.

The moment Mom left the driveway, I hesitantly approached the front door. To my shock, it opened immediately – no bolt was stopping me from heading outside and tasting freedom.

I was in awe. I stood frozen on the porch, staring at the world with a brand-new set of eyes.

But the world didn't interest me. There was only one thing I wanted to do with my newfound freedom, no matter how short it was. I walked, stumbled, ran to the house next door. Hailey's car was in the driveway. She *had* to be home.

Be home. Be there, I prayed in silence.

And there she was, opening the door.

Before I knew it, I was in her arms. She held me so tight I thought I would faint from happiness. Or die from the overwhelming emotions flooding through me.

She was taller than me, and she had this protectiveness about her I had never experienced. It was so different from my mother's hesitant touch. This was how someone should hug the person they loved.

"Alice," she whispered against my ear. "My poor Alice."

That was enough. That was all she had to say. That touch, that feeling, was going to keep me on my feet for all the days to come.

18

A strange but peaceful quiet lingered inside the house. Mom still didn't say much, but she never got upset, angry, or distressed. She allowed me to stay in my room all the time, where I alternated between mourning Dad's death and Hailey's forced absence, and feeling relieved that a dark part of my life was over.

But what I thought about the most were my father's words; that moment had a lasting impact on me. I no longer saw him as my dad, but as a stranger who had kept his secrets far away from this house.

Mom still didn't cook, but things were different. The day that Dad died, she brought hamburgers home. Not McDonald's or Burger King, but real, homecooked hamburgers from a deli nearby. I didn't care what was on them, they were just so good.

The next day, readymade food was delivered to the house by the same local deli and taken upstairs on a tray to my room. The meal consisted of all these nice things I had never eaten before. Gone were the mac-and-cheeses or stale pastas, or any other dish that I had been forced to eat and tasted like feet. Gone were the dry toast and jam days. She brought me peanut butter and jelly sandwiches on freshly baked white bread, and I ate it like it was the best meal I'd ever had.

I never asked questions about the food; I just shoveled it

into my mouth hastily, subconsciously worried that every decent meal could be my last.

She brought potato chips in various flavors, and cookies that were so good I could eat them all day. Was she fattening me up like that witch had done with Hansel and Gretel? I didn't quite understand it, but I didn't care.

Apart from the food, Mom kept to herself downstairs. I could hear her cleaning the house. She worked tirelessly from morning to late in the evening with the television on. Sometimes, music would blare through the house, like in the old days when she still played her records, and I caught myself listening to her footsteps, wondering if she was dancing, because it often sounded like she was.

She didn't drink anymore, or at least not that I could tell. Not once did she hide herself to get wasted. I had seen her withdrawal symptoms improve when she was taking care of Dad, so I assumed the worst part was over.

I never bothered to go downstairs to see the result of her work. She didn't ask me to come take a look, either. Despite her oddly changed behavior, she was still the same woman who had kept me at arm's length my whole life, no matter what she said or did now.

I contemplated whether she remembered what she had told me right after Dad's death, about things changing for the better. Things hadn't changed, or at least not all that much. I was still a prisoner in this house, and the only difference was that I couldn't see Hailey that often because Mom had stopped drinking.

We were still communicating, but it was far less frequent because we both didn't want to risk being caught. I considered it a real possibility that Mom would throw me in the car and drive us off to God-knows-where.

"You have to get out of there," Hailey said. "You're an adult. Your mom has no right to keep you there."

I'm lost without her.

It took a while for Hailey to understand my signing, but she worked it out.

"I have money. You can stay with me."

I don't know this world.

"I'll teach you. It's not that hard. Besides, you already know everything from your TV shows and books. Come on, Alice. *You* have to decide if you want to do this. This is a turning point in your life."

I'm not ready yet.

Hailey understood. She was sympathetic, but she was also extremely impatient. And I hadn't told her the finer details about Dad's behavior. I just couldn't, not like this. This burden was mine to carry for now, but I didn't know what to do with it.

"Let me know when you're ready," Hailey said. "That day will come sooner than you think."

I wanted to believe her so badly, but under Mom's scrutinizing gaze it felt as if I was more isolated than ever.

Mom would leave the house now and then, but never for long. Sometimes she forgot to lock the door, but I was always worried that she might come back sooner than expected and catch me at Hailey's house or Hailey at ours, so I didn't take that risk. Besides, Hailey had to work, so she was often away during the day.

Dad would not have a funeral, and was going to be cremated. Mom explained that this was cheaper than a burial. She would scatter his remains on a grassy field near the crematorium, but there wouldn't be a plaque or memorial for him.

"I won't go to his grave anyhow," she said.

When she came back from one of her trips, she seemed oddly pleased.

"I've been talking to a real estate agent. We'll get a good price for the house. No one seems to care he died at home, so that's something."

So we were moving away. But I didn't want to. I wanted to stay near Hailey. I knew that this discussion would have to come up soon, but I had decided to wait until after the cremation.

"When's he's really gone," she said, "I'll start working on his things. The first thing I want to do is get his stuff out of the way, and then we can decide what we want to keep. I'll give his clothes to charities. His suits are too good to chuck away, and there are plenty of people who can't afford a good pair of shoes."

She dabbled around the house, talking to herself. "A house or an apartment? Big city or small town?"

She never asked me for my opinion. I didn't offer one.

But the cremation didn't come. On the morning it was supposed to happen, she received a phone call from the coroner's office. I was upstairs with a book, but put it aside when Mom raised her voice. My door was wide open, a habit I had grown accustomed to.

"What do you mean they won't allow the cremation?"

Silence.

"Are you kidding me right now?"

Silence.

"Who? When?"

She was still on the phone when the doorbell rang. She hung up quickly and hurried into the hall.

"Shut the door, Alice," she snapped.

I left it open a crack.

The doorbell rang again just before Mom opened it. I couldn't see her face, but I could still imagine her expression used for unwanted visitors.

The police.

"Yes?" she said. "What can I do for you?"

"We'd like to talk to you about your husband, Mrs Jenkins," a man said. "May we come in?"

"Of course."

There were two of them, two men in suits, who entered our house and were taken to the living room. I didn't dare to sneak downstairs, but I did push my bedroom door wide open so I could hear their conversation clearly.

"Coffee? Tea?"

"No, thank you," one said. "We would like to talk about your husband's final days."

"What is there to say?" Mom said, sounding defensive. "He came home sick, he died. End of story."

"I'm afraid it's not that easy, Mrs Jenkins," the other one said. "Your husband did not die of natural causes. He died of an overdose. We received the blood results this morning, and they show an extremely high dosage of opioids in his system, consistent with an unnatural death."

"My husband was in excruciating pain. He took a lot of pills."

"We are not talking 'a lot', Mrs. Jenkins. We're talking a whole bottle, and probably more. Where is the rest of his medication?"

"Gone. I threw it out," Mom said. "Why?"

"We're here to find out if your husband accidentally or deliberately overdosed, or if he was helped into an early grave. What is your opinion on that?"

Mom said nothing.

"Did you have anything to do with his death, Mrs Jenkins?"

"If you're asking me if I killed him on purpose, the answer is no. Why would I? He was going to die anyway; why speed it up?"

"Do you know if your husband may have taken his own life to quicken the process?"

"He might have. How should I know?" Mom said, sounding cold.

"Were you not there with him the whole time?"

"No, I wasn't. I was doing chores, running to the store, that sort of thing. I was there most of the time, but not always."

"Well, the thing is, Mrs Jenkins, that your husband's doctor did prescribe certain medication, but the ones that were found semi-digested in his system after death were not what was prescribed."

"What?" Mom was shocked into silence for a moment. "You *autopsied* him?"

"Yes, we did."

"Why?"

"Normal procedure when foul play is suspected, which was the conclusion reached by the coroner once bloodwork was ordered. The autopsy confirmed his suspicion. Did you know that your husband could have lived two to three more weeks had he not overdosed?"

Silence, followed by, "Yes."

"And you never found it suspicious that he would die so quickly?"

"No."

"Why not?"

"He was exhausted from all the traveling. He told me he had given up. That's what people do, don't they? They just give up when there's no chance of survival."

"On the contrary, Mrs Jenkins. Sometimes they even last longer than originally thought. With some good medical care, your husband could have lived a couple of months longer. His doctor was very surprised that he passed so quickly, to say the least."

"Why would I kill him?" Mom said.

"Medical bills racking up, maybe? The fact that he might still have to be hospitalized if things got worse?"

"He had good medical coverage," Mom objected.

"But that still wouldn't cover everything."

"I'm really sorry, ma'am," the other police officer said, "but it's our job to investigate where he would have gotten that other medication."

"There was only one person in that room," Mom said, "and that was my husband. He wanted to be left alone. He didn't want me there, aside from when I needed to clean up the mess he made."

"Why not? Wouldn't a husband want to see his wife at his side when the end is near?"

"Jack didn't want me to see him suffer. So I left him, as per his request," Mom stammered. "We weren't a loving couple. We had grown apart."

"I see." Silence. "Did you love your husband, Mrs Jenkins?"

Mom hesitated. "We've had our ups and downs, but yes, I loved him until the day he died."

"Then I'm sure this is all a misunderstanding, and you wouldn't mind answering some questions at the police station? Just to get to the bottom of things. We just want to rule out any possible unknowns. Or maybe we've got it all wrong, and the medication he received was on his list."

Mom laughed. "If I had wanted to get rid of my husband, I would have killed him years ago."

The moment she said it, a silence fell on the room.

"I suggest that you don't say anything else without a lawyer present, ma'am."

"Am I under arrest?" Mom asked.

"Yes, ma'am, you are."

"You're insane."

"Give us a minute, ma'am," one of them said. "Please go to the kitchen. Our colleague will stay with you."

I heard some clicking sounds, and then they were talking amongst themselves about what to do next.

"First, talk to her, then see if we can get a search warrant."

Mom was escorted out of the house while I watched from upstairs, hiding in the library room, listening to the sounds of their footsteps. No one came to find me and arrest me too. I didn't dare to head downstairs. I let them go without doing anything.

They were gone.

I was so scared but also relieved they hadn't noticed me. For the first time in my life, being invisible wasn't so bad.

It seemed that for the first time in my life, I was going to be alone for an extended period of time. Mom had been arrested and there was no way she would return immediately. If they really felt something was wrong, they might even keep her there.

What was I going to do? How was I going to get her back? What did I have to do to free her from that situation? Go to the station myself? Tell them who I was? Defend Mom?

No, she would never want that. She'd want me to stay put, to continue life. To stay out of sight.

But I definitely needed help, and the only person I could think of was Hailey.

I fled the house and ran to her house, but her car wasn't there. She was still at work, and I had no idea when she'd be back.

I left a message on her door. *Please come to the house. Please.*

I knew she would recognize my handwriting. I couldn't head downtown to find her; I didn't even remember the name of the clothing store she worked at.

Once home, I paced the kitchen, wondering what to do next. The police said they needed a search warrant, but how and when would they get that? They would need evidence first, right? In all the police shows I had seen, there always had to be a reason to search a house. That had to be true of reality.

So assuming that took a while, and since there were no lives in danger, I could imagine them returning no sooner than tomorrow. Meaning I had the rest of the day to search for evidence myself.

I knew what I had to do. This would be my one chance to figure out what Dad had done, and it felt more important than figuring out how to get Mom back.

For days now, I had pondered Dad's words, but had not dared to go and search for clues. I still sensed that they had be in plain sight. If he was hiding anything, it would be in this house. Where else would he keep it?

I decided to start with the basement, even though I hated it there. As soon as I walked down the stairs and into the now-empty bedroom, I knew this would not be the place. It was devoid of any furniture.

The place in the back where they used to punish me when I was a kid had been cleared out over the years. Everything that used to be stashed there was gone. It was just one big empty space now.

I returned to the ground floor, to the kitchen with its phone that Mom had used to talk to the funeral director while she discussed Dad's funeral. "The simpler, the better. No service. No invitations. No flowers. No cards. No mementos. No grave. No memorial. No ceremony. Just cremate him and scatter him on your lawn for all I care."

She had given him my father's credit card number and confirmed that she didn't want to see his body before the cremation. She was cold and distant.

If the police had spoken to the funeral director and he told them about her odd behavior, that might have fueled their suspicions too.

The kitchen and living room wouldn't be where he would leave anything of value. The one room that had any meaning to him was his bedroom. I remembered his behavior when I had come to speak to him the other night, right before his death. He had shut the door on me.

His personal belongings and some of his clothes were still scattered across the room. Mom had said she would start cleaning up his things after the funeral, but she had been caught by surprise.

I looked around and rummaged through his closet, searching his suits hanging carelessly on various racks. He wouldn't keep anything here for Mom to find.

The locked wooden desk that stood in front of the window drew my attention. There were no papers on top; it was squeaky clean. There was just a silver pen in a velvet box with his name on it, a gift commemorating twenty-five years of service. For his thirtieth anniversary, he had received nothing.

"Thirty years isn't good enough," he had said bitterly.

Behind the desk stood the brown case that he used for traveling, containing documents, paperwork, brochures, and whatever he needed to do his job. Then, I remembered the suitcase with his traveling journals. It stood empty in his closet; the journals were no longer there. I looked at the desk again, which was locked. That would be the only other place he would keep his journals. I knew where he kept the keys, in the bottom drawer of the nightstand, in the same box where he kept his precious gold watch and wedding band.

I found the key and easily opened his desk, where his journals were waiting for me. Stacks of them, all the exact same size. The journals were each made of black leather with a year embossed on the cover, and consisted of thin paper, which made it light to carry and easy to tuck away in a jacket pocket.

For every year that he had traveled, Dad had used the exact same type of journal. I had seen him write in them, always jotting down notes about work. The final one, with the year *1980* on it, wasn't complete.

I took out all the journals and placed them on top of the desk, spreading them out and sorting them by year, from *1947* to *1980*. As I touched the leather, my fingers trembled. I was horrified by the thought that the truth I was looking for lay in front of me, a truth that could destroy what was left of this family.

Before I could start with *1980*, the doorbell rang.

19

I sat frozen as the doorbell rang repeatedly, followed by pounding on the door.

I panicked. I had been discovered. The cops were back, and this time they knew that I was living here. They had come for me after Mom had told them the truth. She would have pointed them to me, or they figured out she had been lying.

I sat down at the top of the stairs and hugged my knees, hiding my face until I heard a familiar voice call out my name.

"Alice, are you there?"

I could have wept with joy. I rushed down the stairs, almost tripping over my own feet, and ran to open the front door.

Hailey immediately took me in her embrace, hugging me as she had done before, but even firmer. She smelled of a sweet, flowery perfume. She wore a beautiful deep-blue dress, and matching shoes with heels, making her even taller.

I pulled back, ashamed of my appearance in my old clothes. I felt disgusting, ugly, and smelly, even though I'd taken a shower a few hours ago. Mom always said to take care of my hygiene, and I'd always done so.

Hailey didn't seem to care. Her fingertip brushed off tears I didn't know I had shed; her voice sounded calm, gentle, and caring.

"Oh, Alice. My poor, sweet Alice. Are you okay?"

I nodded.

She closed the door behind her and stood tall in our hallway. This was the first time she'd been here, and I noticed her looking around curiously.

"Where's your mom? Why am I here? What's going on?"

I started to sign.

"Wow, that's way too fast. Calm down, Alice. What's wrong?"

I grabbed her by the hand and pulled her into the kitchen, where one of my notepads lay on the table. I grabbed a pen off the kitchen counter and wrote quickly.

Mom arrested. Police took her.

"Wait, *what*?"

They think she killed dad.

She was stunned. "Seriously? Why would they think that? He died of cancer, didn't he?"

I nodded. *Overdose.*

"You mean his medication? She gave him more on purpose?"

I nodded and wrote, *Not true!!!*

"Why would she do that when he was already dying?"

I shrugged.

"Is there any evidence?"

I shook my head.

"Oh, my God, Alice, I'm so sorry. She's at the police station now?"

I nodded again.

"Do you want me to call them?"

No! I signed. *No police.*

"They still don't know you're here, do they?"

I shook my head.

"But they'll figure that out sooner or later. It's just a matter of time." She thought for a moment. "Did they say anything about a search warrant or something like that? To look for evidence?"

I wrote down, *Maybe. Tomorrow?*

"Jesus. If they search the house tomorrow, they'll find out you're here too."

I nodded. *They'll take me away.*

"Why would they do that? You're a grown woman."

Think I'm crazy.

"No, they'd never do that."

Yes, they will!

Hailey frowned, pausing for a moment before she spoke gently, reaching for my hand. "Alice... do you think she did it?"

No!! Never!!

"Are you willing to tell them that?"

I shook my head. *She told me no.*

"But the circumstances are serious, and she'll need all the help she can get. Don't you think you're past the point of hiding now?"

I won't go!

"Alice..."

I'm scared!!!!!

Hailey sighed. "I know you are, but these are serious circumstances. Your mom needs you to be there for her."

I know. But I can't.

"Why not?"

She said no.

"And you always do as she says. Right."

It sounded like an accusation, even though Hailey probably didn't mean it like that. It still hurt. Hailey remained quiet for a while, until she finally seemed to make a decision.

"Well, one thing's for sure: If you don't want to be found, then you need to not be here when they search the house. You'll have to come with me while we figure out what to do about your mom. Come on, grab some things."

No. Mom will be so angry.

"I'll talk to her and explain. It's fine. You'll have to trust me on this."

I thought about Hailey's proposal and the consequences of leaving this house for the first time in my life. If I did, I would never find out the truth. Unless I told her.

I can't go with you, I signed.

"What?" she stood bewildered. "Why?"

I took a deep breath. I was so tired, so numb.

My body felt like it was made from pudding, and my legs had trouble keeping me up, but I couldn't rest now. And I also couldn't just leave with my dad's journals, which were sitting in plain sight in his bedroom right now. I needed to know if they were the key to his past. Everything in me screamed that they were. I couldn't just go without them. But I couldn't drag Hailey into this either.

You have to go, I signed. *Please go home.*

"No. What, are you kidding me? You need my help. And you need some food and rest. I won't let you be here all by myself."

I have things to do here.

"What things?"

I can't tell you that.

"Why not?"

Please go.

I walked over to the front door and opened it for her, trying to look firm and determined. She needed to be free from me and my troubles. I'd been stupid to allow her into my life in the first place.

"What are you doing, Alice?" she said, frowning.

Please go. Forget me, I signed.

"Do you really think I can leave, knowing you won't be okay on your own?"

I am not your concern.

She walked to the door, but instead of leaving, she closed it again and walked over to me, cupping my face. "I won't go," she said softly.

I wanted to ask her why not, but her lips stopped me from trying to respond. She *kissed* me. Our lips connected, and then everything else fell away.

It was the softest touch I had ever experienced. No one had ever kissed me before, but if this was what love felt like, I wanted it to last forever. Her hands were in my hair, stroking it as her kiss deepened. I felt my whole body respond to her touch. It was electrifying.

When she let go, we were both panting. I could see her breasts move behind her blue dress, and I wanted nothing more than to undress her, to feel her bare skin beneath those clothes. Suddenly it felt all too warm in the room. I felt dizzy. She reached for me and kissed me again. She could do whatever she wanted with me. I felt safe and warm, almost cozy. This was the best moment of my life. I never wanted it to end.

"This is why I can't let you stay here alone," she whispered in my ear. "I love you. I've loved you from the moment I first saw you."

I love you, I signed. *Don't go.*

I couldn't stop myself. I reached for her hand and pulled her up the stairs. She laughed as she walked with me, probably thinking I was going to take her to bed. But I wasn't. I was going to share my secret with her. I opened my dad's bedroom door and pulled her in with me until we stood in front of his desk. She stared, troubled, at all the notebooks on the table.

"What is this?" she said. "What's going on?"

I stopped her with a single wave of my hand. Another one told her to wait. I ran to my room and came back with a notepad and pen.

She sat down on Dad's bed while I wrote. Her eyes scanned the room, wanting to find out why we were here.

My dad's room.

"Okay?"

His notes.

"His notes? His journals, you mean?"

I nodded, happy she understood.

"Why are they here? What's in them? What do you want with them?"

I started writing but stopped after three words. It was too much to write down. I sighed impatiently, frustrated with myself; I needed time to tell my story. Hailey got up from the bed. She studied me.

"Okay, I get that it's too hard for you to explain, so let's figure this out together, okay?"

Okay.

She pointed at the notebooks. "His notebooks. From his travels?"

Yes, I signed.

"And you have them here because you want to remember him somehow?"

No.

"Then why...?"

Something in there.

"Like what? A message? A secret?"

Maybe. I need to find out. He said things.

"What do you mean? When he was sick?"

I nodded.

"Under the influence or something?"

Another nod.

"What did he say?"

I bit my lip and wrote down the words as well as I could.

I think he may have killed people.

She was shocked to silence. "Are you serious?"

I nodded and let my fingers do the talking. I wrote without thinking.

He talked about it.

"Jesus fuck. Did he say who? Or why?"

No. But it has to do with me. Why I was locked up.

I looked at my hands. My tears flowed freely.

He had wanted to keep this secret from me, but not from Mom. If there was anything I was certain of right now, it was that she was aware of what he'd done.

That had been the subject of their argument. He'd wanted to confess to me, and she tried to prevent him. But he still did – if only in part.

What if Mom had come home ten minutes later that day? Would I have discovered the truth?

"Alice?"

I looked at Hailey, who stood perfectly still, regarding me intently. She was the only one I could trust, the one person who didn't have a stake in all of this. She would never lie to me.

She was all I had left in this world, and if I sent her away now, I would never see her again. So I made my decision.

Those journals screamed at me to be read, and I needed her help to figure this out.

I pointed at the notebooks. They were all I had to go on. Those journals were the only record he had kept.

"You think there's something in these?"

Yes.

I sat her down on the bed and took my time writing it all down, every word Dad had said. She varied between fear and surprise.

"Fuck. Damn it, Alice. If this is true... do you know what that means?" Hailey wasn't as shocked as I had expected her to be, as if she had already believed the worst of my dad, and I had just confirmed it. "If your dad really did something awful, it means that no one in the world knows about it. It means he got away with it for god-knows how many years. And now that he's dead, he won't even be punished for it."

I pointed to the stack of diaries on his desk again and the brown case on the floor that lay open. *I need to know.*

Hailey got up and gently touched the leather binding of one of them. She picked it up and leafed through.

"This is a sales journal. All his sales that he made over the past thirty years or so, right? What else is there?"

Memento, I wrote.

"A memory from his past? Something to hold onto?"

Yeah. But which one?

Hailey's hand roamed over the journals, touching the embossed numbers with her fingertips. "It's like finding a needle in a haystack. There are so many of them."

Hailey's facial expression reflected what was going through my mind. She was obviously stuck between urgently flipping through every book and her disbelief that this was real. I felt the exact same way.

"Do you really believe he killed someone?"

I reached for a pen and notepad. *No. I think he killed several.*

Hailey's mouth fell open.

I need to know if this is real, I wrote. *Or if it was all bullshit.*

"Let's hope for bullshit," she whispered. "I'll help you, no doubt about that, but Alice, these journals could just be memories of his travels. If he really did bad things, would he honestly write them down as a keepsake?"

I took my time writing my answer.

He threw everything else away. Why not these?

"I don't know… It could just be memories of a job that he liked."

He loathed *his job.*

"Oh." She paused. "You are so brave, Alice. Do you know that?"

I shrugged. *If he was a murderer, I want to know.*

"And then what?"

I don't know yet. But not knowing is worse.

Hailey took a deep breath and kicked off her high-heeled shoes. "Okay, then. Let's find out who he really was."

I reached for the very first journal, the one with *1947* embossed in the leather, hoping there would be nothing in it. He had started out that year as a salesman, his very first job. Would he really have done something so awful so soon?

I gave Hailey the year after, *1948*. She pulled her dress up a bit so she could sit cross-legged on the bed, obviously unbothered by the fact that he used to sleep there. I plunked down next to her, opened the journal, and began scanning page by page.

Deep down, I knew he had been telling the truth. Mom's reaction was all the proof I needed.

20

Hailey's regular breathing kept me sane while my fingers walked through the year 1947. I was looking for anything out of the ordinary that might prove that my father was a murderer. A serial killer. An abductor. A rapist.

Anything. Or nothing at all.

We both had no clue what we were looking for, but Hailey never doubted or questioned me about it. She just went at it.

My dad's handwriting was small but legible. I found loads of information on products he had sold, the brand, the price, the contents of promotion packs. He had jotted down names of customers and phone numbers, sometimes only one per day, sometimes up to ten.

As a door-to-door salesman, he would not have any appointments up front, unless the company had provided him with a list, *and* he would have had products in the trunk of his car to sell on the spot. So instead of writing down the names of the customers that he had visited, he had written a list of all the items he had sold that day.

Those who wanted more products or regular visits were kept in a separate section in the back, along with all the sales contracts that he had closed. Later on, he would send those contracts by post, and then by fax or telephone. That had been his routine for over thirty years.

Every day varied, but they all contained similar notes.

Dad had made a habit of writing down the name of the state that he was in on every page. For example, he would go to Chicago in January, stay in a certain area, and go door to door. The week later, he would be in Dallas and do the same.

The weekly notes in every month of 1947 were exactly the same. New states, new cities or towns, new places to visit to sell his products. I noticed that he wasn't particularly fond of big cities. He made notes about those that he loathed.

Never again. Hate this place. Hate the people!!!

But small towns, he liked. *LOVELY food. Great people. Good sales. Will be back.*

I had no clue what other salespeople did, but this journal looked pretty normal. Until I found it: the smallest of clues in the month of June.

There was a brief note scribbled on one day that was different from all the others, with a tiny yellow line marking it. It was the only yellow mark I found.

On June 24th, he arrived in Pennsylvania, where he had spent a week in a place called Milford. On the first day of that week, he wrote the name of the town in full, followed by the name of the state. Milford – Pennsylvania. On the second day, and all the days that followed, he jotted down MIL-PEN, to show that he was still there.

So far, that was the same as all the other weeks. Back in those days, it would have been hard to travel by plane. It wasn't that common yet and quite expensive to do. I remember Mom telling me once that he would be away for weeks at a time, because traveling back and forth took too long. Years later, once flying or train travel became common, his habits changed, and he would come home during the weekends.

During his first year, he was already selling a lot. I saw dates that often marked up to twenty products per day. That week in June, he had flourished. MIL-PEN was obviously a goldmine for him; he sold by the dozens, or so it seemed.

But the number of days he spent selling here was different. Normally he would sell for five days before traveling to another location. But not this week. There were no sales numbers jotted down on days four and five. He had drawn a black cross over the pages. Next to the abbreviation MIL-PEN, he had written down the letters A.B.

Who or what was A.B.?

Was it a town? A suburb? The initials of a person? It could be anything, including a reference to some new product.

When I leafed through the other pages, I didn't find another instance of those letters. None on any of the other pages in that journal. And this was the only week he had used the yellow marker to underline that week's importance.

"What is it?" Hailey said. "What did you find?"

I showed her, while jotting down on my notepad. *Something's not right.*

I pointed at the crossed pages and the yellow marker.

She frowned. "Hm. That's odd."

What does it mean? I signed.

"I don't know. Could be a person, or some reference to a place he visited. It might not mean anything. I honestly have no clue. But it is odd, though. And I think I came across something similar. Look."

She placed her journal on my lap. "You see this? July first to July third, 1948. Three marked days without any sales numbers, all with the letters S.K. added. He was in California at the time, and there are no further markings on any of the other pages. We're onto something."

Initials? I signed.

"Not sure yet."

What else could it be?

"I don't know. Let's find out if there are more."

We quickly checked eight different journals from the fifties, sixties, and seventies, and they all had similar entries. Different states, different dates, two, three or even four days with no sales noted, only letters. I made a list and ranking of the late forties and early fifties, realizing with a shiver running down my spine, that this had been going on for way too long.

1947: A.B., Milford, Pennsylvania, June 30–July 2
1948: S.K., Half Moon Bay, California, July 1–July 3
1949: S.T., Marfa, Texas, March 2–March 3
1950: Q.E., Thurmont, Maryland, April 5–April 8
1951: W.T., Akron, Ohio, Sept 1–Sept 4
1952: H.V., Paoli, Indiana, Aug 10–Aug 14
1953: A.D., Paterson, New Jersey, Nov 2–Nov 3
1954: K.L., Avalon, California, Oct 24–Oct 28

By the time we were finished with the list, I was shaking. I didn't want to believe it, but there it was. There was something so off about all of this, I could hardly touch the journals anymore.

These were initials. They had to be. But whose were they? Why were they important enough to my dad that he had jotted them down in each journal?

"There's no logic in the dates, nor in the locations," Hailey said. "If he really did something awful, he was smart enough to do whatever he did in different places, often thousands of miles away from each other, to avoid getting caught."

I didn't want to think about the people behind those initials. Didn't want to go down that path right now. I didn't want to accept that my dad could have... *murdered* them, while at the same time, I was already starting to accept this new gruesome reality.

The others. That's what he called them. *The others.*

Who had my father really been?

What had he done?

"Are you okay?" Hailey asked.

No.

She hugged me. "I'm so sorry, Alice. Are you sure you still want to pursue this? We can stop now, you know. We can put them away and ignore them for the rest of our lives. We can pretend they never existed. Burn them. Destroy any evidence."

I looked at her bewildered. *Why?*

"Because..." She stopped. "Never mind."

I knew what she was going to say. She was so determined to protect me that she would really take those journals outside and burn them just to save my sanity. But I didn't need saving. I needed the truth. I wanted to know what my dad had done, to whom, and why.

And what all of this had to do with me.

"Okay," Hailey said, before taking a deep breath. "If you're sure, let's get through the list."

She smiled briefly and focused on the list, going over each town with her index finger.

"Okay, so what strikes me as odd is that these are all small towns. Not big, anonymous cities. They're the size of Hays, which is really strange. Why not take to bigger cities, where he wouldn't stand out? He was taking a lot of risks, don't you think?"

I don't know.

"Right, you don't know any other towns or cities."

I smiled. *No.*

"Okay, so if you're in a city like, let's say Chicago, getting away with murder seems easier. You can kill someone, drop the body anywhere and scoot off. But everyone knows each other in a town like this, so strangers would stand out more."

What about police? I signed.

"Police?"

Small town, small police force?

"Ah." Hailey smiled. "Smart. A smaller town might not have the resources to deal with something like this. They might not be able to figure out who the culprit is."

I took my notepad. *You mean the murderer.*

"Right." Hailey looked troubled. "So we're now assuming that he killed people?"

Yes.

"Okay. Assume the worst and hope for the best, right?"

Yes.

But we both knew that we were fooling ourselves.

I gazed at my watch and became aware of the fact that my mom had been gone for hours, and that no one had returned to the house yet. I was done with the journals for now; I didn't want to touch another one today. I was hungry and exhausted.

But there was one thing I needed to know for sure. I was born in 1956, in this very house. I knew he had met my mom in the late forties, but their relationship had obviously not been enough for him to resist doing creepy stuff. Maybe it had even magnified his habits. After all, they hated each other's guts, and hadn't she told me they had married because she was pregnant at the time? She had lost that baby, and two more, before she had me. Even becoming a dad after all these years didn't stop his sick behavior.

I reached for the journal that read *1958*, a few years after my birth, and flipped through it, almost immediately finding what I was looking for. There it was, the evidence that he hadn't stopped after my birth. There was no doubt in my mind that all the others would have the same markings.

I shivered.

"Are you okay?" Hailey asked.

I shook my head. She leaned forward and grabbed my hand, squeezing it gently. "You know, this really doesn't have to mean anything. These markings could just be a list of customers, people he had met along the way that didn't buy anything yet, but who he would go back to later. Or it could still be a town, or an event, or even a seminar or something."

Right.

"Or maybe he went to visit places that had meant something to him."

Uh huh.

"It doesn't have to mean more than that. What if all of this is one big misunderstanding, and your dad simply wanted to keep track of something important to him?"

Affairs?

"Maybe. It really could be anything."

But these weren't affairs. My stomach clenched.

"Alice?" Hailey asked carefully.

I scribbled down what I had to say. *He did something terrible. I just know it.*

Hailey contemplated my words. "You're very sure of this, aren't you?"

Yes. Without a doubt.

"Alright then," she spoke after a slight pause. "I trust your gut feeling."

Thank you.

"What for?"

Believing me.

She smiled. "But what are we going to do, then? If he really did bad things, we need to go to the police. We can't sit on those journals."

And tell them what?

"What your dad told you. Show them these journals. Then it's up to them, but I would assume they would start an investigation. They will figure this out. That's what they do. They're good at that."

Who will believe me?

"Why wouldn't they?"

I'm non-existent. Isolated. Trapped.

"You mean that they will treat you like an–" She stopped. She didn't say it, but I filled in the blank, signing it slowly.

Idiot.

"You are not an idiot, Alice. On the contrary: you grew up in this house isolated, under the strict supervision of your mother and in the shadow of an estranged, odd father."

I will be mocked.

"No, you won't be. I'll explain to them what has been going on over the years."

I'm not normal.

"Yes, you are. Stop putting yourself down. You're smart and intelligent, and they will notice that immediately," she said fiercely. "Listen, we need to figure this out, and I will help you, okay? I will help you learn the truth. I'll support you when we talk to the police. I'll interpret. Trust me. Let's go to them now. I'll drive."

Panic flooded over me as I realized the one complication that I had willfully ignored for the past few hours.

We can't.

Hailey paused, confused. "Why not? I don't understand, Alice. Are you still protecting him? He's dead, what good would that do?"

Not him.

She immediately understood what I was trying to say.

"Alice, did your mom know about this?"

I looked away.

"Alice, tell me the truth."

I took my notepad again. *She knew.*

"Are you sure?"

Yes. She told me.

"Then she belongs in prison too."

No. Yes. I don't know.

"Alice, do you know what you're saying? You're telling me that your mom is aware of what your dad may have done. Were they in on it together?"

I don't know.

"But she didn't do… whatever-this-is with him?"

No. She was always here.

Hailey drew her conclusions based on the scarce info I'd given her. "If she wasn't with him during his travels, she can't have been a direct accomplice. But she still knew, and she never stopped him."

Yes.

"Are you going to confront her?"

No.

"Why not?"

I scribbled down on my pad. *I still love her.*

"Oh."

It was true, and my predicament felt extremely overwhelming. When it came to my mom, I was stuck between love and hate. And I was so scared for her. Of her.

"Really?" she asked.

I nodded, because I couldn't help myself.

"Okay. I respect that, even if I don't understand it. I didn't grow up like you, and I won't pretend to grasp all that you've been through. So, if you want to continue loving her, that's fine."

Thank you.

I loved her, but I feared her, too. And I feared her reaction. If she was released, they would let her go home, and then what? She would find me in this room with these journals, and she would realize what I had done. And then one of two things could happen: Either she would punish me for snooping around and tell me I was an ungrateful little brat before locking me up again for the rest of my life. And, to keep my silence forever, she could even kill me, easily, and the world would be none the wiser. Or she could find me here with the evidence at hand, smile, take it away from me, hug me and tell me that it was all over, and that we were finally free of him for good. I feared the first scenario but yearned for the second.

Still, an inkling of hope clung in me. Could her love for me be the reason she had changed overnight? Or was it her release from fear that had brought on this difference in her?

Had she known all this time what he was capable of and been threatened by him enough to keep quiet? Had he held my existence over her head, blackmailing her? Had he threatened to kill me if she had gone against him?

But why, then, in all these years, had she not gone to the police herself and told them who he was, what he had done? Why keep her silence when she knew the truth? She had ample opportunities, especially when he was out of town traveling. He could have been arrested so many times with no means to return home to kill me.

It didn't make any sense to me.

Unless...

There was one other option I hadn't considered. What if she had known, had somehow been involved in all of this, and had even supported it? People were strange; I learned that from my books and TV-shows. What if some twisted version of her had wanted him to hurt people?

What if her involvement had been so essential that it forced her to kill him after she'd found out he had been blabbing to me? What if killing him was just to keep him from talking even more, to stop me from finding out the truth?

Maybe she didn't kill him to protect me, or to put him out of his misery. Maybe she did it to protect herself. If that were the case, she wouldn't be able to tell the police her reasonings without giving away her secrets. She could only tell them that she gave him the extra dosage of medication to help. Which might actually work. They might show her pity and release her.

Or not.

If she confessed, they would send people to the house to find evidence to lock her up. She would be arrested and charged with murder or manslaughter, or whatever they did in court.

The worst-case scenario would then unfold. They would find me living in this house, and they would wonder who I was and why I had been kept hidden here for so long.

They would quickly figure out I was mute and useless,

and then they would treat me in the worst possible way and handle me like some ignorant young woman who didn't know how the world worked.

They would lock me up. Put me in an insane asylum. Or worse, keep me in a drug-induced stupor, because I had to be the idiot they assumed I was. They would think I was worthless, justifying my non-existence.

This was my future, and it was bleak, dark, and hopeless. I had no future at all. Nothing to look forward to but everlasting darkness.

I stared from the journal to Hailey, who swam in and out of my vision. Panic struck me like a sledgehammer that slammed into me repeatedly. I couldn't stay here. I couldn't live in this house, not with my mom, not on my own. I had to go now, before anyone could find me here.

All the fear and anxiety I had been burying rushed back all at once, overwhelming any sane thought.

No police. No investigation. There was only one thing I could do.

I jumped off the bed, picked up journal after journal and threw them into the open brown case. Hailey's hands were on my shoulders, shaking me.

"What are you doing?" she yelled. "Alice, calm down!"

The panic became so overwhelming that the world started to fade before my eyes. The brown blurred in front of me; I couldn't even close it.

"Alice, look at me. Stop!"

I stopped and looked at Hailey, whose face I barely recognized. Everything turned hazy, including her.

I couldn't breathe. I choked on my own anxiety.

Hailey yelled, but I couldn't make out the words. And then she faded too.

21

Something cold rested on my forehead. Someone held my hand and spoke. The words seemed to have to thread through layer upon layer of fabric to reach my ears, before I could finally understand them.

"You'll be fine, Alice. Just breathe, and you'll be okay, I promise. Just wake up for me, okay? Open your eyes now, or I'll have to call for help."

I finally opened them, and as I looked into Hailey's concerned eyes, the feeling of being choked was gone. My mind had been swimming, and now my body screamed for sleep. Yearned for it. I was exhausted. The many sleepless nights were finally catching up with me.

"Thank God you're back," she said, releasing a sigh that said how worried she had been. "How are you feeling?"

I shrugged, and she smiled.

"That lousy, huh?"

I smiled softly. I was lying on the floor of my dad's room, feeling drained.

"You need some sleep," Hailey said. "I'll gather some of your things, and then you're coming with me, okay? I won't leave you alone in here for one minute longer than I have to."

I nodded, even though I was terrified to leave this sacred territory that I had grown up in. I moved slowly into a sitting position, still dizzy, but feeling better. She ran into the bathroom and came back with a glass of water.

"You had a panic attack."

Sorry.

She handed me my notepad back. I scribbled down the words with trembling fingers. They were barely recognizable. *I can't stay here.*

"Why not?"

Afraid.

"Of what?"

Everything.

I turned to signing next.

I have to go.

"What? Alice, what are you talking about? Our next steps are clear. We obviously have to go to the police."

No. I need to know.

"Know what?"

What he did.

"No, you don't. Not by yourself. The police will figure this out for you."

If they believe me.

"They will. I can translate for you. There are many mute people in this world, Alice. There's nothing wrong with that. Why are you so scared they won't believe you?"

I took my notepad again. *Because people don't like people who are different.*

Hailey frowned and bit her lip, making her look so beautiful my heart leapt.

They will not listen. Trust me.

When she looked at me, I knew I'd gained her understanding.

"You're right," she said. "People don't like those who are different from what they see as normal. But you are not different from any of us. You can hear perfectly fine, and you are more intelligent than the average person. You're streetwise, even if you've never lived outside this house. I'm convinced anyone who gets to know you will see you for who you really are. I'll make sure that they do."

It won't be enough.

Hailey frowned.

I need to do this myself.

"Then what do you want to do?"

I want to leave this house.

"On your own?!"

Yeah.

"Alice, that's impossible. First of all, you've never been out on your own. You wouldn't know where to start, or how to handle this."

That was very true.

"And where would you even begin to search? You can't just go out there and start looking for clues that might not exist. Where would you even start?"

I had an idea, but I let her continue first.

"You're talking about something that may or may not have happened back in the forties and fifties, assuming those markings in your dad's journals are initials. Which they may not be, remember? Where do you begin decades later?"

I reached for my notepad again and carefully wrote down the idea that had begun to take shape in my head before the panic attack knocked me out. It seemed so logical, now that I had time to think about it.

Not the old ones. His latest journals are where I'll start.

Her eyebrows arched in surprise.

"Damn, Alice. Smart thinking. It makes sense to start from there and trace his steps back."

I will tell the police, but not yet.

"Because you want to make sure."

Yes, I signed.

"What about your mom? What if she comes back?"

I'll deal with that later.

"You won't go tell her?"

No.

"So, you're ignoring her for now?"

Yes.

"But you do realize you need to confront her sooner or later, right?"

Later is better.

"Ignoring the problem won't make it go away," she said.

I know. But I'm still going, I signed.

Hailey smiled. "You're stubborn, but I guess that's a good sign."

I shrugged.

"Alright, then," she said after a moment of silence. "Where are we going first?"

We?

"Duh. I need to make some calls and get some things arranged, but my boss owes me some time off. I've been doing a lot of unpaid overtime. I'll fix it."

I gazed at her in bewilderment. *You're coming with me?* I signed.

"Of course I am. I won't let you wander out into the wilds on your own. This isn't exactly a fieldtrip."

I beamed. I could've just kissed her again, but I didn't.

"Promise me something, though."

Yes?

"Once we find proof, we'll go to the police and let them do the rest of the investigation. That's my one condition."

I promise.

"Thank you. You do realize this is insane, right?"

Yeah.

"Good. As long as we agree."

I smiled.

Hailey reached for my hand and squeezed it.

"You're crazily amazing, you know that? And by the way, you do realize that your non-existence will benefit you right now?"

I gazed at her in wonder.

"People who aren't missed aren't searched for. Which means you can travel anywhere you want while remaining under the radar, unless your mom does tell the cops about you and they put out an APB, which is unlikely."

Hailey's words put my existence into a whole new perspective. She was right. Being invisible meant that I could travel wherever I wanted to go, and no one would be the wiser. I could remain a mystery to the world, quickly forgotten by passersby. We were free to go wherever we wanted to.

The thought made a shiver run down my spine. Being invisible sounded great right now.

PART FIVE
On the Road

22

So it was decided. We were going on a road trip together, Hailey and me. I was scared to death, but this was it. My first endeavor in the real world. And I had no idea what I was doing.

While Hailey was on the phone downstairs with her manager, setting things up for her sudden absence – I had no idea what she was telling her, but I didn't hear any shouting or anything, so I figured it would be okay – I was upstairs gathering some things.

I didn't want to take too much, just what was needed. I rummaged through my bedroom, locating the most decent clothes I could find, which wasn't that much, and threw them on the bed.

I knew Mom kept a suitcase up in the attic, so I pushed away my fear and went up one floor, where I found it in a corner all dusty and covered in spiderwebs. I ignored the sensation of cobwebs touching my face, bit back my fear of all the darkest corners that I had never dared to look at too closely and hurried back downstairs.

The suitcase was difficult to open, but I managed to pry the locks, and cleaned it off with a towel from the bathroom. Soon, it was filled with some sweaters, two pairs of jeans that I had hardly ever worn, a couple of old T-shirts, some socks, underwear, and an extra pair of sneakers.

I walked into the library room and debated taking a book

or two, wondering if I would be able to fall asleep without reading at least a little bit. I pulled two thin books from the bookshelves, and packed up some basic hygiene necessities, like sanitary products, my toothbrush, toothpaste, soap, deodorant, and shampoo. And that was it.

Hailey finished her conversation downstairs. I could hear her footsteps creak on the staircase. I had thought about the practicalities, but there was one thing still missing: money.

Mom always kept some cash underneath the mattress in the spare bedroom. I knew a lot of it was lost to her drinking, but there would be at least something left, perhaps enough to pay for a couple of nights in a motel.

Right now, I couldn't envision how this was going to play out. Where would I go first? And how would I handle the situation once I got there? But those were worries for later.

I walked into the spare room and lifted the mattress, revealing two large envelopes filled with money. There was more than I had expected, about five hundred dollars altogether.

Hailey whistled when she saw me grab them.

"Wow," she said. "That'll help, for sure."

I thought about Mom's other hiding place downstairs in the kitchen. She always kept a box of money there in case some delivery guy or the paper boy knocked on the door looking for payment. I felt awful grabbing that money too, but it was a means to an end.

"You're already packed," Hailey said surprised. "How long was I on the phone?"

I smiled. *I don't have much*, I signed.

"You have plenty of strength and determination. That'll get us where we need to go. Anyhow, I arranged things with my manager. She wasn't pleased, but ah well, what could she possibly do when I reminded her of all the time I've put in?"

So you're coming?

"Of course. Wouldn't want to miss this for the world. So, what's next? What else do you need to take?"

Hailey and I walked back to my dad's bedroom. I pointed at the journals and the brown case they usually sat in.

"You want to take them all?" she said.

I nodded.

"Why? We could make notes. They could stay here."

Don't trust anyone.

"Ah. You want them for safekeeping."

Yes.

"Good thinking."

And evidence.

"Uh huh. Okay, so how are we going to go about this? I mean, we can't just start driving, right? We need a plan."

I took my notepad and wrote down, *local newspapers.*

"Yeah, great idea. If anything happened to anyone in one of those towns, there would be gossip."

Yes.

"I'm hungry. Do you have anything to eat?"

Not much.

"Why don't we pack up those journals then and move our investigation to my place? I'd feel a lot safer there. You know, just in case someone *does* come back tonight."

Okay.

We stacked all the journals in the brown case. Hailey closed the lid. I took one last look around Dad's room, ignoring the eerie feeling I might never return. Then closed the door.

We walked to my bedroom, where I said goodbye to every

little detail, without saying it out loud. Hailey would think I was crazy, but I knew every corner and nook of this room.

I walked into the library room next, where I tried to ignore that sinking feeling leaving my favorite books. It really felt as if I was never going to come back. There was no way to know what might happen in the coming days. To know if I would ever be able to return to Hays.

"Are you okay?" Hailey said.

No.

"If you want to cry, that's fine. If you need a hug, let me know."

I turned to her and buried my body in her embrace, feeling fear, anguish, and sadness flush through me, overtaking me. This was a farewell to my old life, and we both knew it.

"It'll be alright," she muttered in my ear. "I promise, it'll be fine."

Her hand stroked my hair, comforting me in a way no one had ever done before. There was something familiar in the gesture, but I couldn't place it. It was too long ago, more like a misty recollection of something that someone had done.

"You'll be fine," she repeated. "Let's get you out of here, okay? Are you ready?"

I brushed my sleeve across my face and nodded. I was ready to go. To leave this house forever.

"Wait. Do you have any ID or something?"

I had no clue. I wasn't sure if I'd ever had one.

"Doesn't matter. Let's go."

Hailey took my bag and guided me out of the house, over our adjoined driveways, to hers. I'd been there before, but it still felt like the furthest I'd ever gone in my life.

* * *

Hailey's house was similar in terms of layout to ours, but completely different in every other way. I noticed that as soon as she showed me in.

What I saw took me by surprise. In my mind's eye, she had this gorgeously decorated house with loads of expensive stuff, but it was exactly the opposite. It was almost devoid of furniture or decoration, as if she'd barely taken the time to make it her home.

Mom, despite all her problems, had always tried to make our house look homely. She would have the walls redone every ten years or so, and she'd hung pictures everywhere. I remembered how much effort she had put into my library room; how comfortable it had been.

I'd always thought that her demeanor didn't match her decoration style, as if I was living with two versions of her at the same time.

Hailey's house was just bare. Not cozy at all. Cold, even. It was hard to imagine anyone living here.

The hallway had one rack for coats and shoes, and one potted plant that looked as if it had died five years ago. Her shoes were scattered over the floor, her coats hung on the rack.

The living room contained two sofas, a mix and match of different colors that didn't seem to fit together whatsoever; a coffee table and two side tables; one cupboard that didn't have any decoration on it; and one empty glass cabinet. That was all. The walls were empty. The wallpaper had obviously not been replaced since she'd moved in. I could see the contours where the previous owners had hung posters and paintings.

There was absolutely nothing personal, as if she'd moved into the house with nothing but a suitcase.

"I'm sorry it isn't much," she said apologetically. "I'm renting this place, and most of my stuff is still in storage. I've been postponing getting it all because it's so much work to get settled in."

Oh.

She looked around. "It's just a place to live, you know."

Not a home?

"Not really. I'm not so sure if I want to make changes to it now, if I'm honest. Since I've moved in, I've hardly found the time to put some decent effort into it. I'm actually looking for a place to buy, so it's pointless spending a lot of money on a rental place, don't you think?"

Buy? I signed.

"Yeah. When I got this job offer, I wasn't so sure Hays would be for me, so I figured I'd rent first to see if I liked the town, spend most of my efforts on my job and go from there."

Do you want to stay?

"Maybe. I'm not sure about that yet, to be honest. I mean, I like my job and the challenge of it, and they've actually offered me a management position, but I... I don't know. I haven't found my way around Hays just yet."

She looked at me. I looked at her.

"You really are the only friend I have in this town. My colleagues are nice and all, but they're not my friends, you know? I'm sure it'll figure itself out at some point. It's not something I need to decide right now."

Hailey had never told me how she had landed this job in Hays, and it didn't matter to me. People moved from town to town all the time. All I knew about her was that she had no living relatives left, and that she liked to live here or there, trying out new things.

She'd been orphaned about four years ago. Her parents were both lost in a car accident, she'd told me, without expanding on the details. No siblings, no aunts and uncles. A grandmother, in a retirement home, who'd been diagnosed with early dementia and who didn't recognize Hailey. She had said it was too painful to go visit her.

I didn't push for details. She hadn't been ready to talk about it, I could sense. So I kept away from the subject. One day, she'd tell me, I knew.

Hailey brought me to the kitchen, where she prepared hot chocolate and popped in some toast. We ate it with butter and cheese, and it was wonderfully sweet and soothing.

"Comfort food; my favorite," she said, eating quickly, before clearing off the large kitchen table so we could take out the journals and get to work.

We'd already decided to start at the newest journal and work backwards, so I picked the one dated *1979*, thinking that *1980* probably didn't have any markers in it, seeing as Dad had already been too sick. Hailey took *1978*.

"Number one: search for clues. Number two: figure out what we're going to do, and how. Number three: get some sleep. We won't leave tonight, but first thing in the morning. Okay?"

Okay.

It only took a couple of minutes to find the familiar clues in *1979*, *1978*, and *1977*. I saw Hailey's fingers tremble when she put a small piece of paper between her journals. This was getting to her, too.

We made a list.

1979: G.H., Lexington, Massachusetts, January 17–19
1978: P.L, Des Moines, Iowa, January 28–30
1977: R.T, Rockton, Illinois, March 1–3

"Where do you want to go?" Hailey asked.

I pointed at *1979*. That was the most recent one, not counting this year, of course. If something had happened in that town, not even two years ago, people would still remember.

"Are you sure 1980 is off the table?" Hailey asked. "I mean, I don't know how sick he was at the beginning of the year, but what if...?"

My eyes fell on the *1980* journal. She did have a point. I had assumed that my dad had been too sick, but what if he hadn't been? What if he had done something to someone earlier this year, as a sort of last act before he was done?

I skimmed page after page until I came to the week of his return home. Nothing. I closed it and let out a sigh of relief, realizing only then that I had really believed him to be capable of doing these gruesome things up until the very last moment.

"Okay, so 1979 it is. Lexington, Massachusetts."

What do we do when we get there? I wrote.

"I've been thinking about that. I've never heard of this town, so I'm assuming that if anything had happened there, it won't have reached the national newspapers. People go missing all the time, and this is a big country, so it would only make the big newspapers if it was someone important."

That's sad, I wrote.

"I know," Hailey said. "But if our theory is right, and there really was something going on with a local man or woman, there would have to have been an investigation. That's our starting point."

We can't just ask questions.

"Which is why we need a cover. How about we're reporters? Or writers, looking for a story, wanting to check the local newspaper records?"

Writers?

"Yeah, we could pretend to be writing a book about the town. And then we happen to bump into this thing."

Will that work?

Hailey smiled. "Trust me, if people are offered a chance in the limelight, they'll take it. Exposure works wonders."

So we're doing this?

"Yeah. I'll have to figure out the route. I've got a map in the car that I can take a look at."

Okay.

"Alice, you look exhausted. Why don't you take a shower first? Follow me."

We walked upstairs, where she showed me the bathroom and a couple of empty bedrooms. I immediately recognized hers, her window looking out onto my own. All the lights in my house were out now; it stood empty and abandoned.

She deliberately showed me the bedroom opposite hers, which did not face my house. She placed my suitcase down, but I kept it closed and sat on the bed. It felt comfortable, but it was still foreign to me. I had never slept in another bed before.

She came back with a bunch of clothes in her arms and placed them on the cupboard against the wall.

"I'm not sure if you'd like to have something to wear that's different from what you're used to, but I figured you could use some of mine. I'm a bit taller than you, but these skirts and dresses might work."

I stared at them in shock. They were so colorful and beautiful, and so foreign. I had never worn a skirt before.

"Have you ever worn clothes like this?" she asked, noticing my shock.

I shook my head.

"God. Alice…"

Her reaction spoke volumes. I burst into tears. She was at my side in a flash, holding me as I wept.

"Your mother has done terrible things to you," she said. "But I swear that I will erase all the bad memories, no matter how long it will take. You are not alone anymore."

I leaned into her, wanting to be with her forever.

She left me in the bathroom, with a large shower, a nice-smelling soap, and shampoo. I set aside my own things and used hers, wanting to smell like her.

I took my time washing my hair and scrubbing my skin, and when I turned off the water and walked out, I noticed a dark purple pair of pajamas and white underwear lying on a chair by the door.

I quickly put them on, went into the spare bedroom, and crawled beneath the blankets, feeling more human than I ever had before.

23

After some sleepless hours, I sat upright in bed. I was so thirsty. My throat was dry, and a headache pressed against the walls of my skull. After a long time of trying to ignore the aching feeling, I finally decided to get out of bed and fetch some water from the bathroom.

The bed creaked as I slipped out, smashing my toe against the nightstand. A loud thud followed as I lost my balance and fell forward, hitting the ground hard. I crawled up and sat dazed on the floor, wondering how I wound up in this position.

Hailey ran in to check on me.

"Are you okay? What happened?"

I'm fine.

I instinctively rubbed the small scar on my wrist like I always did when I got agitated. I didn't tell Hailey that I had been lying wide awake for hours, unaccustomed to this strange bedroom, the windows that felt out of place, and the sounds that were so different than those in my house.

That night in her spare bedroom, I struggled for any chance to find peace and sleep. My nights were never that easy to begin with, often because I was not tired enough, or I was thinking too much. That night was no different. First, I had heard her wander around the house. Then, take a shower. Talk to someone on the phone downstairs. Watch some television. Go upstairs. Use the toilet. Every single move she made, I heard, until she finally crawled into bed, and then the house became quiet.

After she'd fallen asleep – or so I assumed – I listened to every sound coming from outside, quietly wondering if Mom might come home. She didn't.

My conviction that she was not coming back grew with every waking hour. She was still being held at the police station. She may have been charged with something. I wondered what it would be like for her to be locked up in jail. I knew what jail looked like on television, but was it the same in real life?

I imagined her sitting in a small cell with all these women who all had done something bad. Some might be killers; others might be there for petty theft. Could Mom be locked up even if she had done nothing wrong?

Sleep came and went, like waves crashing on the shore – another thing I had only ever seen on TV. Every time I turned, the bed would creak, and the sound of it would wake me. Ah, well.

"Alice, are you okay?" Hailey asked, looking at me bewildered and sleepy-eyed. Even half-awake, she was still beautiful.

I'm fine, I signed, pointing at my toe. *Ouch.*

She smiled and looked at my foot, observing my big left toe. "You bumped it?"

I nodded and rubbed it. *All good*, I signed. *Sorry.*

She looked at me quizzically. "Did you get any sleep?"

A little bit.

"Liar. I couldn't sleep either. Too much stuff going on. Want to come with me to my room?"

I nodded.

"Come on, then."

She pulled me by the arm and took me to her bedroom. "I usually sleep in the middle of the bed, but we can share," she said.

She sat down on the right-hand side, so I took the left. She had a large bed, but sleeping here I'd still be close enough to feel her warmth. Not that I could sleep, however. I was wide awake.

I made a gesture that I wanted to write something down, but there was nothing to use.

"Hang on," she said. "I'll be right back."

When she left, I took the time to observe her room. It was as barren as the rest of the house, but at least it had nice wallpaper. I wasn't sure if she had chosen it herself or if it came with the house.

She returned and gave me a notepad, one with flowers on it that read *Grocery List*, and a pen.

"Here. I'll pick up some notepads in the morning, so you can write while I'm driving."

Okay. Thank you.

She sat down on top of the bed while I tried to write what I wanted to say. I knew she was observing me, but for now, I ignored the feeling she gave me.

"I'm sorry my sign language isn't so good yet," she said, while she watched. "I'm going to work on it."

When I looked up, she pointed at the ASL-book I had given her, which rested on her nightstand. "I've been practicing every night. Here, watch this."

I smiled when she signed, *Are you hungry?*

The movements were a bit clumsy, but she was getting the hang of it. From earlier conversations I knew she was a quick study, but lately we hadn't been able to sign all that much, and it was a skill one had to practice to maintain.

I am, I signed back, rubbing my stomach area. *Very.*

She laughed. "I think I used the right words. I hope I didn't ask you if you wanted to get drunk with me?"

I smiled. *No.*

"Good."

You're doing fine, I signed, putting both thumbs up as a compliment to her.

Thank you, she signed.

I couldn't help but notice her beauty. She seemed so perfect in every way, and I still looked like something the cat had dragged in, with hair too long and pajamas that didn't belong to me. We were not equals, she and I. She must pity me; why else would she help me like this?

"What did you want to write?" she asked, pointing at my notepad.

I want to leave as quickly as possible. I'm afraid the police will come to the house. I don't want to see that. When can we leave?

"Oh." She thought for a moment. "Well, why not leave straight away? It's nearly 6am and here we are, both wide awake. We can get breakfast on the way. I packed some things last night, and so did you, so we might as well go now, if you'd like?"

Yes.

"Okay, then. I'll need a couple of minutes to prepare. Will you be alright here on your own?"

I nodded.

She got off the bed again, picked out some clothes, and moved to the bathroom. I could hear her use the sink. She kept the door open, but I didn't go after her. I wanted to brush my teeth and comb my hair, and freshen up a bit before we left, but I didn't want to do that together.

I slipped off the bed and walked into the spare bedroom

and looked at the pile of clothes she had left for me. My bag was in the room, and I debated between pulling out my own stuff or using hers. It felt awkward dressing like her, but my whole being yearned for normal clothes to wear.

She had a long mirror in the room, so I could see myself full length. I put on a baggy set of sweatpants and a plain, green T-shirt and instantly hated it. My whole life, I'd been wearing clothes like this, and I looked ugly in them.

No more. I decided to wear something of hers. My fingers strolled over the stack of clothes, debating what would look most suitable on me. It had to be something that wouldn't stand out but would also look nice.

I found it. A red dress with white dots. It went below the knee, had short sleeves and a white belt, and looked like one of those dresses women would wear in old movies.

A dress. Was I really going to wear a *dress?*

I looked at myself in the mirror and wondered who this person was. Since yesterday, I'd been going through so many emotions that it dazzled me.

I was no longer just me. I had become Hailey, too. I was wearing her underwear. White, plain but well-fitting, cupping my breasts in a way I had never experienced before. I already felt beautiful standing in front of the mirror, even though it was also awkward seeing myself like this. I didn't have large mirrors at home, so I'd never really known what I looked like.

My old bathroom mirror was small and would show only my face and shoulders, and if I stepped back, I could see my chest, too. I had no clue if my breasts were small, medium-sized, or large, or if they looked different from other women's breasts. I guessed, from the fact that Hailey's bra fit, that we were about the same size.

I slipped on the dress. It fit perfectly. It hugged my body and complemented my skinny appearance instead of making me look starved and exhausted.

Just like that, I had become one of the women on television, who got all dressed up before they went out on a date. I had become Hailey.

She knocked on the half-open door. "Can I come in?"

I stomped my feet to the ground as confirmation that she could. She held her breath as she walked in, wearing a T-shirt and tight jeans.

"Oh, my God, you look so different. You chose the polka-dot dress! I was so hoping you would."

I must have looked startled. She laughed.

"That's what dresses with this pattern are called. They're timeless classics. I love this one, but it looks so much better on you."

Thank you. Thank you for the clothes.

"What?" she said confused.

I pointed at the pile of clothes and repeated, *Thank you.*

"Oh. You're welcome. So are you going to leave your own clothes behind?"

Yes, and burn them, I wrote down.

She laughed out loud. "Good idea."

She walked over and straightened the dress here and there before lifting my hair, examining it. "Have you ever had a decent haircut?"

I shook my head. *Mom.*

"Your mom cut your hair?"

I nodded.

"That's horrible. Come on, I'll take care of it before we take off, if you're okay with that? I don't want people looking at you strangely because your hair is all weird."

Yes.

"I'm not a hairdresser, but I can do a better job than what your mom has been doing. Take off the dress again; I don't want to ruin it."

I changed into my old clothes and walked after Hailey into the bathroom, where I quickly brushed my teeth while she took out a towel, shampoo, and something she called "conditioner". I had never used anything besides the basic shampoo Mom always gave me.

She settled me on a chair in front of the sink and took her time washing and combing my hair. I could feel it hanging low over my shoulders. She picked up a pair of scissors and looked me sternly in the eye.

"Are you sure you trust me?"

I nodded.

"Close your eyes, then, and relax. This will be over soon."

I heard the snipping of scissor blades while I sat with my eyes closed and realized that she could have cut my hair like a man, and I still wouldn't have cared. She did a lot of things with my hair, and I relished every moment of it, feeling strangely at ease.

Then she styled it, using a hairdryer. I could feel her brush it. I wanted this moment to last forever.

"All done. Open your eyes."

She pulled me up and turned me around, and I stared into the mirror at the stranger with hair that couldn't possibly be mine. My brownish-red color stood out in a different way than it had in the past. For the first time in my life, it didn't make me look ugly. It even emphasized the color of my eyes.

"Now put on your dress again."

I did as I was told, and when I walked into the spare bedroom with the large mirror, I didn't recognize myself.

Who was this person that almost looked normal?

"You look stunning," she said happily. "Now nobody will ever be able to say that you're not like everyone else. You're ready to go."

I threw myself into her arms. She wrapped them around me without hesitation and hugged me tight.

"We have to get going if we want to make a decent head start before breakfast. Are you still sure you want to do this?"

Yes.

"Alright, then. Let's go."

I placed all my old clothes on the spare bed and put her clothes in the suitcase. She gave me new toothpaste and a brand-new toothbrush. She also gave me a bottle of shampoo and conditioner, and soap that smelled so nice I just wanted to weep.

I was ready to leave my old life behind. The only things I kept were Mom's money and my books. *Alice in Wonderland* and King were now the only reminders of the life I used to lead.

Where this new one would take me, I did not yet know.

24

Hailey packed our things in her car. I suddenly felt anxious. I had never been in a car before, unless it was when I was far too young to remember. I assumed I would have been driven to the doctor's or hospital appointments, but I couldn't recall either.

"We'll stop in an hour or two for breakfast. That okay with you?"

Yes.

The world was alien to me. Even though I had seen loads of television shows and knew how driving worked, the whole prospect of driving for hours unnerved me no end. I didn't know what it felt like to sit inside a car, let alone be in one for hours in a row. I'd never been in a diner or a restaurant before, either. I didn't even know what coffee tasted like anywhere but at home.

What did people eat for breakfast in the normal world? What would I order, and where? What would it taste like? People on television talked about pancakes or Eggs Benedict, or eggs on toast, but I couldn't imagine those flavors.

The simplest things were new to me; I felt as if I were from a different planet and had to learn everything for the first time.

I hadn't told Hailey of my anxiety, and I was terribly worried that she might back out of our crazy plan once she realized how unprepared I was. I couldn't even fathom how to order a freaking cup of coffee, let alone survive in a world where everything was going by so fast that I'd have to rely on Hailey for every detail. How on earth had I even imagined I could head out there to find out the truth about Dad?

"Are you okay with me driving?" Hailey asked, startling me. "Or would you prefer taking an Amtrak or a flight? Do you know what an Amtrak is? Have you ever seen a plane in real life?"

Yes. No.

"Do you want to fly? We can buy plane tickets with cash. You wouldn't even need an ID if we take one of the cheaper airlines."

No. I made a gesture that looked like pulling the steering wheel of a car, hoping that made sense.

"Okay, got it. Drive it is, then."

She finished putting our suitcases and Dad's case with his journals in the trunk. She closed it, walked back to the house and locked the front door.

"Let's go."

I liked the shape of her car. She called it a "Volkswagen Beetle". I'd seen cars like this on television. It had a round rooftop, part of which was made of glass.

"I just got it last year. Bought it with my first paycheck and some of my parents' inheritance money," she explained. "I've traveled around quite a bit in her."

Her?

"Yeah. I call her Daisy. She's my best friend. Well, she was, until I met you. Come on, get in."

The car seats were soft and comfortable. She turned on the radio before starting the engine.

"What kind of music do you like?" she said, switching

radio stations like Mom used to do at home. "Rock? Jazz? Pop? Classic?"

I shrugged, because I really didn't care.

"Get comfortable," she said, "we're in for a long drive."

She chose a pop music radio station, started the car, and drove it backwards off her driveway. I didn't dare look at my old house. She cracked the windows of the car slightly open, despite the fact it was getting colder outside.

I was so scared when she drove onto the road. We were leaving my old home behind, but it wasn't just that: it was the driving itself. Even this early in the morning, and even in this – according to Hailey – quiet part of Hays, it was already busy.

"We have to stay on this side of that white stripe," she explained. "Follow the lane, that's all you need to do. We'll be on the highway soon, and then there will be more lanes."

I recognized this from television, but this was the first time I was part of the traffic. Hailey drove fast – or maybe I just felt she did – and I didn't feel comfortable looking ahead and seeing all those cars, so I decided to focus on the houses instead.

There were so many of them, and they were all different. Some small, some really big. Some high, some low. Some adjoined, others standing behind gates and fences. It felt as if I was living in one of my favorite TV shows. I had become part of the world I'd only seen on a screen.

Hailey placed a comforting hand on my wrist, sensing my anxiety. "Why don't you focus on the music?" she said, turning up the volume on her car radio.

I took a deep breath and tried to do as she suggested. I looked ahead and concentrated on the songs, the words, the singers. Before long, I'd managed to control my fear, as

I leaned back, half closed my eyes and shut off the outside world.

The voice of a female singer I didn't know came out of the speakers. Her voice was beautiful.

"That's Kate Bush," Hailey said. "The song's called 'Wuthering Heights'. Do you like it?"

I nodded. It was extraordinary. I'd never heard it before. Her voice was high, different.

"Do you like pop music?"

I didn't know, so I shrugged. I didn't really mind either way, as long as there was something to listen to.

Contemporary music was strange to me. I had no clue who was popular and who wasn't, what style of music was in, and who was important. I didn't know the names of modern singers, just the classic ones that my mom had given me albums of, like Elvis Presley or The Jacksons.

The next song, however, I recognized.

It was The Doors, 'Riders on the Storm'. I loved that song. The man's voice was one of my favorites. I had one of their albums. I remembered hearing that the lead singer had died at a very young age, and that he was buried in Paris.

Song after song went by. Sometimes Hailey would hum, other times she just talked. She was rarely quiet, but I liked it. Her talking took away part of my anxiety.

My thoughts wandered from the music to the outside world. I had never even seen anything beyond my own cul-de-sac, let alone past the borders of our little quaint town. Hays was small and insignificant. It was apparently the type of place where people still left their back doors unlocked, and where parents weren't yet afraid to let their teenagers wander outside.

It had always surprised me that my parents had chosen

this quiet town to live in, but at the same time, it was also the best place to avoid any unwanted attention from the law. Nobody would think that something so evil was lurking in their own backyard. That an innocent traveling salesman could set out to hurt someone.

My dad, bizarre as he could act at home, had undoubtedly been charming and witty outside our secluded walls. He wouldn't have been in his line of work for so many years if he hadn't been a trustworthy and convincing person.

"We're about to leave Hays," Hailey said. "Are you still sure about this? We can still turn around."

No.

"I'm just... I'm worried about you."

I'm not.

She glanced aside. "Why not?"

I've got you.

"Okay, then. Let's go."

We pulled up the highway, and suddenly Hailey's VW Beetle was surrounded by other vehicles that drove quickly past us. Sometimes she would go faster and switch lanes; sometimes others did. I looked at every single car, its driver, and its passengers, wondering who these people were and where they were going.

When I saw my first truck in real life, I held my breath. It was huge! They were so big, and so many of the cars were, too. I saw whole families sat in bulky vehicles. I saw pick-up trucks, vans, motorcycles. I didn't know where to look first.

All my fears were gone. I was so excited I wanted to jump up and down on my seat, but that would only distract Hailey, so I kept my excitement to myself.

My heart pounded in my chest, my legs trembled, and my hands fidgeted with the seam of my dress. Music resounded,

Hailey sang or talked, and I felt so damned happy, despite the circumstances that had led us here.

"Alice, are you listening?"

Hailey shook me from my reverie. She laughed when she saw my face.

"You're enjoying this, aren't you?"

I nodded excitedly.

"Okay, listen. I was calculating our route last night, and it's important that you know what's going to happen. Best case scenario, it will take us approximately twenty-five hours to get to Lexington without taking a single break or being stuck in traffic jams. In other words, we'll be on the road for some time, and you know that I can't drive all of those hours in one haul."

Yes?

"Since you can't drive, and I definitely won't let you try, we'll have to take regular stops. I'm thinking we could find a motel along the I-70 or I-71, depending on how far we get. I don't want to stop too early if the traffic is okay, so I was thinking we could sleep somewhere near Saint Louis, which means we'll have a short night ahead of us. And I'd like to leave again early morning to avoid traffic jams around the cities. So, in short, if my calculations are correct, we'll be in Lexington in two days. Are you okay with that? It'll be a long trip."

I don't mind, I signed. Because I really didn't, as long as I was with her. I didn't sign that part.

"If you want to hear some different music, take a look at the cassette tapes I have. They're in a black box behind me between the seats. And you can catch some sleep too if you like. I don't mind the drive, and you don't have to stay awake all the time."

I won't, I signed.

She sped up a bit and switched lanes again. I regretted not being able to speak to her, not to be able to keep her occupied. I didn't pick out a tape, but kept the radio on instead, noticing she liked this type of music.

A plan was shaping inside my head, one that I needed to share with her, but that I would be unable to explain using ASL. So I took out my old notepad and pen and started writing. The first time we took a break, she could read what I had to say.

She didn't ask what I was writing down, but she stopped chatting to let me focus, with only the music filling the car.

25

Around 9am a bit later than first anticipated, we stopped at a busy diner right off the highway, where several trucks and cars were parked.

It was busy, with tons of people – mostly male truckers, but to my surprise there were female truckers, too – walking back and forth through the parking lot for breakfast. Some families with kids were around too, but that was rare. This would be my first time ever eating outdoors, and I was anxious and prickled.

My head buzzed. It was scary to see so many people at once. Hailey reached for my hand and pulled me alongside her, but she let go once we reached the door.

"Just do as I do," she said. "It'll be fine. You need to be amongst people, but you'll get used to it soon."

Nobody really looked at us. We didn't stand out, I guessed, since we were both adults and we were wearing regular clothes. Just two friends having breakfast together. But that still didn't make it easy on me.

I followed Hailey inside and kept my head down as we slipped into a corner seat way in the back, where it wasn't so crowded.

A waitress came to our table about five seconds after we had sat down. "Coffee?" she asked.

"Yes, please," Hailey said. "Thanks."

"Breakfast or early lunch?"

"Breakfast, please."

Who ate lunch this early in the morning?

"Great. We have some breakfast specials." The waitress shoved the menu in my direction, and I scanned it quickly, searching for something familiar. Pancakes. Eggs Benedict. One of those two, for sure.

Hailey watched me debate as my finger strolled between my two options. She smiled and looked at the waitress. "We'll have pancakes and Eggs Benedict, please. And orange juice. Oh, and do you have some strawberries to go with the pancakes? And loads of maple syrup."

I smiled. How did she know I'd never had that before? The waitress briefly looked at me curiously and then left with our order.

"Are you okay?" Hailey said.

I'm okay, I signed. *You?*

"Perfect. It's been a while since I drove so many hours in a row, but it's going great. I'll fill up the tank while we're here. Maybe we could pick up some sandwiches to eat in the car, so we don't have to stop later. I'd like to drive as far as possible today before checking into a motel."

Okay.

"Are you alright sitting here? If not, we can take our food with us and eat it in the car."

I'm fine. I need to learn, I signed.

A woman at the bar noticed my signing. She looked at me and smiled before continuing to eat. I kept my head down. The only person I wanted to focus on right now was Hailey, and all I wanted to do was eat as fast as I could so we could continue our journey.

"You're doing great, Alice. Don't worry about anything else. I'll do the talking," Hailey reassured me. "We make quite the team, don't we?"

Yes, I signed.

"What were you writing earlier?" she asked. "Is it for me to read?"

I showed her my notepad, which now held a bunch of questions for her to answer.

"Okay, let's take a look," she said. "Question number one: 'Have you ever heard of any unsolved murders or disappearances that could match the initials we found in my dad's journal?'"

She thought for a moment. "No, but there are far too many for one person to hear about them all. I read in a newspaper article once that there are hundreds of thousands of people who go missing in the United States every year. A lot of them are never found, and often there is the assumption that they took their own lives or left the country."

Wow.

"Yeah, it's odd to think that people can just disappear, right?"

Like on TV.

"Exactly. TV shows are often based on some kind of reality, I guess. Anyhow, missing persons cases usually aren't big news, except when it's a child, maybe. With adults, there can be so many reasons they go missing. It might take a while before anyone figures out that there's been a crime involved."

Okay.

She read the next question out loud: "'What if he took people that nobody misses?'" she said. "Hm, that's a valid question. If he took people like the homeless, it's likely no one would have any idea they were missing at all, at least not for a while. In that case, it would be even harder to find out what he did. But that scenario won't work here."

What do you mean? I signed.

"Well, we talked about how all these towns in his notebooks are small towns, right? Not cities like New York, or LA, where homeless people or sex workers are common. Towns like that hardly ever have homeless sleeping on the streets."

So it has to be someone regular? I wrote down.

"Yeah. But in that case, there will have been a police investigation or newspaper articles. Let's, for the sake of argument, assume that your dad killed someone. In that case, he might have left the body or made it disappear. It all depends on what he's done, and who he's done it to."

Yeah.

"How about we start with the local newspapers?" Hailey proposed. "Every town has its own library, so there will be newspapers there. We'll read those first, focusing on the days of the week that were marked in his journal. That will be our starting point. We can't just go to the police asking questions, and I want to keep a low profile. Speak to as few people as possible. But we can still find the right people to talk to."

How? I signed.

"Gossip always spreads quickly in local diners. If I wanted to find out more about one of my clients at the store, I'd go to the diner across the street. Everyone always knows everyone in places like this, so if something did happen, people will want to talk about it. Clothing stores work well too. While trying on clothes, they'll discuss the latest gossip. It's the same with restaurants and hotels."

Okay. I trust you.

"Thank you."

Hailey placed her hand on my wrist, before pulling it away quickly when the woman at the bar gazed at us again.

This time, she wasn't smiling. Her eyes narrowed and she seemed to notice something that wasn't there, something between Hailey and me. She turned to the men next to her, and immediately several heads turned towards us. Hailey ignored them, but I didn't glance away, daring them to speak up. I was done being invisible, and with Hailey by my side, I felt stronger than ever.

They looked away first.

When the food arrived, I looked wide-eyed at the huge feast the waitress set before us. First was the stack of pancakes: six of them, thick, fluffy, and smelling delicious, covered with strawberries and bananas. Maple syrup was brought in a small pitcher. She also placed a small bowl of whipped cream on the table.

"You have to pour the maple syrup over the pancakes," Hailey explained. "It's very sweet, so try it first."

She had the Eggs Benedict, but before we dug in, she said, "Let's share the food. We'll switch plates. What do you want to try first?"

I pointed at the pancakes.

"Great. Enjoy."

As soon as I had my first taste of pancakes, my world changed forever. After years of dry toast and jam, it tasted like heaven. I kept on shoveling food into my mouth, making sure I chewed and swallowed on time.

"Be careful, pancakes can really clog up your throat. Drink plenty of water."

I had coffee, water, and orange juice in front of me, but the latter was too sweet, so Hailey drank it all.

At some point, we switched plates. I *loved* the eggs, but I loved the pancakes more. Hailey laughed while she watched me eat as if I'd never done so in my life.

"Go slowly, we have time."

I took it easier after that. We switched plates again and I finished off the last pancake, savoring the flavor of strawberries and cream. This was the most delicious meal I'd ever eaten.

"Well, if you like this so much, wait until you get your first taste of real Italian food," Hailey said. "I can just imagine us going to all these different restaurants, trying out anything you'd like. A whole new world is opening up for you, Alice. It's so wonderful to see you like this."

Thank you.

We finished eating under the scrutiny of the woman and her companions. I paid in cash, even though Hailey insisted she would, but I refused.

We left the diner and headed into the store to buy sandwiches for the road, as well as candy, cookies, chips, water, and soda. Hailey filled up the tank and walked back into the store to pay.

The woman from the diner approached me. She was tall, bulky, dressed in jeans and an oversized sweater. She smoked and looked rough around the edges. I froze, thinking she would talk to me, but she brushed right past me and whispered something that rang in my ears.

"*Dyke.*"

I didn't know what it meant, but it sounded hurtful and insulting. I stared after her feeling dirty and upset for reasons I couldn't explain. Tears that I couldn't stop streamed down my face.

Hailey returned. I quickly ran my hand past my face and got into the car, unable to look at her. I felt so filthy, but I didn't understand why.

"Are you okay?" she asked, looking at me troubled.

Tired, I signed.

She didn't push the subject. She started the car and drove off the parking lot. The last person I saw was the woman from the diner, standing by her truck, smoking another cigarette as she raised her middle finger to wave us goodbye.

26

After some long hours on the road, Hailey yawned. We were still listening to the same pop music station. Some songs were totally new to me, while others sounded familiar.

I missed my books. I missed my room. I missed television. The excitement of being on the road was now replaced by boredom, especially since we were on highways the whole time. Everything just looked the same, like one long road that seemed to go on forever.

It gave me plenty of time to think, but I didn't want to think anymore, and I regretted not taking more books with me for the ride. But that would have been rude towards Hailey.

We stopped a couple of times to pee, get some more food, fill the car with gas, and relax a bit. Hailey deliberately chose places that weren't busy, and she always parked the car way in the back after filling it up.

We sat on a picnic bench at one point and ate our food, watching the sunset. It started to turn chilly, and I shivered in my dress and jacket.

"It's getting colder at night," Hailey said, nodding at the colorful trees that formed a natural barrier around the parking lot. "With this beautiful weather, you'd forget what time of the year it is. I brought you some trousers, too. If you'd like, you can change clothes?"

No. I'm good.

"Let's drive for another two hours, but then I'd like to call it quits for the day and find a place to sleep. Are you okay with that?"

Yeah.

Hailey was getting tired, and I knew it wasn't okay for her to drive for much longer. I couldn't entertain her with words, so I started doodling on my notepad and showing it to her, trying to make her laugh. She cast sideways glances and smiled every time.

Two hours later, in the pitch black of night, we stopped at a Motel 6 that had vacancies. We were checked in at the counter by a grumpy older man who obviously hated his job.

Hailey paid in cash, using the money that I gave her, despite her protests that I would need it later. I had paid for the second round of gas, too, not wanting her to pay for everything. Mom's money would be enough to support this trip, but after that I had no idea how to get more. I didn't want to think about my future predicaments just yet. Looking for a job and earning my own keep seemed impossible right now.

The motel manager handed us the keys and barked that we could get something to eat at the diner next door, using a Motel 6 discount voucher that he dropped on the counter. Another voucher for breakfast was slapped next to it.

"Check-out is before 10am. If you decide to stay longer, I need to know by 7am."

"That won't be necessary, but thanks," Hailey said.

We walked out of the small reception area and back to the car. She parked the vehicle in front of room 524, which was on the ground level, and we took our things out of the car, making sure to leave nothing inside.

There were people everywhere. On the parking lot, walking towards the diner, heading to the motel. There were trucks everywhere too, some with doors open.

I heard noises that I couldn't really distinguish, a guy grunting and a woman moaning. It came from the right and I wanted to turn around to look, but Hailey stopped me before I could. She groaned too, but not in the same way.

"Horny assholes," she muttered under her breath, before shooing me inside our room and shutting the door.

The walls were flimsy; we could hear voices from the adjacent rooms. She bolted the door and shoved a chair beneath the handle. She was nervous, I could tell, but I didn't ask her why. She was obviously hating being here.

I couldn't help but think about Dad, and how many times he had slept in motels like this. He must have hated it as much as we did. The two-bed room was small and damp. It wasn't exactly clean, but the beds seemed okay. The pillows were soft; the mattresses moved beneath our backs.

Hailey sat on the bed next to the window and looked intently at the sheets, obviously checking that they were clean. I was too tired to really care what had happened in this room before we set foot in it. This should have been exciting, but it wasn't. The car had felt safer.

"I want to leave as soon as possible in the morning," she said, "if that's alright."

Yes, please, I signed.

I understood her anxiety. If things were different, and this had been an actual road trip, I would probably have been happy and excited about this new experience. Now, I just wished the night away, so we could leave this place behind us.

"Do you want to get something to eat?" she asked.

I shook my head. The sandwiches we ate earlier had been more than enough.

"Good. To be honest, I'm too tired to care about food right now," she said, yawning.

I'm sorry I can't drive your car, I scribbled down.

"That's okay, Alice. I'm glad that we're here."

Are you?

"Yeah, this is the adventure of a lifetime."

I looked up surprised. *Really?*

"Yep."

Okay.

"Why are you so surprised?"

I thought you'd be used to adventure.

"Ha-ha. Nope. Oh, and Alice? Stop feeling so guilty all the time. I want to be here. This is my choice."

That makes me feel better, I wrote.

She rolled onto her side to look straight at me.

"I've told you before that it's my choice to come with you. You didn't force me or push me into doing something I didn't want to do. I'm happy to be here, okay? I'm glad that I'm your friend. You are important to me."

Am I?

She moved up, sat on the side of her bed while I sat on mine, leaning forward. She took my hands in hers. Her face moved closer to me, and I could see every sparkle in her eyes. My heart pounded faster; I didn't know what to say. My throat dried.

A new fear overwhelmed me, but it was not the type of fear that I had felt before. This was exciting fear – expectation, I guess.

Her hand touched my cheek in such a soft, gentle gesture that I stopped breathing altogether.

"My sweet Alice, you are so special, do you realize that?"

I closed my eyes and inhaled her scent, which reminded me of a summer breeze finding its way through the chill of autumn. She slipped off the bed and sat next to me. I could feel her body slide up against mine.

Her face was just an inch away, so I moved forward and kissed her with my eyes closed. Her lips were soft and moved beneath mine. Her hands cupped my face, intensifying the kiss.

Her mouth opened. I couldn't think. My body took over. I opened my mouth too; our tongues found each other, and we kissed again, but now in a totally different way. The kiss was sweet but heated. I felt her tongue in my mouth. It was the best thing I'd ever experienced.

She let go first and moved backwards, whispering, "Fuck."

My eyes opened and I stared at her in shock, embarrassed and excited at the same time. Her reaction made me think that she was upset. That she would run out of the room, telling me this was all one big mistake. But that didn't happen.

She smiled. She laughed. She radiated excitement. Her lips were swollen, her eyes were shining and her hand moved towards her mouth.

"Oh, wow," she said breathlessly.

Wow indeed. I was so in love.

"This was better than I could have imagined," she whispered. "You are wonderful."

No, I'm not.

"Yes, you are. You have no idea just how special you are, do you?"

She slipped off the bed as if nothing had happened and took off her clothes, leaving only her underwear on. She took her personal items and pajamas from her suitcase and went into the bathroom to change, leaving me stunned. A few moments later, I heard the shower running.

I listened to the sound of water in the bathroom while I fumbled to turn on the television, finding one of my favorite channels. I sat down and watched it, almost forgetting where I was for a moment, until Hailey came back out wearing her pajamas. Her hair hung loose over her shoulders. She had removed her make-up.

She sat down on her bed. "Why don't you change too?" she said. "Leave the dress here, I'll hang it up for you."

I got up, opened the suitcase and took out the same pajamas she had given me yesterday, along with the toiletry bag. I quickly took off the polka-dot dress and placed it gently on the bed, feeling vulnerable in my gifted underwear.

In the bathroom, beneath the strong, hot water stream, I came back to my senses, shaking my head in disbelief. No way a woman like her would be interested in a freak like me. It couldn't possibly be true.

I dried off, put on the pajamas and returned to the room, where I saw the polka-dot dress hanging by the door. Hailey's hands stroked it, while she smelled the fabric, as if she was trying to capture a scent of me.

No, this was definitely not a dream. She was in love with me, too. She turned around and looked at me with darker eyes than usual.

"Would you – I mean – do you mind if we sleep in the same bed tonight? Just to hold each other."

I walked over to her bed and crawled in, and she smiled. She slipped in next to me and we lay side by side, without touching each other. Then I turned to my side facing her, and she did the same. I moved forward and kissed her again. She responded by opening her lips.

I could feel her heat. I knew what we could do. How my fingers could touch that sensitive spot between her legs and hers between mine, but neither of us made the first move. I didn't want to go down that road, or at least not yet. Not when there were so many questions to be answered. I just wanted to kiss her forever, and so I did. We shared a long kiss, before she reached for my hands and held them between hers.

"Goodnight, Alice," she said softly. "If you need anything, just wake me up, okay?"

Goodnight, I signed.

She turned off the light. Within moments, I could hear her regular breathing, could feel it on my skin. She turned onto her other side in her sleep, and I moved against her back after a while to feel her bodily warmth. I fell asleep, spooning the woman I loved.

I woke up when the sunrise peered through the window of the motel room. The drapes were slightly open, and the world was slowly changing from night to morning. It took me a while to figure out where I was, but then it all came back to me.

I was alone in the room.

I shot up, surprised, scared that I had been left alone overnight. And why not? She might have realized that this whole thing we had going was a terrible mistake. She could be on her way back to Hays without me. I wouldn't be surprised, considering what I had already put her through. I wouldn't blame her, either.

I slipped out of bed and looked at the polka-dot dress hanging by the door, trying to figure out what to do next if she had really gone. Going back home was not an option, but I could still hitchhike my way to Lexington. I would continue with my plan with or without her. It would just be ten times harder.

The door opened. Hailey walked into the room carrying coffee and breakfast in a large brown paper bag. I released the breath I didn't know I'd been holding. She looked at me surprised as she placed coffee and food on the table and kissed me on the lips.

"Good morning, sleepyhead, you were out like a light, so I snuck out to get some breakfast. Figured it might be easier to eat here than to head into that crowded diner. It's a full house over there."

I burst into tears.

"Hey, what's wrong?"

Nothing, I signed.

"Oh, my God, you thought I had run out on you, didn't you?"

I said nothing. It was obvious that this was exactly what I had been thinking. She reached for my hands.

"Alice, listen to me. I won't abandon you, no matter what, okay?"

Sorry.

"You have trust issues, and that's normal, but I would never do that to you. Okay?"

Okay.

She let go of my hands, cupped my face and kissed me softly. I was still reeling from her touch when she took the brown paper bag and opened it.

"Let's eat."

The food smelled delicious. The scent reminded me of how hungry I was. I pushed all the negative thoughts from my mind and immediately felt a bit better. At home, I had never been a big breakfast eater, but now it felt like I could eat for two. Hailey gave me a warm bagel. She had brought a plastic knife and two small jars of cream cheese and jelly. The coffee was good too.

Thank you.

"Alice?"

Yeah?

"I loved kissing you."

I loved kissing you, too.

27

We spent another long day on the road, peppered with accidents and jams, going from one problem to the next. This day was a lot more stressful; I could tell by the way Hailey complained about the traffic.

We stopped around 1pm, ate sandwiches while leaning against the car, and ignored the men whistling at us as they walked by. Hailey filled up the tank, and off we went again. Queen was on the radio. Hailey knew the lyrics and chanted along.

I knew that song, loved the band.

"I know the lyrics are all over the place, but *Bohemian Rhapsody* is the best song ever," Hailey said, once the last vocals faded out and the song ended with one single stroke of a key. "Queen is the best."

I know them, I signed. That seemed to please her.

"I wish that we could find a way to get you to speak," she said. "I know you told me that your parents have been taking you to a doctor, but that was ages ago. Times have changed, you know? There could be solutions now. Better doctors. And besides, who says that your condition is medical? It could be something else, like a psychological issue, caused by trauma."

Trauma?

"Yeah, maybe you've experienced something early on in life that brought this on."

I was always mute, I wrote down. She glanced briefly at my written text.

"So your parents said, but is it true?"

I don't know.

"Your parents were terrible, so who says they even bothered taking you to see a doctor?"

I didn't know what to think, but Hailey did have a point. I didn't remember seeing a single doctor my entire life. I've never carried the hope that someone could fix this, not wanting to wait for a miracle. What if I went through the whole ordeal, hoping that someone could help me, but ended up with nothing?

"Once this thing with your dad is over, I'd like to inquire about doctors. Are you okay with that?"

I wanted to say no, but I didn't. If that's what Hailey wanted, then I would do it. I'd do anything for her.

By the time we reached the second Motel 6, much later than we had hoped for, we were exhausted. Hailey was constantly yawning, so obviously tired that she had trouble driving straight.

The problem with not being able to speak was that I couldn't keep her awake. She couldn't look aside all the time to see what I was signing, and she couldn't read notes on my pad, either. All she had was the music to keep her company, and my hand on her wrist whenever I sensed she was getting too tired. I proposed to find another motel and drive longer in the morning, but she insisted that she was fine. As she had booked the room by telephone that morning, she wanted to keep to her schedule.

I paid in cash and signed with my name. The woman at

the reception scrutinized me because I didn't speak, but we ignored her. We received another breakfast discount voucher and were sent on our way. The parking lot was filled with trucks; there were hardly any cars to be seen. Most people were already in their rooms. It was quiet, except for the traffic that was still audible from the nearby highway.

This room was smaller than the previous one, and it only had one bed. I was secretly glad that we would sleep under the same covers again. We dropped our things on the floor and Hailey sighed, running her hands through her hair.

"I'm too tired to eat anything, but we should," she said. "Do you feel like heading to the diner across the street?"

Sure. Or pizza in the room?

She smiled. "Pizza sounds good. Let me check at the reception desk if there's a delivery service. If there is, I'll take a quick shower while we wait for our food."

She went back to the reception area, where she picked up a leaflet of a nearby pizza place, and then she used the telephone in our room to place the order. While she showered, I turned on the TV and flipped channels until I found a sitcom. The room filled with laughter coming from an invisible audience. I lay back on the bed.

Hailey walked out of the bathroom dressed in a towel, while she used another one to dry off her long hair. I couldn't help but stare at her, realizing that this was the first time I had seen her like this. She seemed different, younger, and more relaxed. And I simply could not look away from her.

If she noticed me staring at her, she didn't mention it. She sat on the bed and continued drying her hair, combing through it before allowing the long strands to slide down her bare back.

The towel was firmly placed around her chest and waist, and of course I couldn't see anything, but I still felt something that I had never experienced before. A rush of blood to the head, a feeling between my legs. An urge that I couldn't just ignore. I wanted to see her naked. I wanted to touch her, to hold her. To sleep with her, whatever that would mean. It was as if my natural urges reacted and made me want to kiss her again, but this time in a way that would set her body on fire.

Ashamed of myself, I got up quickly, grabbed my things and ran into the bathroom, closing the door before she could say anything. It took me ten minutes to cool off while hot water pounded down on me. My legs trembled and I resisted the urge to put my fingers between them to relieve myself. I stopped myself, too ashamed to even contemplate doing something like this while she was in the other room.

Who was I? What was I doing? I wasn't supposed to be looking at girls like that. It wasn't natural, and certainly not normal. My mom would tell me that I was crazy and sick, that people weren't supposed to do this. I couldn't understand it myself, let alone try to explain this sudden urge to someone without being able to utter a word. I closed my eyes while I turned the water icy cold, cooling off immediately. It brought me back to my senses.

I dressed in a pair of my old sweatpants and a top, unable to look Hailey in the eye, who was now in her T-shirt and shorts. The pizza was sitting on the table by the door. She opened the box, and the smell permeated my nostrils.

"Right on time," she said. "Come on, let's dig in before it gets cold."

I sat down and started eating, even though I had lost my appetite. I took one slice and chewed on it, while she ate three slices like a famished dog. It made me like her even more. The sensation between my legs was back again.

After the greasy dinner, she pulled back the bedsheets and blankets and slid underneath them, then pointed at my sweatpants. "Are you really going to sleep in that? Take them off, they're way too warm."

I turned red while I did what she told me. She had absolutely no clue what she was doing to me. She punched her pillows, lay back and sunk deep beneath the sheets, stretching her arms and legs.

"God, that feels good. I'm so tired. Would you mind if I fall asleep in a second?"

No, I signed, smiling. *Get some sleep.*

She leaned over, hugged me and kissed me on the lips. No tongue this time, just a small but perfect kiss.

"Night, Alice."

She turned onto her side and was asleep within a matter of moments. My heart pounded as I lay there, staring at the television set without seeing anything. I finally gave up.

Before I turned off the lights, I already knew that I wouldn't be able to sleep a wink, not with her by my side, so close to me. I couldn't stand it. I wanted to touch her, to feel her, to–

No. No! I couldn't add this problem to my already growing list of issues.

But who was I kidding, really?

PART SIX
Lexington

January 17–19, 1980

28

"'Lexington, Massachusetts is a small, cozy town, no more than a tiny dot on the map of the United States. But for anyone interested in the history of the Revolutionary War, the sacred site of the Battle of Lexington is a must-stop destination,'" Hailey read out loud.

I smiled as I listened to her gentle voice, wondering why she had never taken on a career as a schoolteacher. She would have been great at it.

She repositioned herself on the wooden bench in front of the tourist info point, with the leaflet in her hands, trying to protect it from blowing away.

"'One of the first battles of the war took place right here in Lexington, and the people of Lexington are thrilled to share this legacy with you. If you're looking for battle reenactments, this is the place to be. And we hope you'll join us while we honor those who lost their lives on these very grounds.' Eww." She looked at me. "Is this one big cemetery, you think?"

I smiled and shrugged, taking out my notepad. *Isn't everything? Dinos? Native Americans? Etc.?*

"You're right. I didn't think of that. Okay, feeling better already, but don't think we're going to be spending any free time going to one of these things."

We won't.

As soon as we drove into Lexington, it was pretty obvious

what the heart of this town was made of. Hailey pointed out all the statues of famous local people who had fought in the battle that took place here. Some historical buildings had plaques on them, describing why they were significant. Even the tourist shop was decorated with various war memorabilia. We watched as people came in and out, buying what looked to be hats and shirts and replicas, happily chatting about the war as they left again.

The town was quaint but buzzing with activity. It felt like Hays – or at least what I'd seen of it – with its tiny, old buildings, church, town hall, occasional luxury estate, cemeteries, shops, supermarkets, restaurants, and a couple of coffee places.

Time stood still in Lexington, as it did in Hays. The big differences were the scenery and the weather. It was a lot colder here than it had been at home, and I was glad Hailey had dropped a few warm coats in the car last minute. It was fall, and we had to get used to the chill. I wore jeans and sweaters instead of dresses now, again, given to me by Hailey. A bit too large, but doable.

"We should get you some clothes of your own when we arrive," she had remarked in the car, but I didn't want to. I was basking in her clothes, feeling warm, loved, and comfortable.

I immediately took a liking to Lexington because it wasn't as crowded as I had feared it would be. We could walk around and no one would bump into us or try to talk to us. We could just wander, no questions asked, and I felt strangely at ease here, relaxing as soon as we got out of the car.

Hailey seemed to notice this too. She had stopped asking me if I was alright, and when we walked side by side, she no longer felt the need to keep me protected and close to her. Which was a good thing.

"I think our theory is right," Hailey said. "If something terrible happened here, people will know about it. It's odd though, that your dad would take the risk of grabbing someone from this town when all he had to do was head out to Boston and take someone anonymously from the streets."

I know, I signed. *I don't understand.*

"It's almost as if he was challenging people to catch him, or that local townsfolk needed to feel the sense of loss that he would leave behind. Maybe that was the thrill that he needed so badly. Taking an anonymous person was easy, but this would have been more difficult."

I dug out my notepad. *If he did it.*

"We are still assuming that he did, right?" she asked.

For sure.

"Okay."

I remembered some of the notes that we had made before, the list of towns that he had marked every year. What if every town on that list was an insignificant dot on the USA map? Another Hays, another Lexington, with the same type of people living there?

There were no big cities on this list, according to Hailey. He must have chosen them on purpose, to leave a mark on a local community he visited for just a couple of days, traumatized without remorse. If he had any regrets about what he'd done, he would have stopped a long time ago.

If he had done this.

"I'm having second thoughts about our theory though, Alice," Hailey said. "I mean, look at this town. Could he really have done something like that and gotten away with it so easily? If some horrible, unusual crime occurred, someone must have thought about the traveling salesman who'd visited the town that same time, right? I mean, these people still leave their doors open. A stranger must have stood out."

But there are many strangers here all the time, I wrote. *Tourists*.

"Of course." She slapped her forehead. "That makes sense. Stupid me. A lot of the visitors won't have left a trace at all. So many people pay cash."

Uh huh.

"Okay, let's do this, then. I suggest that we check into our hotel first and freshen up before we get started."

Okay.

There were four hotels located on Lexington's main street. All of them were relatively small. Hailey had phoned ahead, using the local information service to find a suitable one. It was right next door to the tourist center.

The building was three floors high and six windows wide. It was right in the middle of the street, surrounded by stores and a few restaurants. All the other roads seemed to lead towards Lexington's long, straight main road, which was obviously the center of the town.

"These people clearly have money," Hailey had said as we drove into the town. "Look at the size of those houses. This is old money."

Old money? I had written.

"Yeah, like wealthy families who have been here hundreds of years, probably migrating from Europe back in the 1600s. You can just smell it."

I didn't know what she meant, but I could make sense of it. These houses were bigger than anything I had ever seen, even though that wasn't saying much. Dad's house had been big too, but it could fit twice in these.

The mansions on the outskirts were large wooden and brick buildings, with huge, well-kept lawns and gardens. There were picket fences all around. The many cars on the driveway were expensive, or so Hailey said. The town had a lake with fishing cabins, a pool, a football club, a tennis club, and two large schools. Poverty was not evident here.

I remembered reading about towns like this. Some television shows were set in such places, and they made me dream about spending my life somewhere similar.

The advantage was that by knowing your neighbors, you could always count on them. The disadvantage was that your neighbors also knew everything about you.

Those living in places like this knew that they needed to accept the unspoken rule that everyone got to meddle in everyone else's life. Secrets were hard to keep, unless you lived so secluded that no one ever entered your house, like my parents had done.

The streets were beautiful, with huge century-old trees gloriously dressed in autumn leaves. It was the first time I could see it in real life, and it made me emotional.

"At least it isn't raining," Hailey said. "And the cold isn't that bad once you get used to it. Do wear your coat, though; you're not used to the outdoors."

She was right. I felt chilly all the time and I felt like I was developing a cold. One of many, I would presume.

"Maybe we can come back here as tourists someday," Hailey said. "Wouldn't that be nice? To just visit without a care in the world."

I knew what she meant. Instead of enjoying my first visit to a real town, I was nervous and agitated, afraid that someone would realize that we had come here for a reason that was different than others.

When we stood in the hotel lobby, waiting to be checked in, I realized why Dad had chosen this town. There were plenty of tourists in line, all with bags in hand, proving that they were here to stay for at least a couple of days.

If Dad had been one of them, perhaps even staying at this very hotel, he would have blended in just as easily. He would act like a nice traveling salesman, might have even chatted with memorial visitors. He would have acted like any other guy, going from door to door with his products, while at the same time prowling the streets for... someone. Something.

Hailey checked us in using her own name. She paid by credit card, at the request of the hotel manager. This wasn't some dingy motel where you could pay cash. They kept records.

I made a mental note to give her cash to repay her, even though it had become clear to me that money didn't seem to be an issue for her. She waved away every objection I made, and said we would deal with that later.

"This is my sister," Hailey said, nodding in my direction. "She is mute, poor thing. We're vacationing here, a well-needed break after our father's passing, but we're combining it with work."

"Oh, I'm so sorry to hear that," the hotel manager said. "If there's anything I can do, please let me know."

"Thank you, that's really nice of you. Actually, I was wondering if you could help us find our way around town a bit? Is there a map or anything that we can use?"

"Of course. What exactly are you looking for?"

Hailey glanced at me. "Well, we are writers, working on a novel about tragic events taking place all over the East Coast."

He looked at me quizzically. "Tragic events?"

"Yes, things that are not your everyday occurrence, like murders or disappearances. Did you know thousands of people go missing yearly, and that no one writes about them? That's what we do."

"I see," he muttered. "You do know there've been plenty of books about the Revolutionary War, and that there have been thousands of such tragedies around here?"

Hailey smiled. "I know, but we're not writing a war book. The events we're looking for should have taken place in the past five years or so."

The hotel manager fidgeted with his wedding ring while he studied Hailey's expression. My heart pounded in my chest. Was he going to believe us, or see through the lie?

"We thought the local library would be a good starting point," Hailey quickly said. "Newspapers would cover those stories, don't you think?"

"Right," the man said. "Let's see. Here's a map of Lexington. If you go all the way down Main, and then turn off on Orchard Road, you'll find the public library adjacent to our town hall. Oh, and the newspaper office is right next door. You could talk to Mark; he's the Senior Editor. He can help you look for stories."

The hotel manager also marked some good places to eat on the map, as well as some memorial sites.

"Everything's close enough to walk," he said. "It will only take you a couple of minutes to go from one place to the other. Oh, and if you want to visit our brand-new mall, drive to the east, up the highway, and take the first exit that reads *Lexington Mall.* Folks go there all the time, even though the local stores complain about the competition. That's progress, for you."

"Thank you," Hailey said, "you've been very helpful."

"Sure. Do you need help with your suitcases? It's two floors up and we don't have an elevator."

"No, we're good," Hailey said. "Oh, and if you think of any tragedies that we could look into, please let me know."

"Of course. Nothing comes to mind right now, but I'll have a think about it," the man said, focusing his attention on the next guests.

"He's lying," Hailey whispered to me.

Huh?

"Did you see how nervous he got when I mentioned what we were here for? He knows something."

I really couldn't see what she was referring to, but that didn't matter. I just wanted to get our things up to our room and get started.

29

We climbed two floors up to our room, which turned out to be light and spacious and held two queen-size beds. The bathroom was huge, with a tub and a shower. We had a view of Main Street, which was relatively calm, though it was only Thursday. Even though I didn't have much experience with people yet, I could spot the tourists immediately, with their cameras and backpacks. Some of them even walked around in shorts, despite the chillier autumn weather.

"Hungry?" Hailey asked.

I nodded.

"Let's have lunch first. Dig into the local community, find out what this town's about. With any luck, we should be able to figure this out quickly."

I didn't really want to leave the room. It felt cozy and comfortable, and I wanted to pretend, if only for a while, that we were tourists, enjoying a nice few days off. But staying here wouldn't bring me the answers that I so desperately needed.

The odd thing was, being here had pushed Dad out of my mind. My life before this seemed like an extended nightmare now, and I had trouble remembering the details of it, as if it had happened to someone else. Had my life before been a television show, and was I now back in reality? It was beginning to feel that way.

I had wondered while driving here how long it would

take me to get used to normal life. No one had once noticed what I had been through. Not a soul out there knew about my life before this except for Hailey. And even her behavior had changed radically over the past few days, going from overly worrisome to seemingly normal.

Sometimes she looked at me as if she was waiting for me to start talking. And I caught myself doing the same thing. I would open my mouth and then realize that I couldn't speak, which I had never done back home.

"Earth to Alice," she said, waving her hand before my eyes.

I blinked, looking at her as I returned to reality.

"Is something wrong?"

No. Just nervous.

"I can't even begin to imagine what you're going through right now. But I promise you that whatever we discover, things will turn out fine. You will get through this, okay? I won't leave you."

Now? Or forever? I signed, but I wasn't so sure that she understood. She hadn't been practicing her ASL since we left, even though the book was in her suitcase.

She placed her arms over my shoulders and pulled me closer to her. I closed my eyes when her hand stroked my face. It felt so good to feel her touch on my skin.

"You are going to be fine," she said softly. Her breath moved the hair covering my ear. "Please believe me."

I believe you.

We kissed gently.

"Let's go."

She reached for my hand and led me out of the room. In the hallway, she let go, and I knew why. Out in the open, we would be monitored and mocked. This had to stay between us for now.

We decided to try out the restaurant that was just a few buildings away from the hotel. The doors stood wide open; the place looked cozy and inviting. A young woman welcomed us and seated us by the window, so we could people watch. It was still early, and there were only two other guests at the restaurant. I assumed they were locals. They wore suits and were having a businesslike conversation.

"Do you have any recommendations?" Hailey said, hardly glancing at the menu.

The girl beamed happily. "I would try one of the omelets; we're famous for them. There are various choices and combinations possible, and you can choose the vegetarian version, too, if you'd like. The house specialty is the most popular one. You can combine any meal with a side dish of fries and or vegetables."

"We'll take two of the house specialty, then, including fries," Hailey said, without asking me. She knew by now that I was crazy about eggs and ate just about anything.

The girl looked curiously at me.

"My sister doesn't have a voice," Hailey explained. "She uses ASL."

"Oh, really? So do I," the girl said excitedly.

She placed down her tray and started signing with me. *Welcome to Lexington. Hope you'll find it enjoyable here.*

I was pleasantly surprised that we had met someone who could speak my language, and I replied happily.

Thank you. It's a lovely place.

What brings you here? she asked, instinctively continuing in sign language. She, of course, didn't know that I could hear perfectly well.

We're just visiting the area, I signed back. *We're doing research.*

Research? What's the topic?

"If you don't mind, you can talk normally," Hailey interrupted us. "Alice can hear perfectly fine, and to be honest, you guys are signing a bit too quickly for me."

"Oh, I'm sorry," the waitress said, looking at Hailey awkwardly. "You don't use ASL then?"

"Not that much." Hailey bit her lip, realizing at the same time as me that we were supposed to be sisters. "Alice is my half-sister. We haven't seen each other in years, but our father passed, and we've been getting closer since."

"Oh, I see," the girl said. "Sorry, I didn't mean to…"

"It's okay; it's an odd situation," Hailey quickly said.

"I'm sorry about my enthusiasm. It's not every day that I get to practice my sign language. My grandfather was deaf, and I learned it to talk with him. He passed a few years ago, and I haven't used it since. Which is a shame, really."

"Sorry to hear that," Hailey said.

"Your sister was just telling me that you guys are researching something. Can I ask what? Maybe I can help?"

Hailey glanced at me; I glanced back.

"We're writers," Hailey said. "We're collaborating on a book together."

"Oh, that is pretty cool. Are you guys from the Midwest? I recognize the accent."

"Yeah, we are," Hailey said surprised. "How did you know?"

"I have some family down there. I don't see them that much, but they kind of talk the same. You guys sure are a long way from home. We usually get people from the Boston area here, but no one from your neck of the woods."

I briefly glanced at Hailey and nodded, giving her permission to talk. The hotel manager had believed us, so this girl probably would too. Or so we hoped.

"My sister and I specialize in researching local mysteries,"

Hailey said. "That's why we're here. We want to write a book about cases and investigations. We've been traveling around towns all over the East Coast finding and writing about unsolved murders or disappearances that have made their mark on communities. You know, the kinds of stories that don't show up on national news but are devastating to the locals."

The waitress reacted excitedly. "We *have* a story just like that."

Hailey and I glanced at each other again. My hands started shaking. I kept them on my lap.

The girl sat down, forgetting all about the menu and our food. "There was this thing last year. We had a disappearance that rocked our community, I can tell you that."

"Oh?"

"Yeah, a local woman vanished without a trace. She disappeared a day before her wedding, so it was quite a thing around here. The local television stations covered the story."

"That's terrible," Hailey said, keeping a straight face. I didn't dare to look at the waitress.

"I believe the case is still open, but everyone around town assumes that she's been murdered and buried somewhere in the woods or something. Some even say her body may be hidden on one of the memorial sites."

"And no one has any clue who might have done it?" Hailey asked.

"Well, some say it was her fiancé. A lot of people believe that theory, to be honest. Or a jealous ex-boyfriend. I mean, it had to be someone she knew, right? There's no other logical explanation."

"What if she left on her own?" Hailey asked. "There are

known cases where people were assumed dead but showed up years later."

"Nah, not her. She was a devoted member of the community. She wouldn't just take off like that."

"Why are you so sure?"

"She had her own business, and it was thriving. Plus, she was marrying her high school sweetheart. Why would she do something like that?"

"But then, why is her fiancé the suspect?"

"Isn't that what all those true crime television shows say? The killer is often the person closest to you?"

My heart pounded in my chest. This was it; this was the one. I just knew it. I could *feel* it. Hailey glanced at me as my hands turned sweaty and I felt like I was choking. It took all I had to keep my emotions intact.

"It sounds fascinating," Hailey said. "When was this exactly? Do you know?"

"Uh, last year, I think? Yeah, that's it. It was early last year, I believe January or February, because they wanted to have a Winter wedding, but not a Christmas one. I recall my mom talking about that."

"Oh. Wow," Hailey said nodding sympathetically.

"I believe they're planning a memorial for her early next year, and I've heard a rumor that they're thinking about declaring her deceased, even though there's some controversy about it. Some people say it's too soon."

"I see," Hailey said.

"It's really sad, you know? People are still reeling over it because things like that never happen around here. I mean, the last murder we had was forty years ago, so it's not like things like this happen every day. And then the whole marriage thing."

"Yeah," Hailey said.

"She vanished on a Thursday, and her wedding was planned that Friday. Some people say that she took her own life because she didn't really want to get married, and that her body will wash up on the shores soon. But everyone who really knew her refuses to accept that theory."

I'm sorry, I signed. *This must have been so hard on her family.*

"It really was, and still is," the young waitress sighed, as if she were personally involved in the matter. The girl obviously enjoyed having this conversation. We had definitely picked the right place.

The people sitting at the other table had ended their conversation and were openly listening in on ours.

"So people are still searching for her, despite it being nearly two years?" Hailey said, pushing the conversation gently forward.

"Oh, yeah. Her fiancé and her parents are still promising rewards to anyone who can lead them to the truth about what really happened to her. But to be fair, a lot of people want to move forward. That's why there's some talk about declaring her dead."

"What's your theory?" Hailey asked.

"Mine?" the waitress said, clearly pleased that Hailey had asked this question, as if she was at center stage of the mystery.

"Yeah. I'd like to know what you think."

"Oh, I don't know," she said. "I didn't know her personally. I knew who she was, obviously. I mean, everyone knows everyone in this town, you know? She was nice, a couple of years older than me, nearly thirty. We went to the same school, a few years apart. She had always been friendly with everyone. She was popular, a business owner. Things were going well for her."

I remembered my dad talking about his job and how he was forced to visit businesses too, in the final years of his life. How he hated doing that.

And this woman had her own business.

What kind of business? I signed.

"She had an ice cream parlor. It was extremely successful, had all these extraordinary flavors, like flowers and fruits. She used to make vanilla ice cream from scratch, and had invented all these homemade chocolate chip flavors, that sort of thing."

"That sounds lovely," Hailey said, keeping her voice straight.

"Yeah, she did everything herself. She grew the business in just a couple years. She even added a whole bunch of new desserts to the menu right before she disappeared. She had just graduated as a pastry baker and was planning to expand her business in that area. She was doing weddings and stuff. So the fact that she would take off doesn't make any sense at all."

Where did she vanish from? I signed.

"Her own store, some time at night, I think? I don't really know the details. Oh, yeah, and that only added to the mystery: whoever did this must have known that she would be working there that night, which only a few people did."

How so?

"That's what I heard."

"Ah."

A man showed up behind the waitress, stopping her before she could say anything else. He looked at her sternly, and then smiled tightly at us, obviously not happy with what was going on. "My apologies," he said, "my daughter has the habit of talking too much about things that she shouldn't be discussing with strangers. We'll leave you to it. Your lunch will be ready soon."

The girl got up reluctantly, but her father glanced at her sternly, ending our conversation abruptly.

"Phew," Hailey said, "that was quite a story."

I watched the waitress and her father argue in the back of the restaurant. The other customers looked at us, obviously curious about who we were.

"Are you reporters?" a woman asked.

"No, writers," Hailey said quickly. "Looking for local true crime stories."

"Ah. Well, you definitely struck gold with this one."

"How so?" Hailey said. "Seems unclear if it's really a crime. It could be anything, really."

"Nope. This one was definitely a crime," a man said. They were seated three tables away in the otherwise still-empty restaurant. Hailey glanced at me, and I nodded. We got up and moved to the table next to them.

"Why are you so sure?" Hailey said.

The man bowed a bit, looking at us conspiratorially, casting a glance aside as if he wanted to make sure the restaurant owner wouldn't hear him gossiping.

"Everyone knew Ginnifer well, I can tell you that, and she would *never* have run off in that way. You hear all these stories in the newspapers about people doing that, but not her. She was too happy. If you look up the term Golden Child, her photo would be next to it.

"The reason why the timing was so odd, was the fact that she'd been working in her shop by herself all day, but behind closed doors. You see, she was making her own wedding cake and desserts. She insisted on doing everything herself.

Which makes sense. I mean, she couldn't have anyone else make them if she was so famous for it, right?"

"Right," Hailey said.

"So the day before the wedding, she was in her shop all day long to prepare the ice cream and wedding cake. As usual, she was alone. She couldn't afford to hire staff yet, as the business had just started picking up steam."

"Okay," Hailey said. "So nobody saw her all day, then?"

"That's right," the woman said, her face turning slightly sad. "Ginnifer was expected at her parents' home at seven that night for rehearsal dinner, but she never showed up, which wasn't like her. So they started searching for her. They found the back door to the ice cream parlor unlocked, but there hadn't been a struggle inside, and nothing was stolen. The machines hadn't been switched off, the equipment wasn't cleaned, and the radio was still playing. Her wedding cake stood unfinished on the counter; the whipped cream, chocolate, and fruit she was going to add sat right next to it."

"But someone must have seen something, right?" Hailey said.

"Not necessarily. The back of the shop leads to a small alley between two buildings, where delivery services usually parked. The police believe someone had parked a car there, snatched her, and drove off. Easy, especially in the dark."

"So this poor woman vanished without a trace, right in the middle of preparing for her own wedding?" Hailey said. "That's so sad."

"And that's the reason this had to be murder," the man said. "She was taken away from where she was safe to be killed elsewhere."

"Why are you so sure she's dead?" Hailey asked. "Maybe she's still alive and locked up somewhere?"

The woman rolled her eyes, as if what Hailey said was stupid. "What idiot would keep someone locked up for years?"

"It's been done before. There are cases where–"

"Young children, maybe, but a grown woman?" the man interrupted her. "Not a chance."

"It could be possible. She could even be in the area."

The man forcefully shook his head. "She's dead. I can *feel* it. I would know if she was still alive."

There was something in his voice that made me look at him more closely. Hailey noticed it, too. She studied him, hesitant when she spoke again.

"Can I ask... Are you related to her?"

The man looked at us sadly. "I'm her uncle. And her godfather."

I felt a cold chill run down my spine. This was *real*. These were real people, suffering. People who had lost someone so valuable to them that it was still destroying them every day of their lives.

I felt my throat choke.

But there was one thing I was certain of: This woman they were talking about? This was *not* my father's victim. She couldn't be. Her name was all wrong.

30

I lost all appetite after that conversation. The waitress and her father hurried up with our food and lingered nearby, as if they wanted to put an end to our discussion. The waitress never spoke to us again, except when she brought the food.

The uncle and his companion finished their food without uttering another word. I regretted sitting next to them, as a silence had fallen across the restaurant. When they got up, I felt relieved. The man dropped money on the table and looked at us. I looked away first.

"Please do not contact her parents or her fiancé," he said. "They've been through a lot already, and I don't want them to feel used. I get that you're here with good intentions, and that you want to write this book about missing persons cases and all, but don't leech off their sadness."

"We'd never do that," Hailey said.

The man smiled. "Young lady, everyone uses everyone to get what they want. And that's okay. Just don't go about it if you can avoid it. Find your info in the newspapers if you must, but don't bother too many people around here. It's an open wound."

"Which is why you've given me all this information yourself?" Hailey guessed.

"You seem like the type of person who'd go to any length to get what you want. Better me than some gossip hounds around town, right?" He cast aside a glance at the young waitress, who walked away embarrassed. "People talk a lot, but no one has the right to do so if they weren't there."

"Then can we talk to you if we have any questions?" Hailey asked.

The man smiled. "Maybe. That will depend on the questions." He dropped a business card on the table.

"We really want to help," Hailey said.

"If that is your intent, then I'd be willing to talk again. But if you're here to earn thousands over my niece's body, I will slap you with a lawsuit so fast you won't know what hit you."

Hailey looked at the card. "You're a lawyer."

"Yes, I am. Have a nice day, ladies."

The two left. The whole discussion left a bad taste in my mouth. We had used the whole "writers" cover as a means to get our hands on information, but now I felt terrible about it. It had people thinking that we were here to make money off their tragedy.

"Don't worry about it," Hailey said. "Let's finish our meals and get out of here."

I didn't want to eat anymore. The food kept sticking in my throat. I got up quickly, smiled briefly at the staff, and walked outside while Hailey paid for our food in cash.

As soon as we were outside, I felt better.

Hailey stood next to me and inhaled. She stuck her hands in her pockets. "Well, we're never going to go back there," she said. "That was the strangest conversation ever, but also a very helpful one. Now we know who we're looking for."

I don't know, I signed, before using my notepad to explain. *The name does not match.*

"Alice, what are you talking about? This is her."

Her name is Jennifer, I wrote down. *Not correct.*

Hailey scrunched her brow at me for a second, then she seemed to understand what I was saying. "Honey, your dad marked the initials 'G.H.' in the journal. This woman's name was Ginnifer, not Jennifer. Ginnifer is spelled with a 'G'."

Oh. Oh, God.

I felt sick all of a sudden. Dizziness overwhelmed me. I had it all wrong. All this time, while they were talking about her, repeating her name, I couldn't help but feel relief that she could *not* be my father's victim, despite the dates and time matching.

Hailey cupped my face, stopping the onset of a panic attack. "Hey, breathe, Alice. Just breathe through this, okay? This still doesn't have to mean anything. We'll figure it out. Keep the faith."

I didn't know what that faith was supposed to be anymore. Was I searching for confirmation of my father's involvement in this disappearance, thus confirming what he had said that night on his deathbed? Or was I still praying, against my better judgment, that we were out here chasing ghosts?

I got a hold of myself, feeling an eerie calm descend over me. What was the point of avoiding reality when this was what we had come for?

I need to know, I signed.

"I know. Come on, let's head to the library next."

Hailey took me by the arm and led me to Cary Memorial Library, which was the biggest of the local Lexington libraries. The building was tall and historical, restored to its original state ten years ago, according to the plaque attached to the wall.

The building was warm, but not too warm. There were students and adults walking around in various layers of clothing, some in T-shirts, others wearing sweaters. Most jackets and coats were off.

We walked over to the counter, where Hailey politely asked to look at the archived local newspapers. The female clerk looked at her surprised, obviously not used to strangers coming in with this request – most people probably came to inquire about the war. There was a large section of the library dedicated to the subject.

"Are you reporters or something?" she asked suspiciously.

Hailey smiled. "No. We're writers."

"Oh. Anything in particular that you're looking for?"

"We'll know it when we see it."

The librarian led us to an area upstairs, where copies of all the local newspapers were kept in large drawers, neatly categorized per date. Today's newspaper was lying on a table; someone was reading it.

She showed us how the papers were categorized and how we could take them out of the drawers without screwing up her system. She explained there was a local one, called *The Lexington Gazette*, and one that was published statewide that often included stories from the area.

"We don't keep the national newspapers here, so if you want to go through those, too, you'll need to go the other section. My colleague can help you if you need anything else. She's sitting right there." She pointed to a corner desk where a woman was skimming through some books.

"The local news is fine," Hailey said. "Thank you."

"How far back do you need to go?"

"Oh, about two years," Hailey said, deliberately not mentioning the January 1979 dates that we were looking for.

"We have newspapers dating back fifty years," the librarian said proudly. "I will set you up at that table. Remember, you're not allowed to copy the papers yourself. The charge is a penny per copy, and you need to ask my colleague."

"Thank you," Hailey said, touching her bag. "That probably won't be necessary. I brought a notepad with me."

"Alright, then. If you need anything else, books or something, I'll be downstairs."

We waited until the librarian was gone before Hailey dug out her notepad with the right date written on it: *G.H., January 17–19, 1979.*

I hadn't told Hailey that I remembered that month clearly. Dad hadn't left after Christmas like usual. My parents had a fierce argument; I don't know what about. As a result, he had decided to stay home for much longer than originally planned. This decision forced Mom to withdraw from her binging sessions. But he stayed until way past New Years, too, which was not his habit. He only left on January 14th. That Sunday night, he flew out to the East coast, though I didn't know at the time where he was going. I never did.

He had been home for a month, and my mom had suffered the whole time. He must have done it on purpose. Staying longer must have been his revenge on her.

The moment he left the house, Mom started drinking again, so I made meals with what was still in the cupboards and brought them to her room. That whole week, she had hardly known I was there. She never even went to the store to get us food.

That week was one of the only times in my life I had debated breaking out of the house and walking to the supermarket myself. By the time I had mentally prepared for it, she came downstairs and acted as if we weren't starving.

When Dad returned on Sunday instead of Friday, he acted all cheerful and happy, and he had brought flowers for my mom. He also apologized profusely for being such an asshole.

If what Hailey and I suspected was true, Dad had traveled to Lexington as planned, where he had worked for three days, and had abducted a young woman on Thursday. This would have been barely four days after he had left our house, after a month of quietly bullying Mom.

How could he do that? Despite all of his flaws, despite the terrible life he had pushed my mom and me into, I couldn't believe that he would be capable of doing this. Despite it all, he had been my dad. My caretaker. The man who had traveled the country for over three decades, who had spent night after night in one sleazy motel room after the other to provide for his family.

It was insane to believe that he was a murderer. What kind of daughter was I to think that he was capable of doing such a gruesome thing? What kind of person was I to assume that, just because he wrote down some initials in his journals, he would be crazy enough to snatch someone in plain sight?

These initials were meaningless. Clients. Conquests. It was so much easier to believe that he had been fucking around, than to assume he was a murderer.

I was a terrible daughter. I wanted to go home *right now*. To talk to Mom. To tell the police that she was a good person, that she would never have killed Dad like they claimed. That I could vouch for her.

Hailey had to drive me home. We had to forget the whole thing. I turned around to tell her when her tense voice silenced me.

"Found it. Fuck."

In a split second, her facial expression and the tone of her voice confirmed my worst fears. A couple of elderly people at the table next to us looked up. The man frowned at Hailey's language.

Hailey tapped her finger on the newspaper article on the table in front of her.

"Shit, Alice. This is it! Listen to this," she said, lowering her voice. "Local well-known bride-to-be Ginnifer Hobbs disappeared January 17th from her ice cream parlor on Main Street. She was expected at that evening's planned rehearsal dinner at 7pm, but never showed up. A search party has been assembled, but there has unfortunately been no sign of Ms Hobbs thus far. Her parents and fiancé have been questioned. At this moment, the police are considering many possibilities, including foul play."

This was the story we had heard at the restaurant.

"The police will be conducting a thorough search of the woods and lake today, January 19th, and are requesting volunteers to join the search party. For further information, please contact the Lexington Police Department and ask for Detective Williams. If you have heard from or seen Ms Hobbs, or if you recall any suspicious activity around her ice cream parlor January 17th, please get in touch with the local police immediately."

Hailey looked at me. "This is huge, Alice."

The article included a photo of a beautiful, red-haired woman smiling at the camera. "This was definitely taken by a professional photographer, probably to promote her business," Hailey said. "Look, that's her ice cream parlor. It looks really cozy."

The woman was picture-perfect, the type of person who could appear on television and be considered stunning by many. I knew the rules of attraction from all the soaps I had watched, and she would have been a perfect candidate to play a major part in them.

She and I shared some features. I was skinny, had fierce

blue eyes, darker hair, and high cheekbones. So did she. That's where the resemblance ended, though. I was pale in comparison to her, but if I were to wear makeup and clothes like her, we could have been considered siblings.

"God, she looks just like you, Alice," Hailey said.

I know, I signed. *This is her.*

"I'm sorry," Hailey said quietly. "The dates match, the person matches. We have a lead now. G.H. *is* Ginnifer Hobbs."

She took another newspaper that was dated a few days later and tapped on the front page.

"Look, the tone of voice has changed. Listen to this."

I prepared myself for what was to come next.

"The police are now convinced of foul play in the disappearance of Ms Hobbs, and continue to question her fiancé, Mark Jacobs, who is considered a person of interest in the matter. Two days before the wedding, the couple were seen arguing in a restaurant, which led law investigators to believe that he might be involved. Ms Hobbs's parents, however, have stated in the press that they do not believe Mr Jacobs had anything to do with Ms Hobbs's disappearance. They stand firmly behind his claims of innocence."

She looked at me.

"Not even her parents believe he was involved."

Because he wasn't, I signed.

If I had still maintained any hope of clearing my father's name, that was now gone. But nobody would believe us if we simply went to the police with what we had so far. This was just not enough.

I need to know what happened to her, to help him, I scribbled down. She looked at my note and frowned.

"How? We don't know where to begin. Besides, you

promised me that we'd only pursue this to the point that you knew the truth and that you would leave the rest up to the police."

This is not enough, I wrote down. *We need more. He needs help.*

Hailey frowned. "You're right. Let's keep searching, then."

31

I was disgusted by the newspaper's change of tone and wrote this down to tell Hailey.

"This is what the press does," she shrugged. "They blow things out of proportion. That's why I hate newspapers and TV news so much. Poor guy. This whole thing must have been so hard for him. I wonder where he is now, and how he's doing."

More articles appeared in the newspapers, but they became shorter and less informative as there was nothing new to talk about. People went about their lives, and search parties were no longer taking place.

"That's what always happens," Hailey said. "A new day brings new drama. Even with something as big as this, people tend to forget."

We hardly found anything in the bigger newspaper. It was as if it didn't matter.

"Even with a woman as pretty and well-known as her, nobody outside of the Lexington borders cares much. Plus, people don't really want to know about the existence of real-life serial killers. They've just gotten over the whole Ted Bundy story. Everyone's just relieved that he's behind bars, you know? Ready to move on."

I didn't know much about Bundy, just the stuff I'd seen on television, but I'd never read about him.

"Okay, so this is what happened," Hailey said. "The

newspaper stopped paying attention. The search has obviously ended; the cops have probably labeled it a cold case by now, and life continued for everyone in this town."

The parlor? I wrote down.

"No idea. Probably gone by now, I guess."

So what now?

"Now we try to figure out the connection," she said. "He must have stayed in town for a couple of days, so people might have remembered him. I'm guessing he was there for work. As a traveling salesman, he would have received a list of places to visit. So if he was there for work, he would have stayed at a local hotel for a while."

I guess.

"And if he was there for the first time, he must have been looking for new clients. But why specifically her?"

The company wanted him to visit local stores. He must have spotted her.

"Aha." Hailey tapped her nose, frowning lightly. "He may have visited the ice cream parlor to sell his products, like he usually would. He must have seen her there. Maybe she was his type. But then what?"

He was always in town for five days.

"That must have given him plenty of time to get to know her routine. To follow her, stalk her, take her, kill her. Bury her or dump her in the lake."

Why didn't the police question him? I wrote.

"Remember how I said that there are plenty of tourists out there who pay cash? There isn't that much to go on. People come and go in places like this all the time. He must have known that he could blend in easily."

But the police should have been able to track him down, I wrote. *Why not question him?*

"Because her fiancé had been their prime suspect from the start," Hailey said. "Tunnel vision; I've read about that. When something seems so obvious, why look for anything else? Most murders happen close to home."

I remembered this TV show called *Columbo*, the one with the weird detective. Almost all murderers were close to their victims. And why not investigate the fiancé, who people saw her arguing with?

"Oh, you're looking into the Ginnifer Hobbs case?" said a voice behind me.

The librarian had returned. I'd been so lost in thought that despite my sensitive hearing, I hadn't heard her coming at all.

I quickly closed the paper, even though she had already seen what I was doing.

"Yes, we are," Hailey said.

"Sad story, isn't it?" she said. "And this whole thing is still not laid to rest. So it's going into your book?"

"Maybe."

"You should take on this story, you know. Ginnifer didn't deserve her fate; neither did her family. And her poor fiancé, well, don't get me started on the injustice of it all."

"Why?" Hailey pushed on.

She shrugged. "You know how it is. He'll never get one moment of peace as long as she's not found. He can't seem to shake off the suspicion, which is really sad. To tell you the truth, it's a miracle the poor man's still living in Lexington, but if he had left, that would probably have been considered a confession. If you ask me, he's stuck in a tough position. He's trying to rebuild his life, but it's hard. A lot of people don't want anything to do with him."

"So I gather you believe his innocence?" Hailey asked.

"Of course I do," she said vehemently. "His parents are good friends of mine; I've watched him grow up. He's a nice guy, genuine and decent. He would never have done this."

"I read somewhere that they had an argument before she disappeared?" Hailey gently prodded.

"That's a load of crap," the librarian said fiercely. "Some local gossip wanted to have her five minutes of fame and cooked up a story about them arguing in the middle of the street. Strange, don't you think, that it was a busy day and nobody else saw it?"

"So her story was debunked?"

"Unfortunately, the reporter on the case didn't want to retract his story, so a lot of locals still don't even know that the story was fake. They never recanted it, and it destroyed poor Mark's reputation."

"And there's no doubt in your mind that he's innocent?"

"Of course not! Those two were crazy about each other. His only problem was he had no solid alibi, and no one who could confirm that he was alone at home all day. That didn't help his case, nor that he was one of the few people who knew that Ginnifer was going to be working at the parlor that day."

"How so?" Hailey asked. "Wouldn't people have known?"

"No. She was very private about her life. No one except a few knew she would be working there. She had kept it a secret that she would do the cake herself."

"Ah. As a surprise," Hailey stated.

"Yeah. The police assumed that Ginnifer must have known her abductor. She always had a habit of locking the back door when she was alone, and since the shop was closed, nobody could enter from the front, either. If she was so careful about her privacy, why should she have opened the back door for a perfect stranger? That speaks against Mark, unfortunately."

"Was he ever arrested?" Hailey asked.

The librarian shook her head as she sat down, happy to continue her story. "He was questioned several times, but in the end there wasn't enough evidence against him. They had to let him go, but they're still keeping tabs on him, so I've heard. Mark still hopes that the truth will be revealed one day, but until that happens, he will never be free."

"That's really sad," Hailey said. "I hope somebody finds out the truth someday."

"I hope so too. This town needs closure."

Hot tears burned behind my eyes. God, what had I done? This made it all too real.

I was the daughter of the man who did this. How could anyone ever make this right? My dad was dead. Dead! He had taken his secrets to the grave with him. There were no markings about burial sites, nowhere to start looking for this poor girl.

And perhaps she was only the first of more than thirty people – women? – to have gone missing. What had he done?!

My stomach churned. I felt sick to the bone, dizzy, distressed. I audibly gasped for air, shoved the chair backwards and fled to the bathroom, where I puked out my lunch until there was nothing left. My body heaved. Tears streamed down my face as I tasted bile.

When I was done, my throat was sore and my mouth tasted disgusting. I could barely stand upright. My legs buckled. I slid down against the wall and stared at my trembling hands, trying to get a grip on myself.

A new panic attack was imminent; I could feel it building

up. This was the second time in a couple of days that I'd felt this way, and it was horrible to experience such a loss of control. I saw red before my eyes. I felt out of this world, as if I weren't even part of it.

The door flew open, but I couldn't see anyone until Hailey slid down by my side and grabbed me by the shoulders.

"Is she alright?" someone asked behind her. I recognized the librarian's voice.

"She's fine, she just has panic attacks sometimes," was Hailey's response as she forced me to look her in the eye. "It'll be alright, Alice," she said. "You're going to be just fine. Trust me on this."

Her voice came from far away. It was hard to hear her words clearly. My head pounded, but my thoughts were slowly gathering themselves again. I needed to get out of this place, this hotel, this town.

I should have burned those journals and forgotten the whole thing. I was wrong from the start: knowing was worse than not knowing at all.

I wanted to disappear from the world, to become as invisible as I used to be before we started this crazy trip. But I knew that those days were long gone.

I rubbed the scar on my wrist without thinking, wanting to touch something that was as familiar to me as my old life had been. I looked at it.

I was still *me*. I was still Alice.

But I was no longer that girl from Hays. We couldn't hide any longer. It was time to find help.

32

The shocked librarian watched us as Hailey took me outside into the fresh air. The newspapers were still on the table where we left them.

I needed to escape the library, so I hung onto Hailey's arm as if I were sick or disabled. My legs weren't able to carry me anywhere for much longer, but I kept on stumbling forward until we reached a bench that looked out onto a park. I sat down gratefully, eager to catch my breath. I closed my eyes and focused on breathing.

"Are you okay? What happened in there?" Hailey asked. Her voice still sounded far away.

She handed me my notepad, which I let slide onto the bench beside me, unable to write anything down. My hands were shaking so much I wouldn't be able to hold a pen.

After catching my breath, I signed the words, hoping that she would understand.

Panic attack. I'm so tired.

"Oh, honey," she said. "It must be so hard being here, but it's almost over. We have to talk to the police now. That's our next step. They have to know. They can reopen the investigation and take it from there."

She was right. This was our endgame. What would be the point of investigating things further when the truth was so blatantly clear in front of us? It would only confirm what we already knew.

But it was not enough. There *had* to be more.

I took my dad's journal from Hailey's bag, opened it on that particular week and looked at the notes that he had made, reading them again with a fresh set of eyes.

I had always been focused on the dates he marked, but now I was looking for something else. I just didn't know what that something was.

Cleaning products, set A.
Vacuum cleaner, type C.
Cleaning products, set D.
Bathroom, set F.
Cleaning products, set C.

The list went on and on. He'd obviously had a good week. Sometimes he would mark that he had to come back later, or that he had to contact the office for more products.

This list was nothing out of the ordinary. It looked the same as all the others of that year.

Until… There it was, at the bottom of a long sales list on Tuesday. A small additional remark was left that we hadn't noticed before, a scribble that was barely readable, at the bottom of the page.

Cleaning products at ICP. Client asked for more. Going back on Thursday.

Hailey stared at me when I pointed it out to her.

This was it, the proof that we needed. This was IT.

"ICP. What the hell is I… Oh, God. Ice Cream Parlor," Hailey said out loud. "I didn't even see that before."

But I did, because I was looking for evidence with a new purpose: proof that would connect Dad to Ginnifer Hobbs. And I found it.

Hailey looked at me, just as stunned as I was that we had found what we were looking for. "Alice, do you know what this means? It links your dad directly to her! He was there that week. He saw her on Tuesday, and he came back on Thursday. They must have agreed to meet up again for whatever it was that she needed. She must have told him she would be working at the parlor. She already knew him, so she would have unlocked the door for him."

I know, I signed sadly, before writing: *We need to tell the police* now.

Hailey got up.

"You're right. We have the journals with the initials and the notes. That should be enough to get them to look into your dad."

Yes.

"But, Alice," she wavered, "do you want to do this yourself? I can do it for you."

No. He was my father.

"I know, but that doesn't mean you have to go there. I can talk to them, tell them everything. About you, about your dad and your mom. You don't have to go with me. You could go back home."

No.

I wasn't prepared for this, but I would never be. I was so scared. Once this got out, once reporters got word of this, my invisible life would forever be over. I would be known as the daughter of a murderer. Perhaps even a serial killer, if they could find enough evidence in his notebooks.

We need to get those journals from the room, I wrote down.

"We can do that later."

No. They're more proof.

"Shouldn't we go tomorrow? It wouldn't hurt to do it a

day later. You're very pale; you're obviously distressed. If you get some sleep first, you'd feel better."

I shook my head. *Now. Please.*

Now that we knew, it felt as if every second counted. I wanted to get this over with; to have the police take over the investigation so I could finally deal with the fallout of my decisions.

Hailey didn't object. She waited patiently until I felt good enough to stand up. We slowly made our way down Main Street to the hotel, where she sat me down on a chair at reception.

"Wait here. I'll be right back."

I remained seated, trying to keep my thoughts together. The hotel manager walked up to me. "Are you okay?" he asked. "Would you like some water?"

I looked at him through teary eyes and nodded. He came back with a glass of water and sat down next to me. "What's wrong?" he asked. "Can I get you something else? Where's your sister?"

I pointed to the ceiling.

"Ah, she went to your room?"

I nodded.

"Are you feeling sick? Do you need a doctor?"

I shook my head. No doctor could ever fix this. All the adrenaline was quickly leaving my body. Perhaps Hailey was right, and I should get some rest first, but now that we knew, it felt as if the truth couldn't be revealed fast enough.

"You've lost your father, right?" he asked. "Your sister said something about it."

I nodded.

"That must have been rough."

I shrugged.

"I lost my wife a few months ago. Cancer. My kids are taking it hard. I know it's none of my business, but have you taken enough time to mourn?"

I didn't say anything. How could I tell this kind man that Dad had not been the type of father he would obviously be?

Hailey rushed down the stairs with Dad's case in hand. She looked startled when she noticed the hotel manager. He got up.

"I hope you ladies are okay," he said. "If you need anything, just let me know, okay?"

"Thank you," Hailey said. "Come on, Alice, let's go."

Arm in arm we walked to the police station near the library. The building had high white ceilings and large windows, and was relatively modern. It was warm inside. We were the only visitors in the reception area.

Two police officers were seated at the front desk. The oldest of the two, who spoke with a deep voice, eyed us curiously. The younger one was tapping away on a typewriter. Behind them were more desks with three other men working.

A radio was playing softly in the background. Pop music. It reminded me of our long drive. I blinked as I tried to stay focused.

"Ladies," the older man said, "what can I do for you?"

"My name is Hailey, and this is my friend Alice," Hailey said. "We come from Hays, Kansas. My friend cannot speak, so I'll be talking for the two of us."

He eyed us curiously, his eyes resting briefly on me. "Okay? And what brings you here today? Hopefully nothing serious, like a theft or anything? We don't have many tourists being robbed, but it does happen."

"We're not tourists," Hailey said. "We came to Lexington with a purpose."

The younger agent stopped typing.

"And that is…?" the older one asked.

Hailey hesitated. "Well, the thing is… we might have some information about the disappearance of Ginnifer Hobbs."

The use of Ginnifer's name immediately caused everyone behind the desk to stop what they were doing. At the back of the room, a man got up and approached us. He was the only one not wearing a uniform.

"Ginnifer Hobbs, you say?" he said. "I'm the investigative officer. What kind of information?"

Hailey took a deep breath and nodded at me. I kept my eyes lowered to the floor.

"We have reason to believe that Alice's father, a man by the name Jack Jenkins, might have had something to do with Ginnifer's disappearance. We can support this claim with evidence."

"I see. I'm Captain Miles, responsible for running this office. Come with me, please," he said, not sounding unfriendly.

He took us behind the reception area to a room with a mirror and brought in enough chairs to seat us all.

I knew what this was; I'd seen it on television. An interrogation room, and people could watch the conversations that took place from the outside in. My heart sank, and it immediately felt as if I was considered a suspect.

"Sit down, ladies," the man said, again not unfriendly. "I'm really sorry that we have to put you in this room for now, but we're having renovations done here and there, and it can get noisy and crowded. Don't worry, you're not under suspicion or anything, and I promise you that nobody is watching us. Can I get you some coffee or tea?"

"Coffee, please," Hailey said.

We glanced at each other before sitting down. The younger police officer from the reception desk came back with coffee and remained standing up, with a notebook in hand. The captain placed another notebook on the table and tapped his pen on it.

I was so nervous my hands were sweating.

"Alice can't speak, but she has perfect hearing, and she can use sign language or notebooks to communicate."

"Do we need an interpreter?"

She looked at me. I nodded. We might need one anyhow, I thought.

"We'll get someone in here to help, but that might take a while," Captain Miles said. "Can you help us in the meantime?"

"Of course. Is it okay that I tell the story instead of Alice?"

"And you are her friend?"

"Yes."

"And you know about her father?"

"Yes, I do. I've never met him, though."

"Okay."

I took my cup in hand to take a drink, but the coffee was still scorching hot. It burned my tongue. I sat it down quickly again, my hands shaking as I did.

"Now, then," Captain Miles said. "Let's start at the beginning. Can you tell us exactly who you are, why you are here, and what kind of new information you might have on Ginnifer Hobbs's disappearance?"

Hailey took a deep breath. "My name is Hailey Sanders, and this is Alice Jenkins. We're next-door neighbors in

Hays, Kansas. Alice's dad used to be a traveling salesman. He traveled all over the country for the past three decades. A few weeks ago, he was diagnosed with stage four cancer and came home to die. He was given opioids and other drugs to relieve the pain. During that process, he confessed in a hallucinatory state of mind to Alice that he might have done something to several people."

The captain looked at me curiously. "You said he was hallucinating?"

Fever and medication, I wrote down.

"Okay. Got it. So what makes you believe that what he said was a confession? And how did his words bring you from Hays to Lexington? Pretty farfetched, isn't it?"

"Actually, sir, it isn't," Hailey said. "We have evidence that something was going on with him."

"What kind of evidence?" the captain asked.

"Mr Jenkins left behind proof of his actions. We came to Lexington to confirm our suspicions."

"Proof?" the younger policeman said, who was obviously not buying it. "Such as?"

Hailey looked at me while she took the 1979 journal from her bag and opened it on the January date. Both policemen looked curiously at the notes.

"Mr Jenkins had a journal for every year that he traveled," she explained, while lifting the brown case on the table and opening it. The policemen looked surprised at all the journals.

"Each and every one of these contains notes that don't match with the rest of the year. One week every time, with a few dates marked differently than all the others."

"And you believe that he did something on those days?" Captain Miles said.

"Yes."

"Okay. And you found a note in January 1979?"

"Yes, we did."

Hailey returned to the Lexington journal and showed the men what she was talking about. She opened the journal in the middle. "You see? He made a habit of noting down where he'd been and what he had sold. Usually the entries look like this: San Diego-California, followed by a list of products that he sold per day. Sometimes a note about a client, or something for his company, but it's always the same."

A silence filled the room. I looked at Hailey, refusing to return the stares of the policemen.

Hailey coughed lightly, before continuing. "But as you can see, on this week, a few days were marked differently. He crossed a couple of days out. And then we have this entry: *G.H., LEX-MAS.* That week, he was right here, in Lexington, and as you can see, these dates that he crossed coincide with the disappearance of Ginnifer Hobbs. Plus, two days before she vanished, he had made an additional remark that stood out to us."

Hailey placed her finger on the mark, which drew their attention. It was in that moment that the policemen started taking us seriously. I could tell the difference in their demeanor.

Captain Miles carefully took the journal from Hailey and leafed through a couple of other months to see if there were any similar notes. He found only these dates marked, just like we had. We hadn't missed anything.

"There are markings like this in all of his journals, dating back to 1947. I'm sure that, should you inquire with all the towns he'd visited during the weeks of those entries, where someone was murdered or went missing."

Hailey's statement was bold, but it had its effect.

The captain obviously believed us. His interest grew. "We've always considered that whoever took Ginnifer was an outsider," he said. "A tourist or a traveler, someone with no connections to this town."

"Then why didn't you investigate that option?" Hailey asked bluntly.

"Do you know how many traveling salesmen we get in this town every week?" the captain said. "Even now, there are over a dozen active. They're a separate breed, you know. They travel from town to town, and most of the time, they pay for their hotel in cash, usually staying only for a couple of days. They're nomads, impossible to keep track of. Mr Jenkins's name didn't even show up on our suspect list."

"The perfect way to do something like this and get away with it for more than thirty years," the younger police officer said softly, as he opened journal after journal. "By the looks of it, he traveled all over the country, which would make it even easier, especially in the fifties, sixties, and seventies."

"Can I keep these for now?" the police captain asked. "We'll need some time to go through them. Can I ask – Mr Jenkins has passed since then?"

"Yes, he has. He died a couple of days ago," Hailey said. "Alice found the journals in his desk drawer after his passing."

The captain's face was troubled, while at the same time exhilarated. If this hypothesis turned out to be correct, it would mean that he could help resolve over thirty missing person cases from all over the country.

"If all of this is true, and I do say *if*, the FBI will have to get involved. For now, though, I want to focus on our own missing person. Is there anything else you can share about your dad? Something that might help us? Do you know why he might have taken Ginnifer? Do you have a picture of him? People around here might recognize him."

I looked at Hailey before taking a brochure from the pocket of my jeans. I had taken it with me before we left, knowing that someone would ask about him at some point. The brochure was about ten years old and in black and white. I had stolen it from the trash can, without my parents knowing, and had kept it in my room.

Dad stared gloomily into the camera. He obviously didn't want to have his picture taken. It was a terrible image, but it was the only photo of him that I had.

"Doesn't look familiar to me," the younger policeman said.

"Nope. We can use it to inquire downtown. Someone will remember him."

"What do we do in the meantime?" Hailey asked.

"We'll need a lot more information than this," Captain Miles said. "We'll need to know about your father, what his habits were, what he was like, and so on. This is going to take a lot more investigation, but we want to focus on finding out if your dad truly was in Lexington at the time, so I'll be sending my officers to all the hotels in town with his name and photo, and then we'll go from there. I'm going to have to ask you to stay in town for now, so we can ask questions whenever we need to."

I nodded, not finding this request abnormal. I had already decided that I wanted to stay here until we received confirmation about his wrongdoings.

Captain Miles looked at me. "You're very brave coming here with this story, Alice," Captain Miles said. "I hope you know how much we appreciate this. This whole case was at a dead end. With your help, we might be able to resolve it. So, thank you."

He got up, took the 1979 journal with him, and left us alone in the room with the other police officer, who started gathering the other journals in Dad's case.

I looked at Hailey, and she looked back at me. We had done the right thing. Now we had to wait it out.

33

The police station was immediately buzzing with activity, much more so than I would have expected. I thought they would handle this quietly, but it quickly became clear that everyone was putting off whatever they'd been working on to focus on Dad.

Hailey and I were the center of attention. Instead of being advised to return to the hotel as I had first expected, we were asked to stay put.

We were taken to the back of the main room, frequently approached by different officers asking questions that we couldn't always answer. Some were about my dad, what kind of person he had been, and why I would think he would do such horrendous things. Others were about Ginnifer, if I had known who she was, or why my dad would have taken her.

An interpreter was on the way, but until that happened it was hard to focus on what they were asking and attempting to answer. I was growing more tired by the minute.

They took photos of me, which I found odd at first, until I realized that someone had noticed the resemblance me and Ginnifer Hobbs. There was something festering beneath the surface of my mind.

The more I tried to block the awful thought that our resemblances were not a coincidence, the more it became apparent. My dad had a certain type, and if they would have had a list of missing women right now to compare us with, they would probably come to the conclusion that they all looked the same.

Just like Bundy had his type, my dad did too.

We saw them examine the journals and dust everything for fingerprints. Not that this would help much, because both Hailey and I had touched them several times. So had the captain and the younger police officer before they realized the importance of them. If there was still something left of my dad's fingerprints, they would be smudgy.

"Look," Hailey said, pointing to the right. "They've blown up your dad's photo. It's hanging in the main area. Everyone's in a frenzy about this. They believe our story. That's a good thing, right?"

But it didn't take long for the first reporter to enter the police station, looking for a good story. He was sent away immediately.

"Gossip is starting to spread," Hailey said. "It won't take them too long to figure out that we've been speaking to some people around town. I wonder when her family will show up."

She'd only just finished uttering those words when the front door flew open. In came an older couple and a woman that looked a lot like Ginnifer. She also looked like me.

"Is it true?" the older woman asked Captain Miles. "Do you have a new suspect?"

"Maybe," he said, trying to shush her. "You'll have to be patient for now, Maggie. We're working on something, but it's still quite fresh and we're uncertain if it'll lead to anything."

"But it's *something*, right?"

"It may be. Please, why don't you go back home and let us do our jobs?"

The woman's gaze scanned the room until she noticed me. She held her breath. Her hand flew before her mouth.

"Who is she?" she asked.

"Maggie, I can't talk to you about this; you know that," Captain Miles said. "Go home, okay? We'll talk soon."

Despite the family's protests, they were guided out of the police station. Captain Miles looked around angrily. "The first person to allow this story to escape our office *again* will be put on suspension. *Nobody* talks about this to *anyone*. Am I clear?"

"Yeah, boss," a man said. The others muttered.

After a couple of hours, we were brought coffee and sandwiches. The food was a nice break from the lengthy wait, but all I wanted was to get some sleep. That was not going to happen straight away, though. It was obvious we would have to stay while they did their jobs. I knew why: they were afraid we'd leave.

All that time, Hailey and I didn't speak much. She was just as tired as I was, and she leaned against me without being too obvious about it.

A woman and a man entered the police station and walked over to us. I could sense they were a different kind of police. They looked friendly but stern.

"You must be Alice," the woman said. "I'm Anna Doyle. I'm a Boston detective, specializing in missing persons. This is my partner, Peter McKinsey. You can understand us, right?"

I nodded while I shook her hand.

"Good. Please call me Anna. And him, Peter."

Captain Miles came over. "Anna, Peter, good to see you here. Are you good to go, or do you guys need some food first?"

"We ate on the way over," Peter said. "We can start right now if you'd like?"

"Start?" Hailey asked.

"We'd like to interview Alice more in-depth," Peter explained. "Alice, since you are not a suspect in this case, I'll need your permission to ask you some questions. Is that alright?"

I nodded again.

"And do we have your permission to record the interview on camera? In case this ever goes to court, we need to have official documentation," Anna said.

"Court? Who would you try?" Hailey blurted out.

"There might be accomplices. It's just a precaution. Your name is Hailey, right?"

"Yeah."

"You're Alice's friend?"

"Yeah." She hesitated. "Her *best* friend."

"Alright, Hailey. I'm afraid you'll have to leave for now, so we can talk to Alice alone. We'll also want to talk to you at a later stage, but since you are not related, this can wait for now. I hope you don't mind?"

"I'm her interpreter."

"Actually, we've brought our own," Anna said.

Another woman came rushing in. She introduced herself as Bridget Landon, a sign language interpreter that the Boston Police Department used for questioning. She showed us an official badge.

Go, I signed to Hailey. *Get some rest.*

"Are you sure? I don't feel comfortable leaving you here by yourself."

I'm not alone. I'll be fine.

"Okay, then. I'll leave you to it for now, but I'll be right there in the hall if you need me."

She glared at the police officers, as if she wanted to show her distrust. I wasn't scared. I knew this had to happen.

"Let's go to my office," Captain Miles said. "Less curious eyes there."

We sat down, the captain, Anna, Peter, and Bridget. Anna set up the camera, and as soon as it started rolling, they all introduced themselves for the record. Anna asked if I could do the same, using sign language.

While I signed, Bridget translated for me.

My name is Alice Jenkins. I live on North Green Road, 66E, Hays, Kansas.

"Can you tell us why you are here, Alice?"

Because I believe that my dad, Jack Jenkins, killed a woman who lived in Lexington by the name of Ginnifer Hobbs.

"What brought you to that theory, Alice? Can you tell us about the circumstances leading to this belief?"

I didn't tell them about my strange life or my mom. I just focused on his deathbed confession and the discoveries in the journals, then explained how we arrived here and found what we were looking for.

"So, to confirm, the reason you came to Lexington," Anna said, "was to find out for a fact that your dad really did what he confessed to?"

Yes.

"You are very brave, Alice."

No, I'm not. I'm scared. And angry.

Anna smiled sympathetically. "I can imagine. Where is your mom in all of this? Why isn't she here with you? Does she know that you are here?"

I hesitated. Now we were getting to the part I wanted to hide, but I knew it had to come out in the open sometime. The part that could get me locked up in an asylum, should they consider me insane after hearing all of this.

I sighed, without making a sound.

"Alice? Are you alright?"

I shrugged.

"What is it? Is it your mom?"

She's in prison, I signed. *Or arrested. Or – I don't know. I haven't spoken to her in days. And no, she is not aware of me coming here.*

"Why is she in prison?" Anna asked.

I caught the startled glances of the police officers and Bridget. I looked straight at Anna, trying to forget the camera pointed at me. I was so scared. I needed Hailey, but she wasn't here.

The police in Hays believe that she gave my dad an overdose of opioids to speed up his death. I don't know where she is right now.

A silence fell before Captain Miles spoke again. "We'll have to check with them." He walked to the door, beckoned a police officer, and spoke to him quietly before shutting the door again.

"Alice, do you believe that she did it?"

No. But she was still arrested.

"Have you spoken to her since?"

No.

"Why not?"

Tears welled up in my eyes. I could feel them slide over my face, to my hands. I shook my head.

"Alice?"

They don't know I exist, I signed.

"Wait a minute… *what?*" Peter said. "What do you mean, they don't know you exist?"

I was kept hidden my entire life.

"I don't understand?" Anna said.

My mom kept me locked up in the house.

"Why?"

I can't speak. She said it was for the best. She said it was to protect me. I looked up. *I am invisible. I am non-existent.*

Captain Miles and Peter shared a glance before the captain left the room. Did he think my story was ridiculous?

"Let's focus on your mom again," Anna said. "Do you believe she was aware of what your dad did?"

I didn't want to say yes or no. I shrugged. *I don't know.*

Captain Miles came back and whispered something to Anna.

"Alice, we've been told that your mom has confessed to the killing of your dad. She called it an act of mercy. She will be charged with manslaughter."

I stared at her in shock. This was not what I had thought would happen, not really.

No!

"I'm afraid it's true. They have her full confession on paper. There will be a trial. I have to repeat my question: was she aware of what your dad might have done? Could this have been a part of her decision to terminate his life?"

I don't know.

"But you do, don't you?"

Maybe. I've… I've heard things.

"Okay, Alice. Thank you."

Will you question her, too?

"Yes, she will be questioned," Anna said. "She will be informed that you are here, and what is happening. They will speak to her in the morning."

I felt icy cold. So cold. I just wanted to sleep. But I knew this was far from over.

This was just the beginning.

PART SEVEN
Ginnifer

34

I wanted this to be over with, but I knew I had no say in the matter. The police weren't done interrogating me. There was a lot more to come.

They were friendly, though. Anna moved a bit closer and placed her hand on my wrist. I looked at her sadly, only realizing then that I was still crying. She gave me a tissue and a few moments to calm down.

My heart pounded as I sat trembling on that chair with that camera still rolling. My legs were shaking, I was nervous that she would continue questioning me about what I'd said.

After a while, she spoke again. "Alice, is there anything else that you want to add to your statement? Anything that could help us further in our investigation? Something that will help us figure out the extent of this matter? Something that can help us find Ginnifer?"

No.

"Are you sure?"

Yes.

"Okay. Now, Alice, I need to ask you a question that is very important. Did you know?"

No!

"Did you ever have a clue?"

No. Not until he rambled on his deathbed.

"Do you really believe that your father did all of these things?"

Without a doubt.

"Because of his character?"

Yes.

"How does that make you feel?"

I'm so angry.

"Do you feel guilty?"

Of course I do. He was my dad, and he did all these terrible things. How could he have done this, and just continue living?

"Hopefully, your mom will be able to shed some light on that," Anna said. "It's obvious you were kept in the dark."

I was always home. Always alone. Dependent on him.

"Do you hate him?"

I had to think about that question. *He must have been sick or something. I don't know.*

"Do you regret coming here?"

No! I signed furiously.

"Because you want to know the truth."

Yes!

"But what is the truth, Alice?"

I don't understand?

"You mentioned briefly that your parents kept you locked up at home because you can't speak, right?"

Yes.

"Why would they do that?"

It's always been like that. It was my life.

"And you've never tried to escape?"

I shook my head. *Where would I go?* I asked sadly.

"You couldn't ask for help?"

No.

"So how did you meet Hailey?"

By chance. She saved me. She was the first person to notice me. She's everything to me.

"Your neighbor, right?"

Yes.

"Okay, Alice. I just have a couple more questions for you, and then it's over."

Okay.

"Did your father ever harm you physically?"

No.

"Sexually?"

No! I thought about my twenty-fourth birthday and Mom's odd reaction, and hesitated. *Not really. I think he tried to, once, maybe. But my mom got in the way.*

I saw the glances between Anna and the other police officers and knew what they were thinking. What if he had been alive today? What if I had become the next Ginnifer?

A shiver ran down my spine. A splitting headache overwhelmed me. I was so tired, my eyes drooped. I just wanted to sit on that chair and sleep.

Anna nodded at the other female officer, who turned the camera off. Bridget sat next to me and held my hands. "You did great," she said. "Well done, Alice. You are amazingly strong, and your ASL is flawless. Did you use it with your parents?"

I shook my head. *They didn't care.*

"Wow. I would have thought you'd learned it at a young age. This is extraordinary."

Then why didn't it feel that way? I wanted to blend in with the white walls, to disappear forever, to drift off to a realm of quiet and peace.

Anna and Peter left, but Bridget and the captain stayed with me.

Where is Hailey? I asked.

"Right outside," Captain Miles said, after Bridget had

translated. "You'll get to see her soon, but we still have to go over some things. Why don't you stay here? I'll get you something to eat and some coffee. Some cake, maybe? Something sweet and sugary; that'll help calm your nerves."

He left the door ajar. I could see the anxiety in the other room grow. Everyone was on the tips of their toes, working overtime to get this done. The panic attack that I had endured at the library was still haunting me physically. Everything ached; I felt sick.

Someone brought a piece of cake and some coffee, but I had trouble eating it. It tasted too sweet and sugary, but it did help to lift some of the exhaustion, so I forced myself to finish it.

"We're just going to have a talk next door, Alice," Bridget said, and she followed the captain outside. This time, they closed the door. I was left in the quiet of the room. I gazed around, trying to figure out what kind of man the captain was.

There was a family picture on his desk. He had pens and paper, a typewriter, a lot of files in cabinets behind him. The office looked well used. The leather sofa was old and tattered. I wanted to go lie down on it, but I didn't care to move.

After another long wait, the Captain, Anna, Peter, and Bridget returned. Hailey walked in behind them, looking tired and bewildered. I was so happy to see her, my heart could have burst.

"Are you okay?" she asked.

I nodded.

It was obvious they had come back for a reason. I was about to hear things that I wouldn't like.

The captain cleared his throat, took a chair, and placed it

in front of me. He made sure that we could look each other in the eye. He had a stack of paper in his hand, which he kept close to him.

The door was standing wide open. Several policemen had stopped what they were doing and looked at us. Hailey sat down next to me and held my hand. She already knew what was coming. I'd never seen her so pale.

The captain's voice was stern.

"Alice, after you came in with your story and your dad's journals, I immediately put my people to work. They've been making lists and dozens of calls to various police stations all over the country. With success, I might add."

Oh, God.

"So far, we've been able to collaborate with fifteen different stations, and they've all confirmed that the dates in your father's journals coincide with a missing person's case around the same time. We've matched the initials in the journals with the names of these women. We've received a dozen or so faxed photos of missing women, dating back to the sixties. I wanted to show you these photos."

He turned around the first picture. A woman that could have been Ginnifer's sister – *my* sister – smiled on a black-and-white sheet of paper.

"This is Phyllis Landers, age thirty-two, mother of one son, married. She went missing in Des Moines on January twenty-eighth, 1978, on her way to pick up her child from school. Her body has not been found."

I inhaled.

The second photo. "This is Rita Thompson. Age thirty-six, widow, one daughter. She vanished from her house in Rockton on March first, 1977. Her body is also missing."

Another would-be sibling.

I swallowed the lump down my throat and stared at my shaking hands.

"Two days before their disappearances, both women bought products from the company that your dad had been working for. We have confirmed this with his office. We're still checking a lot of things with them, but we can confirm that Ginnifer's name appeared on his list of sales last year, January."

I didn't say anything.

"Your father met these women, marked them in his calendar, abducted them, and…" He stopped.

The captain looked at me with pity in his eyes. My vision turned red, the trembling in my legs had returned. Hailey held onto my hand, but her grip felt too tight. I tried to pull myself free, but she didn't notice.

"The FBI has been notified and will take over this case. With all the information that we've gathered right now, and all the evidence that we've yet to find, we're now convinced that we will find a victim in every town that your dad has marked in his journals over the past decades. This will become a nationwide investigation, and a taskforce will be set up that will trace back your father's every move dating back to the day he started work."

He paused.

"I'm really sorry, Alice, but your suspicions were right. Your father was, beyond a doubt, a serial killer, and this is just the beginning."

He looked me sternly in the eye.

"There's more, Alice. Something you might not have considered yet."

Silence. I felt the eyes of everyone in the room those standing in the doorway.

"Alice, due to the obvious similarities between you and the missing women, there is one very important question that I need to ask. One that we need to explore further. Are you sure that your mother really *is* your mother?"

I couldn't hold back the panic any longer. My throat thickened, my hands started shaking beneath Hailey's grip, and the red before my eyes turned into an odd blue, purple, and black.

I slumped forward, in the captain's arms. And then I was on the floor and the people in the room faded into a blur. The captain called out my name. Hailey screamed. Anna called out for help.

My world went dark.

35

I woke up in the silence of a hospital room with Hailey by my side. She was in a deep sleep; it was dark outside. The drapes were open, and I could hear the sound of cars passing by. A siren blared through the night. There was activity outside the room.

The clock above the door told me it was well past midnight. I had been out for hours. Not from the blackout, but from the medication they had pushed into me at the ER, where I had woken up in a state of panic.

The doctor had told me I was exhausted and agitated, and that I urgently needed a good night's sleep, so he gave me a sedative. I had blacked out again almost immediately, until now.

An IV was in my arm and a machine stood next to me, monitoring my heart. My throat was dry and aching. I was so thirsty.

I felt hollow on the inside. Everything came rushing back to me, but it was the captain's words that would never go away.

Are you sure that your mother really is *your mother?*

I *had* known. Somehow, all this time, I had known that something had been very wrong with me. It always had to be something more than just my lack of voice that had made them lock me up. And now I knew what it was.

In the confinement of this room, I could quietly accept

my new reality. That man was not my father. That woman had never been my mother. For some reason or the other, he had taken my real mother. And then, after getting rid of her, he had brought me home to 'Mom'.

I remembered her stories about her miscarriages and the stillborn child. Was it her grief over her inability to conceive that had made him abduct me and take me home with him? How old had I been? When had he taken me? Where and how?

It all made sense now. I was the child of an abducted woman, stolen from my family, probably dead. I was one of those children on the milk cartons that people were searching for without ever finding them.

The very thought that I still had a family out there was too strange to fathom. I should have been happy, but I had never felt so hopeless. I still couldn't remember anything about the first years of my life. Not a single damn thing. All I knew was the house and my life there.

He must have taken me while I was a toddler, or perhaps a bit older. Why did he kill my real mother? Had he wanted *her* or *me*? Had he wanted *me* more than her? Or had it just been his luck that he found his perfect woman, and that she happened to have a baby with her?

I saw a documentary once about people's first memories, sometimes going back as early as the age of two. People really could go back that far and recall some details that were seemingly impossible to remember. Doctors had done something called hypno-regression therapy on them, and they could all remember things from their early years.

But I couldn't see back that far, except for one thing: Since my childhood, I've always had these weird dreams about a different house we used to live in. I had even asked

Mom about it once, but she had brushed it off, claiming it was just a dream.

I was in a small house with a few windows with dark curtains. It only had two rooms; it was tiny. The windows were all high and impossible to reach. There was barely any sunlight. At night, it became pretty dark.

And there was no sound.

Whenever I dreamt about that place, I remembered it being soundless, as if we lived there all by ourselves with no neighbors at all.

I also recalled a woman. She was tall, dark-haired, with blue eyes. My recollection of that woman had become more vivid than ever, ever since I discovered those journals. We looked alike, but I was paler than she was, and my hair was a lot less vibrant. I always believed that she represented the mother I'd never had. A figment of my imagination, perhaps the perfect image of what a real mother should be like.

I never realized that this woman had really existed. I knew now that those missing women did not only resemble me, but also my mother. My *real* mother.

I wanted to remember her so badly, but the memories were too vague, like a recollection of odd dreams I could barely hold onto. I didn't even know before if that woman was real, but she must have been. She was the one who had given birth to me. Who had loved me, if only for a short while.

The woman who had raised me after my abduction, and who had kept me prisoner all those years, was not my birth mother, and I wondered now if she had ever really loved me, or if she'd seen my arrival as a reminder of that what she could never have.

It would explain her behavior towards me, the moments

of love and hate, her erratic actions, the way she kept me cooped up in the house, albeit often reluctantly. But why had she never once tried to save me? She could have gone to the police so easily.

My medical condition had made it easy for them to do this to me. It had helped create this bizarre life where I was forcibly isolated from the outside world. Because I couldn't speak, I couldn't express myself. They had used that as a way of convincing me that isolation was the best thing for me, acting as if it were my condition that forced me to live a hermit's existence, when in fact it had been my father's wrongdoings that made me who I am today.

For the first time, I felt relief. Jack Jenkins was not my father and never had been. I was his victim, not his daughter. That was the only silver lining in this mess.

Hailey stirred and woke up, smiling, relieved when she saw me awake. She leaned over me, stroking my hair gently.

"Hey," she said. "You've been out for a long time. You had us worried. How do you feel?"

So-so, I signed. *I slept well.*

"You needed it badly."

I'm fine now.

"Let me get a doctor."

I stopped her. *No. I need to tell you something.*

"In the morning, when you're feeling better. Right now, you need to rest."

No, it can't wait.

"Okay," she said, "just take it easy, alright? I don't ever want to see you like that again. What is it?"

Mom is not my mom, is she?

Hailey reached for my hand. "No, she isn't. Your – your adoptive mother – was more than likely his accomplice."

Who is my real mom?

"They don't know yet. The FBI arrived tonight, and they have a special task force assigned to the case now. Captain Miles told me that they're currently at your house in Hays, probably tearing it apart for evidence and leads on all the women that he killed. And they've tried to talk to your mom, too. I mean, the woman you raised you, Eileen Jenkins."

Did she say anything?

Hailey looked nervous.

What?

"Captain Miles told me she refuses to talk to anyone before she has a chance to talk to you."

I don't want to talk to her.

"Don't worry; that's not going to happen. If you don't want to, then don't. As far as I'm concerned, she can go to hell."

What happens now?

"This is honestly all I know. They're not exactly forthright with any new information. The national press has already gotten wind of this, so they don't want to share too many details for now."

The door opened. A nurse came in, satisfied to see that I was awake. "How are you feeling?" she said, while she checked my pulse.

I shrugged.

"That's okay, honey," she said in a motherly way. "You've been through a lot; it's no wonder you feel so lousy. Why don't I give you another sedative? You need your rest. Your friend can go home for the night and come back in the morning. How does that sound?"

I was exhausted, but I felt I probably wouldn't be able to sleep due to the thousands of thoughts running through my mind. The nurse didn't wait for an answer. She left and came back with a syringe and injected the fluid into the IV.

"Alice will be out like a light again in a few moments," she said to Hailey. "Come back in the morning. She'll be feeling a lot better then."

"Thank you," Hailey said.

The nurse left us alone. My thoughts were already drifting off again. That stuff she gave me was pretty strong.

Hailey kissed me on the forehead.

"I'll be back," she whispered. "Love you, Alice."

Darkness came and took me away into oblivion.

36

I woke up alone in the hospital room. But it was daylight now, and the rest of the world was obviously wide awake too.

My door was ajar, and a different nurse and a doctor walked in moments after I'd opened my eyes. An IV was still dripping fluids into my arm, but the monitor was removed, and I was feeling a lot better.

"It looks like the worst has passed," the doctor said after taking my vitals and examining me briefly. "You're looking a lot more rested. Can I contact anyone for you?"

My friend, I wrote on the pad next to my bed. *Can you call her?*

"Is that the young lady that was with you when they brought you in yesterday? She's been in the waiting room for hours. I'll go get her," the nurse said.

I was allowed out of bed, and walked on wobbly legs to the bathroom, where I used the toilet and freshened up. One glance in the mirror told me my hair was all over the place. I looked as if a train had run me over. But other than that, I felt more like myself again.

When I came back into the room, the doctor was still there. He looked at me curiously, holding my file in hand. "Can I just ask you a few questions about your mutism?"

I nodded.

"You haven't spoken your entire life?"

I shook my head.

"Have your parents ever taken you to see a specialist?"

I shrugged and used my notepad. *They said they did.*

"But you don't know for sure?"

I shook my head.

"Hm. So you've never had any tests as an adult?"

I reached for my pad. *They said I was born this way. No solution.*

"But you don't know the name or cause of your medical condition?"

I shook my head again.

"Would you mind if I ran a few tests and discussed your case with some of my colleagues back in Boston? I'd like them to take a look at you."

I shrugged again and wrote down on my pad. *Why?*

"Just to confirm a theory, based on the story I heard about what happened to you. I can't make any promises. It's just that I have never seen anyone with your type of mutism before, and the lack of medical explanation behind your case makes me wonder if this has a physical or a psychological cause."

Like trauma? I wrote down.

"Exactly. There are some rare cases where people experience a terrible event that leads to mutism. In that case, we're talking about a condition called psychogenic mutism. And if that diagnosis is confirmed, we might be able to treat it."

Really?

"Oh, yes. But even if there is another explanation, we might still be able to find a solution – or at least a partial one. But I need your permission to pursue my ideas."

Okay, I signed, putting a thumb up, writing while he made some notes in my file. *I believe I have repressed memories of my past. Can you help me recover them?*

The doctor smiled. "I have some people that could help. Leave this with me. I was wondering, though, what you want to do next? As you seem physically fine, I see no reason to keep you here any longer than is necessary. If you want to, I can arrange for you to be discharged now and let you head back to the hotel under the condition that you take plenty of rest. If you can stay in Lexington for a while longer, I can treat you as an outpatient. It's up to you what you want to do."

The hotel, please.

He smiled. "Okay. Your friend will stay too, right?"

I hope so, I wrote down.

The doctor seemed satisfied. "Perfect. I'll have the nurse remove the IV, and I'll arrange those tests."

Hailey walked in just as the doctor left the room. She seemed puzzled. "What's going on? What tests is he talking about?"

I used my notepad. *My voice. He might be able to help.*

"That would be awesome," Hailey said happily. "So what are we going to do? Stick around for a while? Check out the sights?"

Go to the memorial sites, I wrote down.

She laughed. "No, thanks, I've got better things to do with my time."

Like what?

She looked at me. "Oh, I can think of some things to do with you."

I stared at her. My heart pounded in my chest again, but this time it felt good. She closed the door and came over to me, kissing me so intensely that I swayed on my legs. It literally took my breath away.

Never in my life had I thought that kissing someone could

be like this. This was really happening, and I didn't want it to stop. I could smell her perfume, could feel her soft lips on me, could touch her without having to fear being mocked by her. I was so in love.

She let go of me, staring at me in wonder. "Wow," she whispered.

Uh huh.

"You're so amazing, Alice. I can't believe I'm this fortunate to be with you here."

I feel the same way too, I wrote down.

She turned serious. "The thing is, I want to keep our relationship a secret for now. The cops and the feds want to talk to you again. They want to know more details about your life and how we've met, and I want us to focus on getting all that stuff out of the way first, before pursuing this relationship. The sooner that this is over, the sooner we can start our new life together."

You're right. Let's go.

I ate the small breakfast a nurse brought me after removing my IV. Then I got dressed in the clothes Hailey had picked up at the hotel.

We walked out of the room and to the elevator. Hailey made sure to stay as close to me as possible. Her presence made me feel so much better. With her by my side, I could face anything.

When we reached the doors, Hailey stopped. A bunch of vans were parked in front of the building. People were waiting outside. Hailey turned me around.

"Let's use the back entrance," she said, marching me away from the crowd.

37

"The captain wants to talk to us," Hailey said as we exited the hospital through the back door and walked around to the parking lot. She explained that she had picked up her car once I had been transported to the hospital the previous evening.

Okay.

"Do you want to talk to him now, or rest up first? I'm a bit worried those assholes will be stalking the hotel too."

I'm fine. Now is good. Let's go.

From this distance, no one could spot us. She placed my overnight bag in the trunk of her Beetle and helped me get in.

She drove the short distance from the hospital, which lay on the outskirts of town, to the police station while I relaxed. I was doing okay. My legs weren't wobbly anymore and there was no sign of another panic attack coming on. My head was clear again.

The moment she reached the police station, Hailey slowed down. "Shit."

It was a lot busier than yesterday. Apart from curious locals, there were a lot of reporters with television vans that contained antennas and satellite dishes. They were all standing in front of the station entrance, waiting for us.

Hailey quickly turned into a back alley and drove to the other side of the police station. "Captain Miles said this could happen, so he gave me instructions," she said. "He told me to park as closely as possible, and then to leave the car. Shit, shit!"

There were reporters standing at the back entrance, too, but the group was smaller this time.

"Come on," Hailey said. She parked the Beetle tight to the back door, exited the car first, opened my door, and dragged me out.

In an instant, photographers and onlookers showed up and started taking pictures and recording us. Reporters shouted questions at me. They demanded that I show my face, as if they had the right to order me around.

Hailey threw her jacket over my head and steered me to the entrance, blocking me from the vultures. "Get away!" she snapped. "Leave her alone!"

There was a lot of shouting going on. Questions were screamed. I felt people trying to block our way inside. Fortunately, a police officer opened the door, but before we could get in, my arm was pulled backwards. I nearly stumbled. Hailey's jacket slid off my head. I turned, startled.

"Are you Alice Jenkins?" a man asked.

I recognized him from the newspapers. The fiancé, Mark Jacobs. I nodded.

"In, you guys!" the policeman snapped. "You too, Mr Jacobs."

Mr Jacobs slipped inside with us. The police officer locked the door quickly, making sure no reporters could slip in. We followed the police officer to the office in the back. Captain Miles stood when he saw us.

"Mark?" he said, bewildered. "I'm really sorry, but you shouldn't be here. You know that."

"I know, but I needed to see her," he said, nodding at me. "I just – I had to…"

Before I realized what was happening, he pulled me into his arms. I had been so afraid that people would see me as the daughter of a serial killer, blaming me for what he'd done. But Mark Jacobs didn't. He held me tight. I could feel his entire body shake.

"Thank you," he whispered.

I didn't know how to react. He let go of me. I looked at Hailey, who understood my reaction.

"She wants to know why you're thanking her."

"Why? She gave us closure!" he said, confused.

"Closure?" Hailey repeated. "But your fiancé hasn't..."

"Been found? I know. But I – we, our families – at least know now that she didn't run away. That she was murdered."

Hailey and I shared a glance. "You thought she might have still been alive," she said softly.

Mark shook his head. "*I* never did. I could feel that she was gone. We'd been together for so long, you know? We were thick as thieves. But others... Well, I was either a murderer or an adulterer."

"But she's still missing," Hailey said carefully.

"I hope that she'll be found some day," he admitted. "But now I know that she will never come back. It's still hard, but now the healing can start. The not-knowing is worse than knowing that she fell into the hands of this... this..." He stopped and looked at me. "I'm sorry, I know he was your..."

I raised my hands and stopped him.

Don't thank me, I wrote down. *I don't deserve this.*

"Don't you?" Mark said. "Why not? You exposed him. That took a lot of courage. It's incredible what you've done."

I looked at him shyly. When those reporters showed up

at the police station, demanding answers to their thousand questions, I was convinced that my greatest fears were about to come true. That I would be punished for my parents' wrongdoings. The victim's families had every right to be angry at me, even if I turned out to be a victim myself. After all, I had lived with them all this time.

But Mark Jacobs didn't hate me. He was glad. Maybe the others would be relieved too, instead of hating me.

Thank you, I signed.

He hugged me again, then hugged Hailey, too, and took off, crying. He left through the front door, and we could hear the shouts coming from the press.

The captain sighed and beckoned us, ASL interpreter Britney, and Boston police detective Anna, into his office. He closed the door behind us.

"There you have it," he sighed. "The press found out everything because someone at the station leaked the whole story. They know that the feds are on the case and what happened here yesterday. I know who leaked it, and she has been suspended. Unfortunately, that doesn't do us much good right now."

"So Alice's name is out there?"

"Yes."

"Fuck," Hailey said. "This is bad, isn't it?"

"I'm afraid so, but she hasn't been identified as the potential daughter of a victim. That won't take too long either, though. Rumors are spreading like wildfire. I've contacted the Boston FBI assistant director, who is now in charge of the investigation. He confirmed the press is all over your house in Hays, Alice. We can't stop this anymore. All subsequent investigation will now be under nationwide scrutiny. I'm sorry."

That's okay. It was a matter of time.

"It shouldn't have been so soon, but in the end, I guess it was inevitable," he said. "And there's more. Due to the leak, we're being flooded with hundreds of calls from families all over the country, demanding to know if their missing ones are possible victims."

"I think we should release a statement to the press regarding the situation," Anna said. "That might calm them down a bit."

"Or make it worse," Captain Miles countered.

When can I go back to normal life? I signed, which Britney translated for me.

"I hope that leading a normal life will still be possible after all of this," Anna said in all earnest. "A press conference might help. As soon as they figure out you are a victim too, they will leave you alone."

"I don't think she should do a press conference," Hailey said. "It will be too much for her to handle. What if telling her story will only increase the attention? Everyone will want to hear the sad story of the girl without a voice. No, we need to protect her privacy as much as possible."

"They will find out, Hailey. It's just a matter of time," Captain Miles said. "Isn't it better to tackle the issue than to avoid it? If Alice tells her story, the truth can't be twisted into something they'd like it to be."

"You're right," Anna said. "Interesting idea."

No, I signed. *I don't want to do it. I can't.* I paused. *But I know I have to.*

The captain looked at me, a sympathetic smile on his face.

"I know this is hard, Alice, but you are doing the right thing. Why don't you write a statement with Hailey's help, and I will address the press for you. Is that alright, Alice?"

I nodded.

"In meantime, you will need to talk to the FBI. They'll be coming to speak with you in an hour. Are you okay with that?"

I'm fine, I replied.

Hailey looked at me.

"Do you want me to stay while they talk to you?"

"Unfortunately, you won't be allowed to," the captain said. "Bridget will stay as an interpreter, but you are a civilian and therefore not able to attend the interview."

Hailey looked troubled, but she didn't argue.

Anna, Hailey, and I drafted a statement that the captain was going to give in my place. I reread it a couple of times until the words felt comfortable enough. The captain had notified the press of the imminent statement, and they had showed up in droves, or so I was told.

Even though I wasn't the one talking, I had agreed to be there for a photo opportunity, wanting this to be over with. Facing them would be better than having people chase after me to take photos. The press would probably haunt me for months, so I might as well confront them now and get it over with.

Good thing I'm used to people by now, I signed.

We agreed to keep Hailey out of it, in an attempt to keep her name out of the press entirely. Anna and Bridget would stay by my side while the captain stepped into the spotlight to read my statement.

The four of us went outside. I was taken aback by the vast number of reporters. A dozen or so microphones had been set up in front of a speaker's bench. Several cameras were shoved in my face. It was almost too much to bear.

The police captain begged for silence. "Ladies and gentlemen, even though this story is about Alice Jenkins, we have decided that she will not be the one giving a statement today. I will do so in her place. There will be no room for questions right now, as Miss Jenkins needs her rest, and this will be a one-time-only event."

"Why?" a man called out.

The captain looked straight at him. "Because I say so."

I refused to look into the cameras and focused on my hands as the captain read my statement out loud.

"My name is Alice Jenkins. A short while ago, I found out that the man who raised me, Jack Jenkins, whom I have called my father my entire life, and who is now deceased, may have been involved in the disappearances of several women. He revealed this on his deathbed. After his passing, I found evidence in his diaries that suggested he had spoken the truth. This naturally came as a shock to me.

"As a result of his confession, I set out to discover the truth. I came to Lexington, where he supposedly met his last victim. His diary entries matched with the disappearance of Ginnifer Hobbs last year in January. I took the gathered evidence to the police, and this led to a large, combined police and FBI investigation into my father's past, which is ongoing.

"I am very shocked and saddened, but also relieved that my decision to seek the truth has helped bring some clarity and closure for the families left behind. I hope that the full truth will be discovered, and that all of his suspected victims will be identified, so that their families can find closure too."

The police captain stopped and looked at me, smiling encouragingly, before continuing. "During their investigation, the police have found evidence that my real mother and I may have been victims of Jack Jenkins too. I don't know who I am or where I came from, or what he has done to my birth mother, but I am determined to find out, with the help of the police and the FBI.

"I ask you to respect my privacy during this time, and to let the police and FBI do their job. I also ask you to leave the families of Jack Jenkins's victims alone also, so they can find closure and peace. Thank you."

I looked at the captain and took a deep breath. It was done. After a brief silence and a lot of sympathetic nods in my direction, the press burst out in a frenzy of questions and demands.

I turned around and walked back inside the police station with Britney, while Anna and the captain stayed behind to answer further questions about the investigation.

Inside the building, Hailey hugged me. We sank down on the captain's couch. My hands were shaking, but I was doing okay. It was over, at least for now. It wasn't as bad as I had thought it would be. It gave me a sense of relief.

"What now?" Hailey said.

Food, rest, the FBI. Doctors.

She smiled. "After that, I mean."

We go home.

"Is home still home though?"

Where else would we go?

"We could stay here for a while longer. A lot longer."

What?

"Why not? This is such a nice town. Staying here could be good for us."

The very thought of becoming a permanent member of the Lexington community made me want to throw up. Stay here? In this town where that man had murdered an innocent woman? No way.

No.

Hailey frowned.

I want to go somewhere else. With you. I took my notepad. *Do you have to go back to work?*

Hailey smiled. "I could quit. I don't care about Hays, never have. I'm a nomad. How about California? Or do you prefer the East Coast? We can find jobs there, build a good life. You could go to college. Wouldn't that be amazing?"

I will think about it, I signed, even though I had no idea what the East Coast or California would be like. People like me didn't belong in places like that, but my soul would forever be attached to that house in Hays.

We looked up when the captain walked back in.

"Hailey, can I have a quick word?" he said.

"Me? Sure," she said, sounding surprised.

The captain looked at me. "Alice, we're getting some sandwiches for everyone, so why don't you stay here, get some rest, and we'll be right back."

Hailey followed the captain down the hall. He closed the door so I couldn't listen to their conversation.

Confused, I leaned back on the couch and closed my eyes, but sleep didn't come. After a while, Hailey returned looking quite serious. She sank down on the couch next to me, rattled by something.

What's wrong?

"Nothing," she said. "He just wanted to talk things through, before the feds arrive. It's fine. I'm just tired."

Anna walked in carrying a plate of food that she put on the coffee table before us. "Have a good lunch, ladies," she said.

We both took a chair while Hailey unwrapped the food. She was jittery and nervous.

Are you sure you're okay?

"I'm fine," she said, but I could tell that she wasn't.

What's wrong?

She sighed and stopped unfolding the plastic wrap. She dropped her hands, sunk back in her chair and looked at me with an expression I had never seen from her before. I immediately sensed I wouldn't like what she was going to tell me. I placed a hand on her wrist.

Hailey?

She looked away. There was a difference in the air, something intangible. She wasn't telling me everything.

What's wrong? I urged.

Hailey looked up at me with tears in her eyes. "Please believe me when I say that I didn't lie about us," she said. "That's all you need to know."

Wait. What?

38

Hailey paced the room. The sandwiches were long forgotten. She hardly looked at me. This was obviously hard on her.

"It just got out of hand," she said. "I needed to find out the truth. That was all that mattered to me. All that I wanted. You have to believe me that none of this was done deliberately. It just happened."

What did? What's going on?

"I'm not who you think I am."

What?

"I swear that my feelings for you are true. None of it was a lie. I've cared from the moment I saw you, and everything changed."

I don't understand.

I trembled while I signed, not understanding what she was trying to tell me. She cleared her throat.

"My name is Hailey Sanders," she said. "That much is true. And I really was your neighbor. And your friend."

But all the rest wasn't?

"It's complicated."

What did I miss? What is this?

"I lied because the truth – my truth – was too complex to share. And you wouldn't have understood if I told you when we first met."

What truth?!

She swallowed visibly and looked away.

Hailey, tell me!!!

She finally looked back at me.

"I told you my parents had died in a car accident together, but that wasn't true. Dad did die in a crash, but that was fifteen years ago. Since then, it's always been my mom and me."

She stopped.

I waited.

She opened her bag and took out an old photo of her parents. I stared at it in shock. Hailey looked exactly like her father, from her nose to her cheekbones to the color of her hair. She didn't resemble her mother whatsoever.

Her mother resembled me.

"Three years ago, my mom disappeared. A lot of people claimed that she had run off for whatever stupid reason they could think of. But that's not the truth. The truth is that she was more than likely murdered by a traveling salesman, who sold her a vacuum cleaner two days earlier."

I was dumbfounded. Shocked. Stunned.

What are you talking about?!

"You know exactly what I'm talking about. You've known it all your life. You knew that your father, Jack Jenkins, was not the man you thought he was. Something I had figured out three years ago. Only, no one would believe me. I was ridiculed for it."

No. That's impossible.

Hailey hardly looked at me.

"It's the truth, Alice. What you had figured out after his death through his journals, I had discovered through my own research after my mom's disappearance. I just lacked the evidence. And now I've found it, in the 1977 journal. *R.T, Rockton, Illinois, March 1–3*. Do you remember her name, when Captain Miles showed you the picture? Rita Thompson. Age thirty-six, widow, one daughter. That's my mom."

How? How could you know that it was him?!

"I was home that day when your dad came by the house. I was supposed to be in college, but I had been feeling under the weather. I was lying on the living room couch when the doorbell rang and your dad showed up with his sales pitch about these 'excellent' products, and above all, this fancy vacuum cleaner he couldn't stop talking about. My mom was always quite trusting – gullible, maybe – and she invited him in for coffee. Surely such a nice man couldn't do her any harm, right?"

I sat stunned, listening to Hailey's story.

"He was surprised to see me, but he quickly composed himself as he sat down to talk to my mom about all these new products that would make her life so much better. He raved on and on, while eyeing my mom up and down. You see, my mom was a teenager when she had me, so at the time of her disappearance, she was in her mid-thirties, and gorgeous. She had worked night and day to provide for me. After Dad passed, she did everything she could to take care of me. And just as her life was back on track again, and this wonderful man had asked her to marry him, she disappeared. Just like that."

Two days after...

"Exactly."

Hailey paced the room, biting her fingernail as she continued to speak. "There was something off about this salesman. Something that I just couldn't put my finger on. It was the way he looked at her, and how he asked her subtle questions about her life. At one point, I even came to sit at the kitchen table, wanting her to stop babbling. But that was my mom, you know? She was so open about everything, and I just couldn't stop her."

Hailey ran her hands through her hair. "The thing is, after he left, nothing happened. Life just went on. There was no burglary or anything odd, no earthshaking reveal that he was up to something. Until two days later, when I was back in school, she just vanished."

I'm so sorry.

Hailey didn't notice me. She was stuck in her own little world, remembering the time of her mother's disappearance.

"The police told me to wait another day or so, and she would show up on her own. They gave me a ton of reasons why my mom didn't come home that night, too many to recount."

She looked at me. "People do that, apparently, did you know that? They just decide they've had enough and go away. Sometimes they take a train, or hitchhike with some stranger to some godforsaken place they've never been before, only to realize then what they've left behind."

She paused. "I told them she would never do that. She wasn't like that. They still told me to come back the next day. But when her abandoned car was discovered by the railway track, with her purse and keys inside, that started the investigation real quickly."

I sat and listened. What else was I supposed to do?

"For days, they searched for her. A whole group of people, all volunteers. They went through fields and houses, abandoned buildings and God-knows what. But they couldn't find her. She had vanished off the face of the earth."

Hailey bit on another fingernail while remembering.

"They questioned everyone close to her. Her fiancé, her ex, her friends, my grandparents, me... I told them everything I knew about her, every habit, everything she had ever done. But nothing led to a suspect. Until months later."

She looked at me. "It took me a while to remember that strange man who walked into our home two days before her death, Alice. And by that time, it was too difficult to even remember what he looked like. I lost so much precious time."

It wasn't your fault.

"By the time I got to the police with my story, they didn't even bother with it. You know why."

No paper trail.

"Right. Do you know how many traveling salesmen there are in this country? Thousands. And they all drive around towns, trying to sell the same products. Talk about a needle in a haystack, huh? Anyhow, the police promised to look into it, but I knew they had already given up on her. I lived in a small town, with barely any police force to speak of, and they had already moved on. I still don't know to this day if they did it to forget as quickly as possible about her, or because they were simply too stupid to handle her case properly."

So you went out to look for him yourself.

She nods. "It was painfully slow and hard, but I had to. I had to quit college because I didn't have any money left. My mom's life insurance wouldn't pay, because technically she wasn't dead. There was no body – there still isn't. In the eyes of the law, even now, she is still alive."

I'm so...

I stopped. What was I supposed to say when I was still furious that she had lied to me?

"I searched the entire house for the one bit of proof that this man had sold my mom that vacuum cleaner. Maybe a copy of the receipt. Or the warranty. She wasn't good at paperwork, but she kept everything that was of meaning to her. I finally found it, and so I went back to the police, who again promised to look into it. So I waited weeks for a call to tell me they got their guy. It never came."

They didn't investigate.

"They lost it. Can you believe that? Some moron left the only evidence they had somewhere and someone else threw it away."

But you wrote down the company's name?

"I did. And I found them, and called them. I called them fifty-six times, until I finally spoke to a woman who told me the name of the guy who had visited my town, and I asked her to send him by my house again for another big sale."

Did he show up?

"Oh, yeah, he did," Hailey said. "Can you believe the audacity? Your dad came back to my house, and he knocked on the door as if he had not murdered my mom."

How do you know he did?

She blinked. "What?"

How did you know it was him that took her?

"How can you say that, after all you know?"

No. How did YOU know?

She finally understood. "I just knew. I looked into his eyes, saw his whole demeanor, and knew. But he didn't know me. I didn't see any signs of recognition in his gaze; he'd completely forgotten me."

You put yourself in danger.

"I didn't care. My mom had been gone for a long time by then, and he looked at me as if he had never seen me before, so I played along and purchased a long list of products while scrutinizing him the whole time. I gave him her name as his contact, and it must have rattled him, but he never reacted. At the same time, I caught him glancing around the room. I had placed pictures of her everywhere, so he was confronted with the sight of her at every turn. He even asked about her. I told him she was dead. He never asked any of the details."

When was this?

She didn't reply.

She paced the room again and gnawed on a third fingernail as she continued to explain herself.

"My first thought was to kill him right there and then. People like that don't confess when you point a gun at them, you know. I've read all the reports on Ted Bundy. He mocked every single victim. This guy would too. He'd rather take the truth to the grave with him, I could feel it. So I didn't hurt him. But I never showed him I knew who he was."

And then what?

"I could tell something was off. He was different. Pale, sickly, skinnier. He coughed a lot, looked like he was going to be sick all the time. So I asked him about it. He told me flat out he was dying. I was in shock, to say the least. And furious. I felt defeated. If he died, he would take the truth about my mom's death to the grave."

I thought about the timeframe. About when this must have taken place. If Jack had already known at that time that he was going to die. He had told me he'd been sick for a long time. When he came home to die, he had reached the final stage. But he must have known he was going to die a lot sooner.

"Then, all of the sudden, he started telling me about his

family. About how he had a wife and a daughter he was going to leave behind, and how his daughter was going to be so upset. What a great bond he had with her, and how it was such a shame that I had lost that connection with my mom."

I was dumbfounded. *No...*

"He started talking about the value of a relationship between a mother and her daughter, and how it was so important for them to stay together for as long as possible. How there was nothing as precious as that bond. I saw red, Alice. That look on his face when he spoke. It was – he knew that I knew. He could feel it, the hidden rage, my anger, my anguish, my grief. And he *liked* it, Alice. He *loved* it."

I was shocked. If I'd had a voice, I would not have even been able use it.

"He looked me straight in the eye and told me bluntly that I should accept the fact I would never see my mom again, but that, if I wanted to, he could do me a favor and send me on my merry way."

Kill you?

She nodded. "I ran outside the house and waited for him to come out too. He did, carrying his bags with him. He wished me a nice day, got into his car, and drove off. But not before I got a good look at his license plate number. It took me another week and a lot of phone calls to find out where he lived."

The police?

Hailey shrugged. "What good would that have done? They still wouldn't have believed me. No one did. So I took matters into my own hands."

You came to Hays.

"I did, yes. I came to Hays to kill him, Alice."

I held my breath.

"I was so angry with myself for not doing it at the house. I'd had the perfect opportunity, and I didn't grab it. But I wasn't going to let that happen again. So I drove to Hays and moved into a small motel in the center of town. I stayed there for days, wondering how I was going to kill him without getting caught, trying to work out the perfect plan."

But he was already dying.

"I didn't care. I wanted to see the fear in his eyes. That was all that mattered to me, no matter how long it took. I decided to stay in Hays, and I bided my time. And the right opportunity came when your neighbors left, something the motel owner told me about. I had told him I was planning on renting a place in Hays. He helped me secure it, and so I moved in."

Did you ever work in that store?

Hailey smiled. "That wasn't a lie. I needed the money, but I wasn't really that good at it. I was too busy thinking about the million ways I was going to kill your dad. But meeting you changed everything for me."

I don't–

"I told you my feelings for you were real, Alice. They are. The moment I met you and we connected, I immediately started to realize that there was something wrong. It wasn't just the fact that you were mute and locked up in that house. There was something so off about it all, a sense that I had only felt once before."

On the day you met my dad.

"Yeah, and I will blame myself for not warning my mom about him for the rest of my life."

You didn't know.

"But I did. And I didn't act on it."

What could you have done?

She shrugged lightly. "That's what the police said too, when I admitted the truth this morning."

They already knew?

"Yeah. I showed them the journal, her initials, and my town."

I didn't ask the details. I couldn't. I didn't want to remember how she skimmed through those journals with me, finally discovering the proof she had wanted for so long. It must have been so hard for her to accept that her gut feeling had been right. Poor Hailey.

"Please don't hate me."

I don't.

"But you're upset."

I don't know how I feel.

"I know I should have said something, but there was never a good time or place, and when we got here, I needed to focus on you, and finding the evidence to prove his involvement. I couldn't just drop this on you out of the blue."

I sighed. *I can't be angry. You saved me.*

Hailey smiled gently. "No, Alice. You saved yourself when you went on this journey. You, alone, figured it out. I just tagged along and admired you for pushing through."

You still should have told me sooner.

"I know, but what was I going to say? 'Hey, I'm the daughter of one of your dad's victims. Nice to meet you.' Would you have believed me?"

I don't know.

"You needed to figure this out on your own, Alice. Besides, I am indebted to you, more than you know."

I looked at her inquisitively.

"You gave me closure. Just like Ginnifer, my mom's body will most likely never be found, but I know now that she is never coming back. I can close the door to my past and lock it, and build a future for myself from here on out. Do you realize how valuable that is?"

I know.

She moved towards me.

"Can I hold you?"

Yes.

The next moment, I was in her arms, resting my head against her shoulder. She hugged me protectively. I was still angry, but more than anything, I was sad.

"Right now, all that matters is you," she muttered against my hair. "Now that you've found some form of closure, we can move to the next stage of healing."

I looked at her and signed. *I don't understand.*

"What I'm saying is that it isn't over yet. There are reasons for your mutism, and I believe there is a way of healing you. Your doctor, at the hospital, thinks so too. We discussed it last night."

How?

"The doctors are saying that you might be repressing terrible memories from things that happened to you as a child."

Like what?

"It's clear now that your father isn't really your dad. And he might have done… I can't say it out loud, but what if he harmed you, too?" She stopped and took a deep breath. "I believe, without a doubt, that this trauma is causing your mutism."

But I don't remember it.

"The doctor said they can help you figure this out, if you

are willing to go the distance. There are specialized therapists who can help you to dig into your past, and if you still want me there, I'll be with you every step of the way."

You still lied to me, I signed.

Hailey cupped my face and kissed me. It was the most beautiful kiss ever. I loved her, despite the lies. And I understood why she had withheld the truth from me. I would probably have done the same.

She looked at me as if she had read my mind.

"Alice, listen to me. I've fallen in love with you because of who you are, and that will never change. You are a crazily amazing, beautiful woman, and I want to be with you. If you will continue to let me in. Please. I love you so much."

I kissed her.

Because I loved her, too, and there was nothing I wanted more in this lifetime, than a lifetime spent with her.

PART SEVEN
The Truth

39

Eileen

I was led into a small room, where several people were waiting for me. The prison warden – a fifty-something firm-looking man – FBI-agent Andy Fitzgerald, who we all called Fitz since we had gotten so close, and the prison's head guard, who never really introduced himself.

I was nervous, even though I had Hailey by my side – she had not left me since Lexington, now three weeks ago. She was still my interpreter, but more than that, she was also my girlfriend. She was the most patient woman I'd ever met, and I could not imagine a single day without her.

This would be the first time since her arrest that I would get to see my adoptive mother – if she had ever really been that. I still didn't know how to refer to her. My caretaker? My watchdog? Had I been her prisoner, or her protégé?

Who was she really?

"Ms Jenkins," the warden said, shaking my hand. "I've heard so much about you and your bravery. Welcome. It's an honor."

I nodded and smiled briefly. Over the past weeks, I had gotten used to people's reaction to what had happened to me, but it still felt odd to suddenly be so highly regarded after a lifetime of invisibility.

"How is she doing?" Hailey asked. "Does she know Alice is coming to see her?"

"Yes. We've prepared her for this visit. At first, she adamantly refused to see you, Ms Jenkins, but then she changed her mind and insisted on talking to you."

"Did she say why?"

"No. We're guessing she'll leave that up to you."

I didn't know if Mom wanting to see me made me feel any better. I was still stuck between my desire to run away right now and confronting her with our recently discovered drama.

"She's changed a lot since you last saw her, Ms Jenkins," the warden said. "She has hardly eaten since she's been charged with accessory to murder. We keep her under suicide watch; she can't sleep with the lights out."

"Is she starving herself?" Agent Fitzgerald asked.

"She still eats, but just the bare minimum. It's enough to keep her alive, but there have been talks about admitting her to the psych ward."

Or she's faking it to get out of here, I thought.

"We don't allow any sharp objects near her, and she's only allowed to stay in a windowless room with a mattress on the floor. We can't take enough precautions with her, not when there are so many people who want to talk to her about her husband."

I didn't respond.

"Our psychiatrists are observing her, but we hope that things will improve once she speaks to Ms Jenkins."

He looked at me.

"My advice is to handle the situation cautiously. We're not sure if she's faking her state of mind or if it's legitimate. She's a mystery to us."

"We understand," Hailey said, looking at me.

Ready, I signed.

I had agreed to see her because we all knew that it needed to be done. This woman had so many secrets buried inside of her, things that people needed to know. Stories that would help families to bury their dead, to grieve. But the problem was that no one really knew the extent of her knowledge, or if she was even aware of what her husband was doing.

The one thing I did know was that she was aware of who my birthmother had been, and what Dad – Jack Jenkins – had done to her. There was no way that she could *not* know. And that was exactly why I was here. Even if she could only tell me half of the story, it would at least help me to figure this out.

But if she decided to keep silent for the rest of her life, she would take the truth to the grave. And if there was one thing I could not stand for, it was not knowing what Jack Jenkins had done to my real mother, or where he had buried her.

"Ready?" the warden asked.

I nodded.

"Let's go."

Hailey, Fitz, and I were taken down a long hall to a small room in the back. More guards were watching us, but none spoke.

The door opened. Fitz walked in first, Hailey went second, and I was last. The door shut behind me; a hard clunking sound rang.

Eileen sat in a small room with a guard in uniform standing nearby. Her wrist was cuffed to the table. The table itself was bolted to the floor. No one would be able to overturn it, no matter how strong they were.

The room felt too small and claustrophobic, but I knew I wouldn't leave. I had mentally prepared myself for this moment. It was time to confront her.

Her face lit up when she saw me. She was smaller than she'd ever been, all skin and bones, barely noticeable in that dark room with one light glued to the ceiling. She seemed sickly. The contrast could not have been any greater.

Over the past three weeks, I had mentally and physically taken huge leaps. I had people supporting and guiding me every step down the long and winding road I had to take. There was no way back for me now, no return to that house in Hays and the library room Eileen had created for me.

I had gained some weight, had basked in the sun, had my hair cut and wore the tiniest dash of makeup, so I wouldn't look so pale. I had received medical and physical care, but most of all, I had been mentally taken care of.

The Lexington locals had taken me under their wing, and they cared for me like one big, warm family. I was in close contact with Ginnifer's family, and Mark, who had been there every step of the way. I still didn't feel I deserved it, but they offered it to me nonetheless.

I was being treated in Boston *and* Lexington by several doctors and had gone through a variety of extensive tests that proved that my mutism was not physical, but psychological. The problem was that I still couldn't make a single sound.

They said to be patient. To hang on. That it would get better. I just needed to give it time. I trusted them.

Every step forward was a step in the right direction, but the nights remained filled with dark dreams I couldn't explain nor understand, and I woke up with my heart pounding several times per night, scratching the scar on my wrist that reminded me of a life lost.

Moving forward also meant facing my past. I was going through retrograde therapy, a type of hypnosis that was supposed to bring back my earliest memories, so I could finally understand what had happened to me before I came to the Jenkins house. I wasn't there yet, but I felt I was on the brink of discovery. We could all feel it. I just wasn't so sure I was going to be able to deal with what had been done to me.

My therapist was adamant about me confronting Eileen. He fully supported it, calling her "the gateway to my memories". Since Jack was already dead, he would never be able to fill in the blanks, but maybe she could trigger me enough to get past the mental barrier that kept me from discovering my past. It was at his recommendation that we set up this meeting.

The FBI was eager to work with me on their case. The investigation went painstakingly slow, as they had over thirty years to cover. People inquired daily if their missing daughter could be one of Jack's victims. There were still so many missing women out there, and no one really knew if that one murder per year was all he committed. He could have committed so many more, and we would be none the wiser.

A special task force was working with Brightsweep Industries during the long, tedious process of retracing Jack's whole life. All the paperwork was out there somewhere, but the puzzle was too big for just a few people, so they had dozens of people working on what was now called one of the biggest serial killer cases of all time.

But the one person that could save weeks of investigation was sitting in front of me, facing me.

"Just her," Eileen said, when she noticed the others. "I only want to speak to my daughter."

"She's not your daughter," Hailey retorted.

Eileen looked at her, smiling lightly. "Ah, the neighbor. Finally, we meet."

"I can't say it's a pleasure to meet you," Hailey replied, having obvious trouble holding her composure.

"Well, I'm happy to meet you. I've heard you've been taking care of my daughter. I'm glad she has you. Well, at least for now."

"What's that supposed to mean?" Hailey said, balling her fists.

Eileen looked her in the eye and cocked her head slightly. "Why are you taking such an interest in my daughter if the rumors that Jack took your mother are true. Is that why you're so attached to my little girl? Do you feel a connection to her that no one else gets to share?"

Stop it!!!!! I signed, and banged on the table, halting them both before this would get too far. *Just stop it!!*

Mom was taken aback. "Sorry."

I turned to Hailey. *You need to leave.*

"No. I'm staying with you. I need to translate."

"Oh, but we don't need any translation," Eileen said. "I understand sign language."

I stared at her. *What?*

She smiled lightly and shrugged.

I turned towards Fitz and Hailey, knowing all too well that Eileen would not speak when they were here.

Go, I signed.

Fitz turned to Hailey. "You go; I'll stay. I won't endanger Alice, I promise. But you are too closely involved."

Hailey opened her mouth to protest but ultimately sagged her shoulders and left. I knew she would be right outside, looking at us from behind the mirror, along with several FBI-agents, the warden, and his guards.

I sat opposite Eileen. She moved her hands forward as far as she could, but I pulled mine back. If she had been a real mother to me, I would have called the look in her eyes love. Now, I didn't know what it was.

"How have you been?" she asked.

Fine.

"Still no voice?"

No.

"But you do have one. It's just a matter of time before you find it. Maybe I can help you with that."

I don't need your help.

"Then why are you here?"

To get answers.

"What kind of answers? Where his women are buried? I don't know, Alice. I have no clue."

But you knew.

"Yes."

And you let it happen.

"Yes, I did."

Why?

"I had no choice."

Bullshit.

"I wish it were. By the time I realized what was going on, it was too late."

Why?

"He blackmailed me with the one thing I had always wanted in life but could never have."

I looked at her, at a loss.

"Love."

I made a question mark.

"You, my sweet Alice," she said softly. "He brought you home, told me the truth and gave you to me, knowing all too well that I would never give you up after losing all of my children."

You said you didn't care about them.

She smiled softly. "Of course I did. Any mother would care about losing her unborn child. I'm not a monster. I have feelings, just like everyone else. But I am ashamed to admit that I hated you, too."

Why?

"Because of who you are."

Who am I, then?

"His most prized possession. And his worst nightmare."

She leaned forward again, and this time, when she placed her hands on my wrists, I didn't pull back.

She was dressed in orange prison clothes, but suddenly she didn't look so sad. I caught a glimpse of the way she had looked in better days, before the alcohol had taken over and turned her into what she had become.

And, God forgive me, deep down, I still loved her. Despite all she had done to me, there was a part of me that wanted to see her as my mother. But she wasn't. She had been my prison guard for too long.

I pulled back.

She flinched.

"I'm sure you and your people want to know about him, but I don't know any more than you do. He never gave details, except for the one time when he brought you home. And, to be frank, I'm still unsure if that was the truth. He liked to play these games. He would say one thing, and then the next day, he would twist it all around."

So he lied to you, too?

"All the time. Well, when we spoke. As you know, we didn't really talk for years, not after he had killed your mother."

She paused. "It's odd to think about him now. His name is probably out there in the press, next to the most notorious criminals of all time. I'm not so sure if that was his heart's desire, but then again, he's dead, so who cares?"

Do you care?

"I care about those women."

But you could have saved them.

"I know. That is my biggest regret."

Why didn't you stop him?

"For you, of course, Alice. To protect you. If the truth came out, your life would be ruined. That's what I believed, at least. I could see the headlines: Serial killer's daughter spends the rest of her life hiding in shame. I couldn't have that."

So you let him murder people?

"Yes. For you."

I felt nauseous.

Eileen looked at her hands. "I'm sorry you hate me so much. I guess I deserve that. The world despises me for keeping my mouth shut. But in the end, all I really wanted was to protect you. If that makes me a bad person, then so be it."

Who is my mother? I signed.

She didn't say anything.

I took my notepad and scribbled down my next question. I was so angry.

The FBI couldn't find her, nor a trace of me. I was never reported missing. Who was she? Who was I?!

"Is that important?"

Yes!!!!!

"I was your mother."

No. Tell me who she was.

"I won't."

Why not?

"As long as you don't know, you'll always be my daughter."

I hate you.

I got up and walked to the door. Fitz banged it, looking upset at Eileen, who sat stoically on her seat.

"Don't you have any respect?" he spat.

She shrugged.

I banged on the door. It opened. This would be the last time I would see this woman, and that was fine by me. I couldn't stand being in the same room as her any longer.

"Alice!" she called after me. "Your name was always Alice. It never changed."

I turned around and signed angrily. *You lie!!!! What is my real name?*

She didn't say anything.

I walked out.

"Your mother's name was Elizabeth Lane!" she shouted after me. "He called her Lizzy. Lizzy Lane. And she was special to him. Once you've figured that out, you'll know the truth."

I turned around one last time. *Where?*

She smiled quietly. "Home."

The door shut.

40

Elizabeth

Elizabeth Lane was twenty-two years old and lived in Stockton, Kansas, a thriving town near Kansas City. The town was expanding but still remained small enough for people to leave their backdoors open and feel safe.

She had just gotten married to Joshua Jackson, a banker. He was a friend of the family, the son of one of her father's oldest friends.

Elizabeth had everything going for her. She was a stay-at-home wife, and they were planning a big family. She had always wanted to be a young mother, and after moving into their big, brand-new house, she was ready for it.

But all of that changed when Elizabeth walked into her bank on a bright Tuesday morning and a man followed her in. Elizabeth waited patiently in line to request a withdrawal from her account, and she looked around curiously at the other clients waiting for their turn.

She knew everyone in town, but the man behind her now was a stranger to her. He looked uneasy, standing there with a check in his hand, smiling nervously while he gazed at his watch.

"Are you a local?" he asked.

She saw his lips move and knew the words he was saying, but she couldn't hear his voice. She had been deaf since birth.

"Are you a local?" he repeated.

Elizabeth was not used to strangers speaking to her, and she felt nervous. She didn't know how to handle herself when an unknown person came up to her, especially if they didn't know American Sign Language.

The man looked at her curiously and continued speaking to her. She could make out his words by reading his lips.

"Do you live here?"

I can't hear you, Elizabeth signed, hoping the man would understand. He looked at her with an expression that she could only describe as curious shock.

The bank teller knew her. He slipped from his chair and walked over to them. She could see him speak to the stranger, probably explaining that Elizabeth was deaf, but that she could read lips and used ASL.

The stranger looked at her again.

"I'm sorry," he said, speaking slowly. "I didn't mean to startle you."

She waved slightly with her hand, to show that she wasn't bothered by it. The man faced forward again and so did she, now that the bank teller had returned to his seat. The stranger dug a piece of paper from his pocket and wrote something on it, which he gave to her.

I'm sorry. I didn't know you were deaf. Are you a local?

She looked at him and nodded, taking over the paper and pen. *Why do you ask?*

I'm looking for a nice place to have lunch. I'm not from around here, he wrote.

Oh?

I'm traveling. On my way to my pregnant wife. Got lost.

Elizabeth's eyes opened wide. She was always cautious about talking to strangers, but this man had some innocence about him. He looked pretty young, too; couldn't have been more than thirty, she guessed. He had a bit of a limp. She glanced at his leg. He winked when he caught her doing so.

The War, he wrote down.

Elizabeth didn't know how to react. There were several people in Stockton who had gone off to war in Europe, but it was a touchy subject. No one wanted to be reminded of those horrible days, only ten years ago.

He brought his hand to his chest and said slowly, "I'm Tom."

"Elizabeth," she said in a way she had been taught as a child. She could say some words, but she never heard them herself. It was more of a humming sound that came from her chest.

He waved her goodbye and walked up to the desk, while she walked up to hers. He had another conversation with the clerk serving him, too, but she forgot all about him when she requested money from her own account, as always, writing down exactly what she needed.

Tom left the bank before she did. She looked around to spot him, but he had already gone. Elizabeth shrugged and started walking the short distance home.

When she got home, she went inside and locked the doors, as always. Joshua had advised her to do this, since she couldn't hear anyone come in. She went about her daily routine, counting down the days until her husband would come home from Kansas City, where he stayed throughout the week.

Two days later, right before sunset, her doorbell rang. Elizabeth only knew because of the alarm system with a light signal her husband had installed, which alerted her that there was someone at the door.

Elizabeth walked to the front door, but when she unlocked it, there was no one there. Surprised, she looked left and right, but the street was as quiet as always, and there were no cars in sight. She shrugged, closed the door, and walked back into the kitchen. Worried, she checked her back door too, to find it unlocked. Did she forgot to lock it earlier, when she went out back with the garbage? Frowning, she locked it.

Hours later, she went to bed at her regular time. She shut off all the lights, found her usual sleeping position, and soon fell asleep. Only to awaken a little while later to a hand roughly shoved over her mouth. A man shone a flashlight in her face and struck her over the head.

Elizabeth wasn't knocked out, but she was dazed. He tied her up by the ankles and wrists, lifted her off the bed and carried her down the stairs. He took her to the back of the house, to his car which was parked in the dark on the driveway. The terrace lights were out, as was the porch light. He had prepared for this.

He dumped her in the trunk of his car and shut the lid, ignoring her desperate silent pleas. He hadn't blindfolded her, but she couldn't quite see his face. He got in the driver's seat and started driving.

Elizabeth tried to keep track of the time she was in that car, but it was hard to focus, especially because she was so scared. The only thing she could recall later on was that the drive had been relatively short, and that it had taken her over bumpy roads.

When the car stopped, he opened the trunk and lifted her out. She could barely see in the dark. All she could make out were some big trees, and what appeared to be a cabin. Nothing looked familiar, but in the moonlight she was able to catch a look at the man's face and it was clear he was the stranger from the bank She felt cold fear grab her heart and squeeze it until it knocked the wind out of her.

The stranger – she couldn't remember his name – took her inside and set her on the cabin floor. He knelt before her but kept her tied up.

"Look at me," he said slowly. "I won't kill you if you do as I say. Do you understand?"

She caught most of it, but it was still hard to focus.

"I will release you if you don't attempt to escape. If you try anything, I will keep you tied up here. Nod if you understand."

He spoke faster this time, but she still understood. She nodded.

He untied her and took her to the small, damp room in the back, where a mattress lay on the floor.

Nooo! Elizabeth tried to scream, but he held his hand over her mouth and dragged her to the mattress, forcing her down.

Without so much as an inkling of mercy, he forced her legs open and raped her. He paid no attention to her silent screams, and did not care that her body went limp.

He continued to force himself on her every couple of hours throughout the night and the next few days, while telling her that no one would come for her. She was at his beck and call, a toy for him to use.

She would be dependent on him for survival. If she didn't do as he said, he would not feed her. If she behaved as he demanded, she would be rewarded. He wrote all of his rules on a piece of paper that he left with her before he went away. She was horrified that he would leave her there to die.

He was gone for five days but had left just enough food for her to survive, consisting of potato chips, fruit and chocolate bars. She used her time to try to escape. She did everything she could to open the door, but the bolted locks were too strong, and the wood was too firm. The windows were too high and too small. She couldn't get out.

Something told her he had used this cabin before, but he never admitted as much.

When he arrived carrying bags of food and water, she could have wept with relief, only to realize that he had returned to assault her again. He stayed with her for two more days and nights, leaving her broken and desperate. Again, he forced himself on her until she wanted to die.

But she didn't. The thought of her husband and her family kept her on her feet. She would not give up, because then they would never know what had happened to her.

This repeated for months. She assumed he lived close to her prison, but too far to pop in every day. Which was a good thing. He brought her books and magazines, but never newspapers. He brought her canned foods, dry toast, jam, water, and sometimes orange juice. He even installed a toilet in the backroom, replacing the bucket she'd been using until then.

At some point, the frequency of his visits started to change. He came only briefly now, but his sexual assaults were worse. He would be rough with her, demand things of her a man should not ask of anyone, and it left her broken.

But she knew that after she had given him what he wanted, he would leave, and she wouldn't see him for another week. She tried to keep track of the days, weeks, and months she had been kept prisoner, but she didn't know how long it had been. She guessed at least a year.

She recognized spring by the singing of the birds, summer from the heat beating against the wood, fall from the rain, winter from the snow on the windows.

Elizabeth thought it would last forever.

Until her period stopped.

He was furious. She thought he was going to kill her right there and then, or force the fetus out of her, but he did nothing but continue to rape her, albeit softer and gentler this time, while his hand rubbed her flat belly.

In the weeks that followed, she realized that he wanted to keep this baby. Her despair grew. If he forced her to have his child, it would bind her forever to him.

She didn't want to give birth to this child, but she had no choice. She didn't want to get rid of it herself, too afraid she would die in the process. So she did nothing.

Her belly grew, and his assaults continued.

Nine months later, she gave birth to a baby girl, completely alone. It was a Wednesday night.

41

Alice

A girl named Alice woke up one day to watch her mommy sob once again without words, making only grunts as she tried to express herself. Her mommy didn't speak. She communicated through gestures, which the little girl didn't always understand.

Her lack of speech narrowed the girl's already small world. The child had no one to talk to except for her daddy, who came back occasionally to bring food, water, and clothes. When he wasn't there, she only had her mommy. The days were long, the nights often longer. Her mommy was sparse with light in the confinement of their narrow home and would often turn it off before it was even dark outside, something the girl could tell by the sunlight streaming through the gaps in the wooden walls.

They had one narrow window, far above the little girl's head, and she would yearn to see the outside world, but she was never allowed to. She couldn't, even if she had wanted to. Both she and her mommy were too small to be able to peek through it.

The little girl had figured out a long time ago that something was wrong. That she wasn't supposed to live in this dark, damp place where she was chronically sick, waiting for an inkling of light with every passing day. Her eyes ached from the lack of natural light; she always felt cold. But her hearing was sharp, and she waited for any sound that would betray her father's arrival.

There were days she didn't hear a single noise, except for her mother's silent screams and the dripping water on the roof during a rainy day. Sometimes it was too hot, so her mommy would sigh and groan throughout the day, expressing her discomfort with gestures.

The girl had figured out that her mom was unable to hear anything. She wouldn't be startled at the sound of a mouse running over the wooden floor, or the cackling of some bird outside the narrow window. Or the rustling of leaves when a wind blew through the woods.

"This is your home," her daddy had said some time ago. "Right here, in these woods, in the heart of the forest. You should call yourself lucky, Alice. There are so many people who would kill to live here, surrounded by nature."

But then why, if life was so amazing here, did her daddy not stay with them too? He was gone so many times, for so long. Sometimes she wondered if they would be able to survive alone if he never returned.

She was always relieved when he came, but when he did, she could see a change in her mommy's behavior. She didn't understand, because Daddy always brought gifts with him. Toys and books with colorful pictures for her, and books with many words in them and no pictures for Mommy.

Mommy didn't like Daddy, or her. She would look at her with an odd expression, as if it was her fault that they were cooped up in here together. She would make these wild gestures that Alice simply did not comprehend, and she had stopped making sense of them because the hand movements simply went too fast.

When Daddy came, their world brightened up a bit. The little girl began to believe that it was her mommy's fault they were stuck in this dark, damp place. Her father confirmed it.

"Your mom is stubborn, Alice," he would say when he arrived with boxes and boxes of canned goods and water. Sometimes he would bring cookies and candy, as well, but that was rare. "All I want is for her to love me. But no, she doesn't want to. Isn't that a shame?"

"Yes, daddy," the girl would say, because that was the only time she could use her voice.

"You should tell your mommy to love your daddy more. Maybe we could move away from the forest then, and we could always be together."

So the girl turned to her mom, with anger written all over her face and accusation in her eyes. "Why won't you love Daddy more?"

Of course, Mommy wouldn't respond. Perhaps she didn't even understand her daughter's words. After all, they were spoken in the dark.

"Why don't you go to sleep, Alice?" Daddy would say once the groceries were put on the shelves in the back of the room. "Right in that corner over there." He would point at the small mattress she would often lie on with her dolls.

"Do I have to already, Daddy?"

He smiled. "Yes, Alice. There are things I need to discuss with your mommy."

So Alice sat on the mattress in the far corner of the room she shared with her mommy.

"Look away now, Alice," Daddy would say.

So Alice did. But she always looked again when Daddy no longer paid attention to her.

Alice didn't like it when Daddy was at the cabin. Mommy would start screaming soundlessly as soon as Daddy approached her. He would put his hand over her mouth to stop the odd sounds that escaped her mouth, and he would hush something in her ear that would stop the crying.

Then Mommy and Daddy would lay down on the bigger mattress by the door, and he would throw a blanket over them. Even in the dark, Alice could see their movements, but she didn't understand them. There would be muffled sounds that she only heard when he was there, and she would push her hands over her ears so she wouldn't hear them. Her mommy's sounds were the worst.

Alice didn't like those moments, and as she grew older, it became harder to understand what was happening. One thing she knew was this: her mommy hated her daddy. She was afraid of him too. But her daddy loved her mommy more than anything in this world.

"Why won't you love me?" he would say. "Why won't you accept what I've given you? I could give you such a good life. Such a nice, beautiful, and rich existence. We would be so good together, you and I, and our daughter. We could start all over again, far away from here. I would treat you like a queen. Doesn't Alice deserve a better life than this?"

Her mommy wouldn't – couldn't – respond. She just wept and curled into herself after daddy moved off the bed, and she would remain unresponsive, which angered him.

"Suit yourself, then," he would snap.

He would grab his things, unlock the door, and head outside. The sound of the slamming door and rattling keys were followed by a roaring sound. It would become quiet after that.

The little girl didn't understand why her mommy didn't just do as he asked. Now, they were being punished for her refusal to love him. Mommy fought, struggled, cried, and screamed; she never gave Daddy the love that he sought so desperately. And that was the reason why they were forever stuck in the dark.

Daddy would sometimes wait for days to return, even with simple things, like a light bulb. Mommy had thrashed around and struck it by accident with her arm, sending them into the dark. He was so mad after she broke it that he said "go fuck yourself" to her, whatever that meant, and left. It took days for Alice's eyes to get used to the dusk that became their routine after that.

Mommy was worried too, after that visit, probably fearing as much as Alice that he would never come back. When he did, with the light bulb and a spare, she didn't struggle when he pulled her onto the bed. The little girl still hated the muffled sounds they made, even if they weren't as bad as before.

The little girl didn't understand why her daddy would do these mean things, when he was always so good to her. He brought candy, chocolate, and cookies. He gave her more toys and books. That could only be a sign of love, right?

That night, he stayed. It was rare he did, and Alice felt oddly happy that she wasn't alone for once. He came to lie by her side on the smaller mattress and held her in his arms. She rested her head against his chest. His arms felt so protective and caring, and she never wanted him to leave again.

"Why won't she love me back, Alice?" Daddy whispered against her hair.

"I don't know, Daddy," the little girl whispered back.

"I don't deserve it. I've been so good, but she just won't

listen to me, will she. She treats me so cold, and all I want is to have her by my side forever. I want her to trust me, so we can live together in a big, warm house. I would give up everything for her, if only she would do the same."

"I want a big house too, Daddy," the little girl said.

He seemed pleased. "You are so sweet, my darling Alice. Please don't stop loving me. I'm doing this all for the both of you. Love shouldn't be so hard."

The little girl smiled when he pecked her on the forehead and held her even closer to him. His hands roamed over her back, and she felt strangely comforted, since Mommy never did that. When he looked into her eyes, she noticed sadness.

"I have to go now," he said, "but I'll be back soon, I promise."

"Can't I go with you?"

"No. Not yet. But soon. Once your mommy changes her mind. Go to sleep now, Alice."

He moved up from the mattress and left the little girl alone in the dark. She had never felt so cold.

When she woke up the next morning, the little girl found her mommy sitting on the floor, watching her. There was something odd about it, different than other times. She made those gestures again, but Alice could not make sense of them.

She moved and grabbed the little girl by her arm while making awful sounds that seemed almost unbearable to listen to, forcing her up. Alice didn't know what she meant, but then she could feel her mommy's hands roam all over her body.

"Stop it!" Alice screamed.

Mommy mouthed things to her. Slowly but surely, Alice understood what she was trying to say.

Hurt. Are you hurt?

Alice couldn't make sense of it. Why would she be hurt?

"No," she said, and she caught mommy looking at her mouth, reading what she was saying.

All of the sudden, the sounds, the gestures, and her mommy's behavior started to make sense. She saw her hands move in the same manner, as if every gesture had a separate meaning.

"No," she repeated, gesturing at her mommy's hands. "No."

Mommy understood. She moved her hand.

"No," the little girl said again, copying the gesture. "No."

Her mommy started laughing, with sounds escaping her mouth. *No.* The sign was repeated, then followed by other signs. Her mommy would painstakingly show her word after word.

She stood and dug a book from beneath a pile of unread books that Daddy had brought them and showed it to her. Alice couldn't read, so she didn't know what the words said, but as soon as the book lay open on the ground, it became obvious what it was. She recognized the signs her mommy was making. This book would help her read.

That day, a bond formed between them that had not been there before, and in the days that followed, Alice came to understand more of her mommy than she had ever before. She picked the words up really quickly, and by the end of the week, she had learned whole sentences. After all, they had nothing else to do.

When Daddy came back, he was shocked to find Alice and her mommy communicating.

"Mommy is teaching me how to speak to her," Alice said excitedly as she threw herself to her daddy's arms. "Isn't that amazing?"

"It is," Daddy said, but Alice could tell he didn't like it. "Let me speak to your mommy. Go sit on the mattress."

Alice was confused. Shouldn't Daddy be happy?

Her gained happiness dwindled quickly when she saw him pull Mommy to the mattress. He didn't bother turning off the light, nor did he pull the blanket over them. He pulled off Mommy's trousers and then he moved over her, making shocking gestures. When her mommy tried to fight back, she could hear him bark at her.

"Why? She'll find out quickly enough. Or did you think I'm going to stick to just you?"

Alice knew that this was his way of punishing them both. She still didn't know what he did to her mommy, but it was bad enough that her mommy would cry and try to get away. His hands weren't loving, his arms weren't around her to protect her. They were there to hold her down.

When he was done, he moved off the mattress, turn around and walked over to Alice, who sat quietly in her corner, her arms around her knees.

"I'll be back tonight," he said with a rough voice. "And then it's your turn. You need to learn, kiddo. It's time."

After he left, mommy crawled to her with tears flowing down her face.

I'm sorry, she signed.

She got up on shaking legs and moved to the shelf of canned food and just stood there. Alice didn't know what to do. Was she supposed to comfort her mom, or be angry with her for not listening to Daddy in the first place?

She was so scared. She had seen something in Daddy's eyes she didn't like. What did he mean when he said that it was her turn? What was he going to do?

Mommy didn't sign another word. But she did the oddest

thing. She opened a can of beans, but instead of eating them, she chucked them on the wooden floor. She then removed the entire lid and touched the sharp side.

"Daddy is going to be so mad that you spilled food," Alice whispered. "He doesn't like that."

Her mommy looked at her sadly, and then she smiled softly. She knelt down by Alice's side, took both wrists in her hands and kissed them. Then she took the lid of the can and, while holding Alice's right wrist tight, sliced through it from left to right until blood flowed freely from it.

The cut was deep, and it took her mommy a lot of effort to slice through the skin, nerves, and muscle. It stung; Alice screamed. She stared in shock at the cut and the blood that streamed onto the floor. Mommy took her other wrist next and tried to cut it too, but this time, Alice fought back.

She pushed her mommy away in time, so that the sharp edge cut into the air instead of her skin. With one wrist bleeding and the other one unharmed, Alice got on her knees and tried to flee. But the room was small and there was nowhere to go.

Mommy then started making wild gestures, just as she had done in the past, before Alice could understand her. The little girl picked up only a few words.

Daddy. Dangerous. Gone. No, we can't go.

Her mommy seemed to realize that Alice had no intention of listening to her, and she became frantic. She tried to catch Alice, tried to stop her from running through the room. Tried to talk to her.

But Alice wouldn't listen.

Her mind became foggy and her thoughts blurry when she realized what her mommy was trying to do. She was trying to kill her. And so, she ran around the room for her life, until her legs could no longer carry her, and the loss of blood exhausted her.

Her mommy lifted her up and placed her on the mattress. Alice could barely keep her eyes open, but she struggled for as long as she could, knowing even then that she would never wake up again if she succumbed to the darkness.

Through a blur, she watched her mommy sit on the mattress beside her, with the sharp lid of the can slashing through her own wrists. She laid down then and held Alice next to her, and even though she couldn't speak, her very presence was comforting and gentle.

The last thing Alice saw before she passed out was Daddy entering the room. The last thing she heard were his shouts of anguish.

42

Jack

Jack's throat burned when he saw what had happened during his short visit to a neighboring town for groceries. His love, Lizzy, lying dead on the filthy mattress. Their daughter unconscious in her arms.

It didn't take a doctor to see that Lizzy was gone. Her eyes were wide open; her blood had pooled on the mattress and floor. She had bled out. But Alice was still alive. She had one cut wrist, one that had remained untouched. The cut hadn't been deep enough. That had saved her life.

Jack sank by the mattress and buried his face between his hands, screaming in anger when he realized he had lost his one true love.

He thought of the many times he had come here to make love to her, of her resistance to love him, of her reluctance to share their child's love with him. And now she was gone. Here she was, dead at his feet, leaving him their child who looked so much like her.

His thoughts immediately started to rearrange themselves. He had enough experience with death to not be rattled by it anymore. That didn't mean that this didn't cause him heartbreak. He was a broken man.

He set out to work. He lifted up Alice, wrapped her wrist to stop the bleeding, and placed her on the mattress. Then he pulled the bedsheets from the mattress and rolled Lizzy in them until she was no longer visible. When he wiped his brow and looked at Alice's still body, he saw her eyes were open. She was awake but obviously confused.

"Mommy?" she whispered.

Jack didn't even have to think for one second. He rushed over to her, knelt, and looked at her firmly.

"Your mommy is dead."

"Dead?"

Alice stared at him with those big eyes he had come to love so much. They were Lizzy's eyes. In fact, she looked so much like her mother, it tore him apart. A thought popped into his mind. He had lost Lizzy, but he could keep Alice. He just had to play his cards right.

But what could he do? He had to kill her, too. That was, in fact, the most logical thing to do. Keeping her here would be the death of her. No five-year old could survive on their own, not even one as smart as Alice. But taking her with him would not be possible without his wife's help.

He couldn't kill her. It would break all bonds with Lizzy. No matter what she'd done, he still needed her. So he made up his mind.

"Listen very closely to me, Alice," he finally said. "Your mommy killed herself after she tried to kill you. She was not a good person. Do you understand?"

Alice looked at him with large eyes.

"Do you get that, Alice?"

She nodded.

"Good. Now, if you do everything I say, I will get you out of here. You can go home with me, to that big house I have always talked about. But only if you do exactly as I tell you. Do you understand what I'm saying, Alice? If you ever speak a single word to anyone, you will die."

His daughter, born in this shack in the woods, stared at him with a haunting look on her face that he would never forget.

He pulled Alice up and dragged her to her mother's wrapped and still body, pointing at her.

"If you speak, you will end up like her. Do you get that, Alice? You don't say a word."

Her eyes dwelled on the white sheets around her mother's body, bloodstains already visible through the cloth, then looked to her father.

She nodded.

"Wait here."

He carried Lizzy's body outside and shoved it in the trunk of his car. He marched back into the house; Alice sat where he had left her.

"Get in the car. Front seat."

She hesitated. He pulled her up and dragged her outside, opened the passenger side door, and pushed her in. She sat nervously on the seat, her gaze bewildered.

"Buckle up," he barked, but she didn't move.

He realized only then that she had never seen a car in her life and had no clue what he meant. He leaned over her and buckled her in. Alice cringed when he accidentally touched her, just like Lizzy always did.

That was the moment he realized why Lizzy had chosen this moment to try and end their lives.

He drove quietly to a small lake nearby, where he grabbed rocks from the ground and ropes from the back of his truck, and attached them to Lizzy's body.

He knew the area well. He used to live here as a kid, had

grown up near the lake. His dead parents' house was only three miles away. He'd left there after they had died in an accident. He had known Lizzy's parents too, since they came to his father's store once in a while for fishing gear.

He had met Lizzy once when she was just a kid, and he was already a traveling salesman. He returned here once a year, selling vacuum cleaners to people he grew up with. When he saw Lizzy, all grown up, there was no doubt in his mind that she was the one he would keep.

He had dreamt of keeping someone for a long time but never thought he would be able to do so. Until he found the perfect spot and the perfect woman.

A small boat with an outboard motor lingered on the edge of the lake. It was late November, and no one ever came here when it was this cold. He carried Lizzy into the boat and then went back to the truck to fetch Alice.

"Sit next to your mom," he said.

He started the motor and drove the boat to the center of the lake. It was getting dark fast now, but the white sheets seemed to reflect in the moonlight.

Once they reached the center of the lake, he looked at Alice. "Say goodbye to your mom now. But before you do, remember she abandoned you. She chose this fate, not me. She tried to kill you, too. So if you ever mourn her, remember the moment that she sliced your wrist and sentenced you to death."

Alice didn't speak a single word as he slipped Lizzy's body into the water. It lingered just a moment above the surface before she was gone, weighed down by the rocks. Alice stared at the water wide eyed, shivering from the cold. She had never been outside in her life, but she didn't seem to care about her surroundings.

He grabbed her by both arms and squeezed her hard. She didn't scream when he lifted her up and held her over the edge of the boat.

"If you want to die, I will let go of you. But if you want to live, I will give you a new life. What's it going to be?"

She made a gesture. He didn't understand.

"Speak to me," he said. "Use your tongue."

But she didn't. Not anymore. She stared at him with those big eyes and remained quiet. He sat her back in the boat and started the motor.

"Her name is Alice."

That was all Jack said when he came home with the little girl, dressed in sweatpants, a T-shirt, and a large sweater that didn't match the rest of her clothes. Her hair was all cluttered and she was filthy. Eileen reacted startled and confused. He had never told her he had kept one of them.

"She's mine."

That's all he said. *She's mine.*

"I'm keeping her. Her mother's dead. She's got no one else. So she's your daughter now. Your responsibility."

Jack knew how his wife would react. She would take an immediate liking to the little, half-orphaned girl in her filthy clothes, raggedy hair, and scared eyes standing in her living room. She would wonder what it would be like to finally have a daughter.

Jack loved his wife in his own way. But she could never give him what he needed. She was just his wife, nothing more, nothing less.

"You should be happy," he said, knowing all too well that she would be conflicted between a strange desire to keep this child and to throw her outside. "You wanted a kid. Now you have one."

"What's your name?" Eileen asked the child, but the girl did not reply.

It was only then that Jack realized the child could no longer speak. She had become mute, just like her mother.

43

Hailey

Hailey watched Alice practice her speech, but there were still no words coming out. It was frustrating to see her like this, but she knew that someday, it would all come back.

And then what?

She didn't know where to go from here. All that she knew was that Alice needed her, and she would never let her down. She had done that too many times before, and Alice didn't even know it.

"How's it going?" Fitz said, who was still residing in Lexington to work on the "Traveling Killer Case", as they called it now.

"Okay, I guess. But she's still not talking. It's as if something's still holding her back."

"I'm not a psychiatrist, but my guess is that she's holding herself back," Fitz said. "There's still something missing in this whole puzzle. She just doesn't know what that is yet."

"She should be getting better by now, though. I mean, Eileen told her who her real mother is, and she's recalling early memories of her captivity. We know that her mom was from Stockton, her family has been tracked down. Her grandparents have contacted her and are on their way. She has a family now. What else is missing?"

"I don't know," Fitz said. "But it will come."

"At least the house has been sold. That's something," Hailey said. "Well below market price, but she obviously didn't care. Thank you for finding that real estate agent for her. That definitely helped. I'm so glad they also took care of selling their furniture and stuff. I was surprised she didn't want any of it, not even her books."

"Well, finding out those precious books were her captive mother's definitely changed her perspective on things," Fitz said. "That man must have been the coldest son of a bitch ever."

"He was," Hailey said.

"Have you guys been talking about what you'll do next? The lease on the Lexington apartment is ending soon, so you guys have to make a decision."

"We've been talking about moving to Boston, but that seems too crowded for her, so we're looking into smaller towns in the area. We really like it here, but it's best for everyone to move on, now that the worst of the storm has passed. You're going away soon now too, aren't you?" Hailey asked.

"Yep. The case is nearly over. We've tracked every victim, so we're packing up soon and going back to Boston. Hey, if you need a place to stay there, let me know. I can always put you up at my place."

"That's really kind of you, but no, thanks. You need your space and so do we. Now that the press has finally backed down, Alice stands a chance of starting a new life, and I'd like to help her with that."

"You're the best, Hailey," Fitz said. "She was so lucky to have you around, you know? All this time you've been pushing yourself to the background, wanting to help her. That's really sweet of you."

"Yeah well, I had to," Hailey said.

"What do you mean by that?"

"The moment I saw her, I knew I would do anything for her," Hailey confessed. "I've never seen anyone like her. She's unique."

"Yeah, I know. But now it's time for her to become one of many millions of people. Normal life is standing on her doorstep. She just needs to grab that opportunity with both hands. Oh, and remember what I told you: If you ever think about joining the FBI, call me and I'll put in a word for you. You'd be good at it."

Hailey smiled. "Maybe someday."

Fitz waved goodbye and took off. Hailey waited for the session to finish and hugged Alice when she came out.

"How'd it go?"

So-so. I'm frustrated.

"I can imagine. It'll come."

Hungry?

"Very. Let's go grab some lunch."

Hailey placed her arm around Alice and took her out into the winter cold. It had just turned February, and the nights were still long and dark. They'd been here for months now, staying in the furnished rental apartment Captain Miles had arranged for them.

Weeks had turned into months, and Hailey had seen her girlfriend grow tired and weary of Lexington. At first, everyone had been really accepting about them staying, but as the months went on and everyone else picked up their normal lives, they could both see what others were saying about them. What Alice had always feared.

She really is his daughter. And he killed Ginnifer Hobbs.

Alice had difficulty accepting the fact that she was his

flesh and blood. She had hoped and prayed that Eileen had been lying, but when all evidence led to Elizabeth Lane, who had been abducted years prior to Alice's birth, she couldn't deny it any longer.

The regression therapy was bringing back a lot of memories that Alice didn't really want to remember, but she still insisted on proceeding with the sessions, if only to find out why her mom had tried to kill her.

One step forward. Two steps back.

That night, as Hailey lay in bed beside her girlfriend, she closed her eyes and focused on Alice's even breathing. She took sleeping aids to get through the nights, but Hailey didn't. She didn't want to.

Not sleeping was her punishment, her atonement for what she had done. The nights were the only time she allowed herself to think about those rare moments she had encountered Eileen Jenkins on the driveway of her home, adjacent to Hailey's.

The first time came after Eileen had caught her talking to Alice through the bedroom window. She had confronted her then, demanding to know who she was and what the hell she thought she was doing.

"Do you have any idea how disturbed my daughter is?" she had snapped.

"Your daughter is perfectly fine," Hailey had said. "What I would like to know is why you keep her locked up like a prisoner. I wonder what the police would have to say about that."

"Don't you dare meddle in our business!" Eileen had snapped.

"Afraid of what they might discover?"

"Stay away."

"Or else what?"

Eileen hadn't said anything further, and just stomped away. After that, Hailey's talks with Alice continued unopposed.

The second time came when Jack was already home, dying. Hailey had been on her way out when Eileen stormed out of the house, distraught.

"What's wrong?" Hailey had asked. "Is Alice okay?"

Eileen had snapped her neck towards Hailey so fast it must have hurt. "What do you care?"

"I care about her."

"Why?"

"She's my friend. I'd do anything for her."

Eileen looked at her quizzically. "Anything, huh?"

"Anything."

"Hm," was all she said before she walked back to the house.

The third and final time came early in the morning. Hailey was still in bed when there was a hard knock on the door. Eileen was bouncing on the wood.

Hailey stormed downstairs, horrified that something had happened to Alice.

"I gave her a sleeping pill last night," Eileen said. "Her father, he…"

"What did he do to her?!" Hailey interrupted.

"Nothing yet, but I'm afraid."

"That fucking asshole. He's doing it again, isn't he?"

Eileen's bewildered reaction said enough. Hailey bit her tongue.

"I knew it," Eileen said slyly. "You came here on purpose. It was too convenient, all of it. You moving in here, sucking up to my daughter. Who the hell are you?"

Hailey knew she couldn't lie any longer. She took her parents' picture from her purse and showed it to Eileen. The look on her face said it all.

"When?"

"Three years ago."

"Fuck."

"You knew?!"

Eileen said nothing.

"Where is Alice now?"

"Still asleep."

"And him?"

"Downstairs. Wanna see him?"

"Yes."

"Come with me."

Before she knew it, Hailey entered the smelly basement room and witnessed Jack Jenkins's suffering. Eileen stood back and allowed her to take her time.

His was a painful, slow death, but it couldn't be slow enough, as far as Hailey was concerned. His lungs struggled to take each breath, as many as he could before the end finally came. He fought so hard to stay alive, even when the cancer was eating him from the inside out. He wouldn't give up the fight, even through unbearable pain. Why would he want to continue living if another day was so painful?

Go, she begged in silence. *Go, so we're finally rid of you.*

He opened his eyes and looked at her. He recognized her. He was scared.

"No," he stammered. "No... *Go!*"

But she wouldn't. She sat down and watched him catch his breath one more time. And then one more. And then another one.

She was trapped between the urgency to kill him and the desperate craving to watch him die that long, painful death. But the longer he lived, the more time he had to fuck up the life of the one person she loved the most.

She sat for half an hour, waiting for him to die.

He wouldn't. Even when he could barely speak, he just would *not* die. He defied her, even now.

A crooked smile played on his face. "W-Water," he hissed.

He stretched his skinny hand with the cracked skin as he pointed at the glass standing on a table by the bed. He couldn't reach it on his own, not in his current state.

She didn't give it to him.

"Water. *Now.*"

She refused.

"Water!!!" he roared loudly.

She didn't move.

"I'll tell her *everything*," he said.

She stood on trembling feet. She turned around and looked at Eileen, who stood in the doorway with a filthy-looking glass and a cup of crushed pills in her left palm.

"Your choice," she said. "But if you do this, it'll be over."

Hailey poured the crushed pills in the water and went back to him. Jack gulped the liquid down, pulling a face at the taste of it. He stopped halfway.

"Drink it all," she said, and she placed her hand behind his head, forcing him up while holding the glass to his lips. "Every last drop."

He looked her in the eye as he drank. He smiled when he was done. He stayed awake for as long as he could, but then his eyelids drooped and he sunk away into a comatose sleep he would never wake from.

She stood and left the room, where Eileen was waiting for her.

"Happy now?" she said.

Hailey nodded.

Jack died two hours later.

Epilogue

I tried so hard to feel something, but my emotions had been all over the place for the past months.

I was a stranger to myself. A new person, who had to reinvent who she was and where she would go from here. An orphan with a surrogate mother who would serve life in prison, whom she never wanted to see again.

People all around were wearing scarves and hats and preparing for Valentine's Day. It was halfway through February already, but I could barely recall the days, let alone keep track of the seasons. I wanted so much to be part of them, but I had never felt so alone in my life.

I sat down on a bench and watched couples strolling by. Normal people with normal lives. People with problems who had managed to move on.

Like Mark, who had lost his fiancée but was now seeing someone new.

Like Ginnifer's parents and sister who had come to accept their daughter and sister was never coming back.

Like the parents, families, and friends of the people my birth-father had killed.

Like Elizabeth's parents, who were trying to figure out my place in their world.

Who was I in this scheme of things? And would I ever be able to find my place in a world that no longer felt hostile but still strange?

Hailey approached, her hands stuffed in her jacket pockets. "You okay?" she asked.

I nodded. Our usual routine.

"Ready to go?"

We had packed up our things and were supposed to drive all the way to the East Coast, where we would pick out a new town to settle in. I had enough money to last a lifetime, thanks to the inheritance that I was allowed to keep, the sale of the house, and the money my new grandparents had wired me. We had met a couple of times, and I liked them, but I wasn't so sure if they were ready to have me in their lives. They'd move on too.

Ready, I signed, and got up, saying goodbye to Lexington *and* Hays. I was done with the past, ready for the future.

As we walked to Hailey's Volkswagen Beetle, which we hadn't used since those days back in October, I suddenly felt a chill run down my spine. This didn't feel right. Nothing felt right.

"What is it?" Hailey asked, opening the driver's door.

Something tugged at the back of my mind, a nagging sensation that I shouldn't be here with her.

I loved her so much, but I also loved her *too* much. From the moment we first met, until this very second, I had loved her so much it hurt.

I loved her so much that I wanted to keep her with me for the rest of my life. To hold her so tight that she would never leave me.

Escape me...

I remembered Jack Jenkins gazing at my mom inside that cabin. I remembered him assaulting her while I was in the room, not caring that I saw.

I remembered the way he had looked at me.

What if some day, I would look at Hailey the same way? I was, after all, his daughter.

I let go of the door, turned around, and started walking away.

"Alice?" she called after me. "Alice!"

I didn't look back.

She came after me, stopped me, came to stand in front of me.

I swallowed. My throat felt thick and clogged, and I had trouble focusing, but this *had* to be done.

"I... am... his... daughter," I forced out of my throat. It sounded raw and strange. But the words were mine.

She let go of me.

I smiled weakly and walked away.